GU0087042

Madatan

Through the dark cold and the empty desolation,
The wave cry, the wind cry, the vast waters
Of the petrel and the porpoise. In my end is my beginning.

T. S. ELIOT
East Coker. Four Quartets.

PETER CARTER

Madatan

ILLUSTRATED BY VICTOR G. AMBRUS

London
OXFORD UNIVERSITY PRESS
1974

Oxford University Press, Ely House, London W. 1

GLASGOW   NEW YORK   TORONTO   MELBOURNE   WELLINGTON
CAPE TOWN   IBADAN   NAIROBI   DAR ES SALAAM   LUSAKA   ADDIS ABABA
DELHI   BOMBAY   CALCUTTA   MADRAS   KARACHI   LAHORE   DACCA
KUALA LUMPUR   SINGAPORE   HONG KONG   TOKYO

ISBN 0 19 271359 0
© Peter Carter 1974
First published 1974

For my sister, Catherine

Printed in Great Britain by T. & A. Constable Ltd., Hopetoun Street, Edinburgh

Foreword

Madaah is Celtic for fox. Madatan means little fox.

The Norse expansion began in the eighth century. From their base on Orkney the Norsemen raided first Ireland, then England. Lindisfarne was destroyed in 793, Jarrow and Monkwearmouth in 794.

Aethelred was King of Northumbria during this period. He was as ruthless as shown here. He was murdered in 796.

The Church in Northumbria remained strong and stable until the final collapse of the kingdom around 840. York was a centre of learning known throughout Europe.

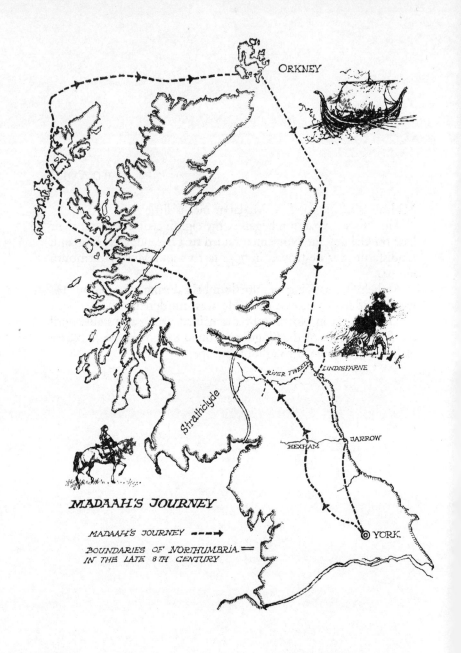

ORKNEY

River Tweed

LINDISFARNE

Strathclyde

JARROW

HEXHAM

YORK.

MADAAH'S JOURNEY

MADAAH'S JOURNEY ‐‐‐‐▶

BOUNDARIES OF NORTHUMBRIA
IN THE LATE 8TH CENTURY

PART ONE

Chapter 1

All day the gale from the Atlantic had swept the shores of the island, and all day Madaah had crouched against the wall of the fort, looking out to sea.

As the daylight faded he began to feel afraid, again. He clung to the rough stones, his eyes sore with the salt spray, until at last all he could see was a line of foam crawling over the rocky beach like white fingers. Finally he turned and jumped down. The dogs growled as he shoved his way among them to sleep, but he ignored their bad temper, as he did their rank smell, little different from his own.

The wind cried along the wall, and poked cold fingers through its holes. Madaah lay very still. Down by the shore he thought he heard the water-horse come, dripping from the sea. He thought of its wet mane of seaweed, and its dead, drowned eyes, and through the howl of the gale he heard its six legs pounding on the shore. He thought, too, of the dark pool in the hills, and of the thing that surely lived there stirring in its black depths . . . then he fell asleep, clutching to him the sword his father had left when he had gone to Sheppey, four days ago.

The dogs woke him with their growls, and he started up, grasping the sword. It was dawn and the gale still screamed against the sky. He ran up the little tower. At first the wind blinded him. He shielded his eyes and squinted out. The sea was terrifying. The waves crashed on the rocks with a huge Boom! and from the cave where the water-horse lived came a dreadful throaty gurgle. Madaah knew his father would not be coming home that day. Sadly he turned and jumped back into the broch.

There was still oatmeal left so he made porridge, running to the burn for water. When he had finished eating, the dogs licked the plate and he wiped it dry with moss. Then he took out his soft wedge of sandstone and began to sharpen the sword. There was little blade to sharpen because it was broken, but Madaah liked the feel of the hilt with its wreathed ornament of snakes, and the feel of it gave him confidence and a sense of power. This, he knew, came from the sword's magic, put there by the great magician who had made it far away, across the rim of the world.

It had taken many spells to subdue that magical power. Madaah had sat for hours, weaving his own magic, and thinking of the drowned man who had brought the sword to his island, but for a long time the sword had obeyed its other magic and had twisted in his hand when he swung it, living and venomous, obeying the will of the serpents on the hilt. Not until Madaah had killed a snake and bound its skin round them had the sword understood who was its master and grown docile in his hand.

Now Madaah could sharpen it without fear of cutting himself. It was a precious sword, made of a dark heavy substance as hard as rock. There was none other like it in the world.

The dogs looked at him as he worked on the sword, all the time singing the sword spell. He pointed the sword at them and they grew uneasy and turned away. Madaah laughed at the power the sword had, and which he had through the sword.

The gale blew and blew, and Madaah sang the song of the boat to bring his father safely home. He looked at the small sheep in the pen and he sang the song of the sheep. He ate more oatmeal and longed for his father to come home, and then it grew dark again and he wriggled among the dogs and slept. Once, during the night, he woke and heard his mother calling him from the water-fall where her spirit had gone when she died, but he was afraid to go out in the dark, and his mother called him in vain. He fell asleep again, and when he woke his father had been gone six days, but the gale had died, and the world was full of stillness.

He ate quickly, then took the sword and called the dogs. Behind the fort was the black hill Mamdorcha. On its peak he would sing the boat-song and his father would come home. He ran up the hill and paused by the water-fall to call to his mother. She did not answer, but a bird with white barred wings flew out and fluttered over his head and Madaah knew it was his mother. He felt happy and ran lightly to the crest of the hill and looked down on the island and its bays, fretted by the sea. He could see the few dark houses of his father's people. Women were working by the shore gathering sea-weed for the fields. There were only women and children and a few old men down there. The men had gone to Sheppey with his father to bring in the village sheep from the summer grazing. Madaah lay in the heather and gazed down. In the rain-washed sky the little bird flew overhead and gave small chinking cries. Madaah looked up. 'Greetings, Mother!' he cried. And then, when he turned to sea again, he saw the boat.

His first thought was of his father and he leaped to his feet. But then he paused. The boat was big, bigger than anything he had ever seen before that had been made by man. Legs stuck out from its side, like water beetles, and then he realised that the legs were oars, a bank of them on either side, fighting against the swell. As the boat inched into the bay, metal flashed in the sun and the long oars rose and fell as the boat steadied herself on the tide.

He stared wide-eyed, then began to move down the hill. As he descended, the boat was grounding on the shore. Figures were leaping from it and heading over the sand-dunes to the houses. It was then that Madaah felt the first flutter of fear. There was something about the way the figures were moving, about their speed and urgency, that was frightening, although he hardly knew why. But by a cluster of rocks he paused. The sword in his hand was the most precious thing the tribe possessed. It was worth more than the sheep, or the goats, or the dogs, or the loom; it was worth more, even, than the great millstones that broke down the sharp oats. They kept men alive but the sword had the power of death, although no man had seen it used except on the animals. Who knew, Madaah thought, but that the strangers might not desire the sword as much as he? He stooped by some boulders and thrust the sword into the black peaty soil. For a moment he felt a tremor of uneasiness—would the sword stay there? Would the snakes on the handle remember their master and lie coiled there and wait for him? Or, deep in the darkness, would they begin to wriggle and squirm, remembering their old home in the cool earth, and glide away, taking the sword's magic with them?

Reluctantly Madaah moved away. He knew no spells for this. To hide his confusion he called sharply to the dogs and ran down to the sea and the long ship.

He heard the first scream as he crossed the burn where the cultivated land began. Quite instinctively he ran forward and saw a crumpled figure, face down on the rough path. From where he stood he could see the figure had white hair, and Madaah knew

that it was Blind Brin, the oldest and wisest man on the island. A man was stooping over him and Madaah thought he was leaning down to help. Then the man struck at Brin, and then again, and as Madaah stared, amazed, the man raised his head, and then Madaah screamed.

The man was not a man! Its head was long and pointed, and horns swept up from it. From underneath the horns a mass of tangled hair swung and trembled. Then Madaah knew that the figure was a monster, come from the sea to kill all men. As he stood, sick and helpless, the monster gave a great cry and ran at him. Madaah saw with disgust the hair on the creature's face and caught a stench of the sea and rotten fish, and then the monster struck him, and he fell, fathoms deep, into darkness.

The snakes had escaped from the sword. They had wriggled from the peat, down the hill, across the stream, and into his mouth and his head, and there they writhed, biting at him angrily. One was in his stomach, twisting and turning, and one was round his throat. Madaah cried for his father, but he was dead, drowned beneath the waves, and the monsters with their horned heads sat in the fort, laughing and feasting.

He woke. A light blazed in his eyes. It was the sun. He tried to turn but the snake round his throat stiffened and held him. his head boomed and roared and it was the sea in his head. A white blur jigged before his eyes and he remembered Blind Brin, lying on the path, and then a black cloud swept overhead and he thought it was the spirits of the dead come to take the old man, as they had taken his mother; but he smelt smoke and knew that the Fire-Gods had come to war with the sea, and the snakes, and the monsters.

When he woke again, the sun was sinking. He stared round vacantly. The monsters were still there, Brin still lay on the path but he had been joined by others, Lame Gavin, Niala the potter; there were more but he turned away. The monsters had made a fire. They stood by it idly, or lay on their sides, laughing and shouting.

Madaah began to fall sidewards. He felt a sharp constriction round his throat and his head was pulled sharply back. Slowly he turned and saw the face of Moida, Lame Gavin's wife. They were tied together by a rope which ran from his neck to hers, and then on to others he could not identify. Moida was staring blindly in front of her and her mouth was opening and closing in a jerky way. Madaah giggled. Moving his mouth hurt him, and he coughed as he caught a mouthful of smoke from the burning houses. The hours passed and the fire glowed the brighter as the darkness thickened. Once a shape loomed out of the night and Moida screamed, a thick animal cry which went on until she was

5

kicked into silence. The moon rose, steady and peaceful. By the fire strange shapes howled and whooped, but among the terrors, Madaah slept.

He woke again to the morning sun. His head ached and his eyes were swollen, and the rope tied round his neck had rubbed it raw. He peered round vaguely. The fire still smouldered and a few men moved round it. Madaah called to them, hoarsely, and pointed to his mouth. The men stared at him, and then one laughed and threw him a piece of meat. Madaah looked at it, shook his head and pointed again to his mouth. One of the men walked to him and casually threw a bowl of water across his face, shouting something, but what it was, Madaah had no way of telling.

Some of the water caught his cracked lips and it revived him a little. Although he had difficulty in focusing, he stared at the men. That they were men there was no doubt. The monsters of the previous night had been the creations of his own mind, born out of fear and despair. Who these men were he had no idea, nor from where they had come. That there were other people in the world he knew. On islands nearby there were small groups, living as Madaah's own people did, growing oats, raising sheep, and fishing; somewhere to the East, Blind Brin had said, was another land, but no one had ever been there, and no one had ever come from there. The sense of strangeness was too much for Madaah, and his mind drifted away into a daydream and he was back again in the quiet straggle of houses, peaceful under the summer sky.

A kick brought him to his senses. He rose with the other captives. A man pushed him forward and with the others he stumbled forward to the shore, and to the ship.

Until that moment the biggest boat Madaah had ever seen had been his father's, a canoe of animal hide stretched over wicker, with a crude sail. To his eyes this new boat was enormous, long and sleek, with bows that curved upwards in a fine sweep and ended in the head of an eagle, cruel and rapacious. It looked as if the ocean had created it, and Madaah felt a prickle of admiration and awe. They walked under the shadow of the prow and waited, knee deep in the rising tide. A man pushed a plank over the side and they shuffled awkwardly on board and stumbled down the ship; the women shocked and silent, the children crying, and Madaah, neither man nor child, silent but watchful.

6

The boat was hollow inside. Rough seats were strutted against the sides and the oars were stacked by the seats. The raiders climbed in and took their seats and held the oars high. As the tide rose, the boat rose with it, trembling now with motion. Then the men heaved on the oars, the eagle's head swung away from the land, and Madaah felt that he was seeing the last of his home, his father, the black hill Mamdorcha, and all the days of his childhood. The great ship faced the open sea. Behind them smoke from the houses, smouldering yet, curled along the beach. The men heaved at their oars and the shore fell away. The last thing Madaah saw was the white head of Blind Brin, the greatest magician in the world.

Chapter 2

Away from the shore the ship heeled as the waves chopped at it. The raiders hauled up a sail. It was ragged and stained, with a single eye painted on it, which stared coldly and malevolently at the horizon. The men shipped their oars and sprawled on the benches. They looked sullen and dispirited. There was little talk or laughter. One of them stared at Madaah who opened his mouth, like a fledgling bird. The man scowled but Madaah was made bold by thirst and he rubbed his thickened tongue over his lips. Someone, Madaah did not know who, shouted, and the man brought water. Madaah drank deeply, peering at the man over the rim of the bowl. When he had finished, he opened his mouth again and rubbed his stomach. The man's face went dark with anger. He cried something harsh and unintelligible, and suddenly struck Madaah in the face. Madaah fell back and lay very still. The man stared down for a moment, then turned away.

Towards evening the captives were thrown lumps of meat. The others left it but Madaah fell on his like a dog. Then, as night fell, they drifted into a silent bay and the men went on shore, taking the women with them. Madaah was left with three children. They were tied by the neck to the tiller. Madaah tried to gnaw through the rope but the thick tar made him sick and at last he fell asleep, like an exhausted animal.

At dawn the men returned, alone. Later, at sea, he was untied and kicked forward. He was given sand and a rag, and set to work scouring rusty helmets. He could see the shores of distant islands, a familiar tumble of rock and peat, bordered with white sand and bright grass, and once, far out to sea, he saw the glint of a sail in the immensity of the ocean. He scoured and scrubbed all day. At noon he was given a lump of stale fish and then turned back to work. As he scrubbed, he began to look carefully at the men on the boat. They were big, with huge strong limbs, and matted

8

beards, but, behind their massive strength, they looked worn and exhausted. One or two looked really ill, with sores around their mouths, and they all had boils.

Some of Madaah's fears were ebbing away, and with it some of his awe. Yesterday the men had seemed to be monsters from another world. Today he could see them for what they were, savage, strong, unpredictable, but still men. The ship too, for all its grace, was worn. The sail was tattered and the ropes frayed, and water seeped into the ship through gaping seams.

Deep inside himself Madaah felt the stirring of contempt. The raiders were clumsy and uncontrolled, always crashing into things, as if they thought that objects would move for them, whereas his own people were quick and graceful, recognising that the world was full of life, unseen and delicate, but to be treated with the respect that all life deserved.

But all these men had swords, great flakes of dark metal that seemed to Madaah the work of wizards, like his own sword buried in Mamdorcha, and that frightened him. One blow from those dark blades had destroyed Brin, for all his invisible shield of magic. That night, while the children whimpered beside him, the thought came to him that perhaps these men knew the wizard who made the swords! And that thought beckoned a more horrible one; perhaps that wizard exchanged swords for slaves— why else should the raiders have come, and why else should they be sailing on, and on, towards what everyone knew was the end of the world? That night Madaah was afraid as he had never been afraid before.

The sun rose and fell, and at night the narrow moon shone. The children died of exposure and bad food, and at last only Madaah remained, accepting, and enduring. Little by little he moved towards the men and they accepted him as they might a stray dog, sometimes throwing him scraps of food, sometimes kicking him, but never driving him away altogether.

He began to learn their language. At first he had found it hard to believe that their harsh cries could mean anything, but, out of the jumble of noise, sounds with meaning began to emerge; 'irsmeddel' meant food, a good word! 'svard' meant sword, and sword meant power. Olaf, Eric, Sven, were the names of men, and Olaf was the most important name. He was the master of the ship, and the sail's single eye was painted after his maimed face. And the name of the men was Norsemen.

Using his quick ear, and quicker mind, Madaah began to use the words he heard, and this staggered the men. When he spoke, they looked at him in amazement, as if a dog had begun to speak. For a while he got no rest. Always someone would be prodding him: 'Speak!' they would command. And he would shout a jumble of words, and they would howl with laughter, and give him food, or their thick sour beer. Madaah began to like the Norsemen, and now, when they sighted a settlement, he went with them, screeching and howling, blind to the blood and the fire. And he held a knife of iron.

One day he stood balanced at the prow of the ship. They had turned North. For the first time they had lost sight of land and before them was an infinity of water. The wind was cold and there was a smell of winter in the air. Madaah shivered and then heard a harsh laugh behind him. He turned and saw Eric, a big red-haired man behind him.

'You like it,' Eric asked. 'The sea?'

Madaah did not, but he was careful in his answer. Of all the men on board Eric was the most unpredictable. Madaah had seen him change from laughter to murderous rage in seconds, although no one knew why.

Madaah steered clear of the question. 'When will we reach land?' he asked in his broken Norse.

'When we reach it. Who knows when that will be.' Eric waved his huge hand vaguely.

'Doesn't Olaf know?' Madaah looked furtively over his shoulder as he spoke. He was horribly afraid of Olaf.

'No one knows.'

Madaah stared at the tumbling waters. 'What land are we going to?' he asked.

'To Orkney, where else?'

'Oh, Orkney.' Madaah tried to look wise. He glanced sideways at Eric. The big Norseman looked less bad-tempered than usual. 'What is Orkney, Eric?'

Eric spat over the side of the boat and stared moodily ahead. 'It is an island, boy. It is the winter's place of all the Norsemen. The Sea-Kings have their halls there. Ya, there are a hundred ships and a thousand men. There is plenty food, plenty beer. I have spent good winters there, but now . . .' His voice died away. A mood of deep melancholy seemed to be taking hold of him. His voice rose and fell in a sad chant. 'I have sailed to Orkney in ships full of gold and silver and slaves. I have lived like an earl on wine and meat, I have lived like the Gods themselves. But now. . . .' He shrugged. 'What do we take? Hard tales and wounds. Almost I wish we do not get there. It will be a race I think, anyway.'

Madaah looked at the empty ocean. 'Who are we racing, Eric?'

'Look' Eric pointed his long arm to the North East. High up in the sky grey clouds were turning and twisting slowly, trailing long curtains of rain across the sea.

'Those are the storm-maidens,' Eric hissed, 'Look, their hair trails down to reach us.'

A cold breath seemed to blow across Madaah's neck. The clouds were obviously grey spectres. He could see, yes, he could see their hair—fool that he was to think it was rain!—and he could see their arms and their cold eyes. He wished he had not asked what the storm-maidens were. It was a thing he had begun to notice. First there was nothing, then someone said a word, and then a thing appeared. Words were true magic, he thought.

'Will they catch us, Eric?' he cried.

Eric grinned sourly. 'Don't worry about the storm-maidens, think of the frost giants!'

Madaah's heart jumped. Frost giants! Always it seemed there was something new to be learned, and always it seemed the new was bad. But men were not helpless. Wise men had learned how to ward off the evil in the world. Madaah turned to the grey waters and opened his hands and called on the great lord of the ocean to spread his hair and calm the waves, and he called on the good spirits of the air to blow away the storm-maidens.

Eric stood by looking puzzled, and dangerous.

'It is a charm, Eric,' Madaah said, 'To take us safe to Orkney.'

His explanation did not take away Eric's scowl. The Norseman gave him a hard stare, then turned away down the boat. When Madaah glanced after him a moment later, he saw Eric talking to Olaf. There was something about the way Eric's head was tilted toward Olaf that made Madaah uneasy. He stood uncertainly for a moment and then went to the mast. The crew had gathered round the tiller and there was a good deal of talk and head-wagging. He began fiddling nervously with a rope, anxious to show goodwill. His action by the mast only seemed to disturb the men more, and he heard a murmur behind him. He felt a foot on his back and turned to see Olaf above him.

B

Olaf jerked his head and Madaah rose obediently.

'What is this you sing?' Olaf asked.

Madaah cleared his throat which had gone dry. 'A song—a charm, to take us to Orkney. My father taught it me.'

Olaf's face was sullen. 'Your father was a wizard?'

'No, Brin was the wise man. He had white hair. He was killed, you—they—someone killed him. . . .' Madaah's voice died away.

'Wizards are evil, they have great power.'

'Not Brin, he was good.' Madaah thought of the harmless Brin with his spells for the sheep and sickness. 'The charms are good.'

Olaf took Madaah by the throat. 'If the song you sang was good, we will go safe to Orkney.'

'Yes, Olaf.'

'If they are bad—'

'Good, they are good!'

The hand round his throat tightened. 'Good,' Madaah squawked.

He was heaved off his feet and over the side of the boat. The water slashed at his face and then he was back in the boat. He stared at Olaf's face, at the blind shrunken eye like a snake's, set in withered membrane.

'If they are bad,' Olaf growled, and dropped him.

Madaah backed away to the prow of the ship and squatted. The crew stood by Olaf at the tiller and every eye seemed aimed at himself. The ship rose and fell, and the sky grew darker. Madaah began to realise that one could never really know what fear was. There was always something worse than what one knew.

Snow, falling wetly on his face woke Madaah. He lay, chilled, staring at the sky. At first the wheeling flakes bewildered him, merging with his dreams of a moment ago, dreams of his home and his father.

He rose and peered over the prow, into the whirl of snow. Then he turned and looked down the ship. Under the tent which was put up at night the Norsemen lay in crumpled heaps. Beyond the tent, at the tiller, was a dark shape, and Madaah thought he could see Olaf's harsh face with its single eye staring through the darkness at him.

The water knocked against the side of the ship. It sounded like a summons, and for a moment Madaah saw himself, a white face gleaming in the water before the waves engulfed him for ever.

12

He rubbed his hand across his face. The dark figure at the tiller
had made no move, and that stillness was more frightening than
violence. Without consciously willing it, Madaah found himself
moving down the ship.

The boat had a light sprinkling of snow on it and Madaah
could see every detail with strange clarity; a leg stuck out from
under the tent and he saw the worn leather of the sandal, the
frayed legging, a stain of old, dried blood. He climbed on the ship's
side and moved along to Olaf. The night was quiet, peaceful
almost, but behind Madaah, as he moved, a line of footprints
appeared, as though a dark spirit followed him.

At the stern a dark shape loomed over him. 'Olaf!' Madaah
whispered. 'Olaf!'

13

There was no answer.

'Olaf?' Young as he was Madaah heard the pleading note in his voice and despised himself for it, but it was there when he spoke again.

'The snow, it does no harm. It is not a storm, eh?'

The silent figure above him rocked slightly with the movement of the ship.

'Olaf!' Madaah cried, and clutched at the master's feet, and, as he did so, the figure slid forward, a cold arm fell across his neck, a cold cheek was pressed to his, and for one brief moment a vacant eye stared blindly at him, and then they rolled together into the scupper, Madaah sick with terror, Olaf dead.

For a moment Madaah was trapped under the body, and then, with a frantic convulsion, he wriggled free. A scream bubbled to his throat but he fought it back. Olaf's collapse had not roused the crew. The ship rocked a little as the prow swung free, and the sail rattled as it lost the wind, otherwise the night was as still and peaceful as before.

Madaah backed away from the body, but then he bent and dragged Olaf up a little and jammed his arm over the tiller. Then he turned and went forward, Olaf's sightless eyes following him through the snow.

For a while Olaf's hand, dead as alive, kept the ship's bows onto the waves, but the tiller clattered and the ship lurched as it swung off course. Madaah heard voices from the tent, and one called, 'Olaf!' Madaah closed his eyes tightly. A shaggy head appeared from the tent and cried loudly, 'Olaf, the ship!'

The voice cracked with alarm and a man heaved himself from the tent. All the men were awake now and Madaah heard the stamping of feet and cries of fear. He wrapped his rough coat around himself and peered over its edge. The tent was down and he could see the length of the ship. A thin grey light was filtering through the darkness, and he could see the Norsemen clustered round the tiller and around Olaf's crumpled body. As he watched, they turned and looked at him.

The men at one end of the boat, and the youth at the prow stared at each other. One of the men started forward, but some-one, Madaah could not see who, grabbed his shoulder and stopped him. Then Olaf's body was raised and heaved over the side. There was no sound at his departure.

The men in the stern talked together for a few minutes, then

Eric began to move down the ship towards the huddled youth. He came to within a few feet and stopped, his tall gaunt figure, wrapped in ragged wool, swaying with the ship. Madaah stared unwinkingly upwards, and under his coat his hand tightened on his knife. If he was to die, he would die fighting, and not slip passively into eternity as the women and children had. That he had some control over his destiny he had learned from the Norsemen. Let Eric be the first to know!

'Olaf is dead.'

'Yes,' Madaah forced the words out.

'We have—' Eric gestured with his thumb.

'Yes.'

Eric nodded. His red eyes flickered uneasily. 'He was our leader; now he is dead.'

'Yes, he is dead.'

The big Norseman gave a deep racking cough. 'He struck you and now he is gone, as if he had never been.' He shook his head as if he was trying to comprehend a truth that was beyond him and yet one that should be obvious.

The small, dark boy stared at Eric, not knowing what to do, or say. Eric had a bundle under his arm and with a sudden movement he swung it up. Under it was Olaf's sword. Now, thought Madaah, I am to die. He grasped his knife and then, to his amazement, Eric threw the sword at his feet and backed away with a nervous shuffle.

'Take us safely to Orkney!' he cried.

Chapter 3

Madaah reached forward and pulled the sword towards him. The 'Widow Maker' Olaf had called it, and it had made many widows in its time. There was no ornament on the hilt, and the blade was dinted and hacked, though sharp. This was power, he thought, this and the ability to wield it, but there were other sorts of power. What had led Eric to give him the sword? And why was Eric frightened? Madaah began to drift into dream as the thoughts flickered through his mind. He dreamt of Blind Brin. He, too, had power: to make the dead rest easy, to make the oats grow, to bring the fish each year in great shoals. Madaah dreamt of Brin dancing, clad in a seal-skin with sea-weed over his white hair, then, in the dream, Brin changed, and it was he, Madaah, who danced and controlled the spirits of the sea, and the air, and the land.

Two days later they sighted land. By noon the mass of an island had killed the wind. Wearily the Norsemen unshipped their oars and rowed against the tide up a huge bay, studded with pillars of rock, and shrouded with a soft, subtle mist. Madaah stood at the prow as they moved slowly into the bay. He stared eagerly at the withered cliffs which frowned above them, but the land was silent, and seemed as remote now as when he had first heard its name.

Before dusk the prow grated on a shingled beach, and the men threw out the anchor stone. A few hundred yards up the beach was another ship, canted at an angle that made it look oddly defeated. A few men gathered idly around Madaah's ship, and as the crew jumped ashore, there was a little half hearted joking. Madaah felt depressed. He stared through the gloom at the two ships, the handful of weary men, and the barren moors beyond. Was this all? Then he shrugged. More boasting, the Norsemen's speciality.

The men had made a fire and he moved over to it, staggering

a little as his body still answered the endless movement of the sea. He crouched by the flames, clutching Olaf's sword—*his* sword now. He liked the way the men had given way to him, and he liked more the way they kept their distance. It was a sign of his power over them. He shivered with excitement at the thought of it. Where his power came from, he did not know, but he was beginning to believe in it, and his belief was giving him power.

The men from the other boat drifted over to the fire. They

talked across the flames. It was despondent talk, of bad luck and bad weather, of lean pickings from fat lands, of sickness, and death, high hopes and low achievements.

Eric was sitting across from Madaah, deep in talk with a man from the other ship. Once Eric pointed furtively at Madaah and the other man stared across the fire. His face was heavy and expressionless but he nodded sharply, then rose and went into the night. When he had gone, Madaah went round the fire to Eric, who moved uneasily.

'What now, Eric?' he asked. He had chosen the words carefully. To show ignorance was to show weakness, and to show weakness was death in this world.

Eric muttered something which he couldn't catch. 'Speak up!' he commanded boldly.

Eric scowled, but answered. 'Why, we are here; what next can there be?'

'But what will you do now you are here?' Madaah artfully stressed the word 'you.'

'Can't you tell me, Wizard?'

Ah, Madaah thought, 'Wizard', that was the word. That was the word that gave power, as words did. 'Do you want me to tell you?' he asked.

Eric looked wary and hunted. 'No!' he said and went into the night. Behind him, Madaah laughed softly.

The men dragged the tent from the ship and slept under it that night. The next morning they huddled again around the fire, looking irresolute and uncertain. When they spoke though, it was in a different tone from the previous night. They boasted of their bravery and strength and of their exploits of the summer, but it was vain-glorious talk, as men talk to keep up their spirits when something unpleasant is to happen to them.

About noon Madaah heard his name called by an unfamiliar voice. He turned to see a man standing a few yards away. It was the man Eric had been talking to the night before. He waved his hand and as Madaah walked towards him, he turned and moved up the shingle. Madaah followed him. Away from the men, on a bank of turf, the man faced Madaah.

'My name is Thorold,' he said.

Madaah nodded casually.

'That is my ship. Thorold pointed a long dirty finger at the beach. Madaah glanced at the shore indifferently.

18

'Is it true that you are a wizard?'

Madaah nodded. Who was he to deny it?

Thorold spoke again. 'You are very young. Still . . .' His voice tailed away and he looked baffled. It was a thing that Madaah had noticed about the Norsemen. Faced with something practical, they did it, and well, but when they were up against something intangible, they seemed to lose confidence. But Madaah had confidence enough now for both.

'Speak!' he commanded.

Thorold bit his lip. 'I have a fair ship,' he cried. 'She rides the waves like a swan, and she is mine, my own. Her sail is like an eagle's wing—' Madaah closed his eyes as the voice droned on. He had heard this many times before, from Eric and Olaf, but he wagged his head in agreement as Thorold, finished now with his ship, cried his own praises. Madaah nodded on and on; yes, indeed, Thorold was a great warrior, yes, a great seaman too. Indeed Thorold had gone south that summer to Ireland (where was that, he wondered?) and killed with his own hands one of the black wizards who ruled there, (who were they?) and smashed with his club the crosses they placed everywhere. But then Madaah began to listen more carefully. Thorold's voice had altered. It became dull and heavy.

'What man can fight the Gods? Tell me what I must do? For all that I am brave and have my fine ship, this summer's raiding has come to nothing. And this for the second year.'

Madaah, amazed, saw that Thorold's eyes were filled with tears. He patted him on the shoulder, although his eyes were full of contempt. Children! 'I will help,' he said. He thought carefully of what to do. The Earth was, certainly, full of spirits, and they could be talked to, but whether they would answer was another matter. He thought of Brin and what the old man had done when working magic. He had danced and sung, but then the whole tribe had been with him, dancing and singing too; many people with one mind. Brin had fasted for days before seeing visions, or he had sat naked by the sea, day after day, before some spirit possessed him, and spoke through him in a strange howling voice. Then he remembered how Brin had a bag of bones, which he rolled on the sand. There had been messages there, for he who knew how to read them. That would do.

He went to the beach and gathered some pebbles, and a gull's feather, then went back to the Norseman. He threw the stones in the air and looked at them carefully. There was no message that he could read. Thorold stood by him, his mouth agape. Madaah closed his eyes and thought hard. He had to say something. Slowly he waved the feather and said in his own language, 'Thorold is a fool, Thorold is a fool, Thorold is a fool.' But as he did so, something strange began to happen. A picture formed slowly in his mind. He saw a boat, a black Norse ship. Thorold was standing at the prow. The ship was sailing to an island and a man in a rough gown with his hair cut queerly was on the beach holding a cross. Thorold leaped from the ship and slashed the man down. The man fell into the waves. Then the picture went.

Madaah shivered. Thorold's heavy face was before him, but it seemed less real than the picture. He looked at Thorold gravely. 'You have done a great wrong,' he said. He raised his hand as Thorold opened his mouth to speak. 'I will not say what the wrong was, that will make it live again.'

Thorold looked frightened. 'Tell me what I must do!'

Madaah had an inspiration. 'You must fast for three days. Give your food to the spirits.'

Thorold nodded reluctantly. That encouraged Madaah.

'Go to the rocks and sacrifice to the god of the sea. Give him—' he thought hard for a moment—'Give him gold!'

Thorold looked depressed, but Madaah went on remorselessly. 'Take your sword and bury it deep in the ground where no one will ever find it.'

The Norseman opened his mouth wide. 'These are great things you ask.'

Madaah nodded coldly. 'But you have done great evil, and you must give to the sea, the earth, and the air.'

The big man sighed deeply and nodded. Madaah added, casually, 'I ask nothing for myself.'

Thorold hesitated, then sighed again. He fumbled in a purse and threw down an object, then stalked away. Madaah picked up the object and gazed at it curiously. It was a little brooch of silver. On it was a carving. The brooch was so worn it was hard to tell quite what the carving was. A man? Yes! He seemed to be hanging from something—a tree was it? His arms were outstretched, Madaah spun it in the air, and it gave a dull wink; curious! Curious too, about the picture in his mind; perhaps the demons of Orkney were in the mist, ready to enter a willing mind and play their evil games there. Beware!

He sauntered down to the beach. Eric looked at him grimly.

'Have you given good counsel, Wizard?'

Madaah smiled. 'Yes. And now Thorold will rid himself of evil and prosper. Eric, where is the great fleet of ships you told me of, and where are the great Halls of the sea-kings? They are not here.'

'Can't you see them with your magic eyes?'

In his turn Madaah was sour. Eric was growing bold. He began to hum tunelessly. As he did so, he pointed the feather at Eric and began to wave it in a circle. The big man cleared his throat and said, hastily, 'The harbour is over there.' He pointed across the dull moors behind them.

'Then why are we here?' Madaah was surprised.

'Because . . . because . . .' Eric's voice faltered and he looked down at his feet. Madaah's eyes narrowed as he realised that Eric was ashamed, and he realised, too, Eric and he himself and all the others were ragged and dirty and worn. And poor. And for the first time he noticed that Eric's hair was streaked with grey.

'We go now,' said Eric.

Madaah had assumed that they would sail to the harbour, but the crew gathered their possessions and struck inland. 'We will sail her around later,' Eric said. He sounded bitter, as if he was sick of the sight of the sea, and the ship.

They climbed over the moor and onto the black peat hags where even the heather would not grow. Once Madaah looked back. A figure was scurrying over the dunes, carrying a sword. He could just make out that it was Thorold, and he laughed delightedly. At first the men were jocular. They strode along and boasted in their braggart way but a mist crawled in from the sea and cowled them, and their voices died away. They came to a rough cairn. Each man flung a stone on it, and then they began to move downhill, squelching through the peat. Then they dropped under the mist and below them was a huge bay, cradled in arms of black rock, and on its shore, fenced from the sea by a long line of ships lay at last Stromness, the great meeting place of the northern raiders.

Madaah was staggered by the sight. He had begun to believe that Stromness would be nothing, a mere village like his own, but this was the biggest thing he had ever seen, bigger than he could have imagined. His heart leapt with excitement. But as they made their way down to the shore, through rough fields, he began to feel frightened, and the nearer the harbour came, the more formidable his companions seemed and the smaller he, himself, seemed to shrink, until as they entered the settlement, he was trotting at Eric's heels like a puppy behind its master.

At first they walked between huts, rough structures of turf and stone slabs, but then they came to a square and Madaah stopped dead, truly amazed. Facing the sea was a hall. To his eyes it was like the work of gods rather than men. It was made of stone, and carved. It was some forty feet long. Outside it was a wooden post, carved with a wreath of some strange plant, and at the bottom was the remains of a man.

Around the square were other, smaller halls, and huts, and even stalls, where men stood, haggling and bargaining. Madaah had never seen so many people, and the sight shocked him, half numbing his mind. Most of the men were like Eric and Thorold, big and raw-boned, but here and there, looking wretched and cowed, were men like Madaah himself. One man he saw had a face such as he had never seen before; triangular and dark, but with a golden gleam under the skin, and with strange eyes, hooded at the corners. The Norsemen stood in the square before the hall. Often men shouted to them, and once someone called drunkenly at Eric. Madaah did not catch the words but Eric's face flushed.

Finally Eric shook his tangled hair and strode to the Hall, Madaah with the others followed him.

The first thing Madaah noticed was the smell. Men and dogs, stale food and sour beer had created it from waste and rot, and Madaah, straight from weeks in an open boat, felt as if a foul blanket had been dragged over his head. He coughed and gulped. His eyes smarted and he rubbed them, leaving a smudge of dirt underneath. When they had cleared, he saw that they were in the centre of the hall, and that from round the walls a score of men were looking at them. There was a mind-splitting noise, but Eric raised his harsh voice.

'I am Eric Ericsonn, of Oseberg. The ravens know my sword. I am one of those whom Olaf led, Olaf the Widow-Maker.'

So far as Madaah could tell, no-one was listening to Eric, but he seemed undaunted and bellowed on: 'They have known me in the land of the Rus, and the Frisians know my name. Now the black ship rests on land, and I am here.'

Eric's persistence was wearing down the noise in the hall. The men were falling silent as, red-faced, he bellowed his own praises, but as silence fell, Eric faltered, as though embarrassed. Then, as his voice died away, another voice spoke from the gloom.

'I see you, Eric Ericsonn. Welcome to this house.'

A man walked from the gloom of the hall. He was smaller than the normal Norseman, but fat, sleek with good living, and finely dressed. Around one thick arm was a bracelet of gold and his belt was held together by a silver snake. The man raised his arm. 'I welcome Eric Ericsonn and his companions. Give them drink!'

There was a cry from the men—was it one of welcome? Or was

there something else behind it—a note of mockery, of malice? Madaah found himself clutching a cup of horn, full of dark, bitter beer. The man poured some of his drink onto the ground. 'Ragnar gives the first drink to Odin, God of Battle,' he cried. 'The second he pledges to Eric the Brave.'

He drank to the sound of a great shout from the watchers. Then Eric raised his cup, 'And I drink to Ragnar the Wise and the Brave, and to his house, and' Eric turned with dignity, 'to all here.'

They drank, and when Madaah looked up from his cup he saw that Ragnar was sitting on a little stool, looking up at them. It seemed to be an act of humility, or was it, Madaah wondered, one of sly contempt, a false prostration, a mockery of manners before the ragged crew?

Ragnar looked up at Eric and smiled. 'You have had good raiding?'

The Hall was silent and again Madaah felt something cruel in the air, as if the men in the hall waited with pleasure for an admission of failure.

'It has been a hard season,' Eric said.

'You are modest, Eric. Surely you have brought me gold and silver and slaves, as you and Olaf promised when you took my fine ship in the Spring.'

Eric spread his arms wide, then let them drop wearily.

'No, Ragnar. The gods were not with us. A gale caught us a week out, and we were on the ocean for many days. We lost men in Ireland when the soldiers caught us on the beach. The slaves died. Olaf is dead. It has been a hard time for us.'

Ragnar was still smiling. 'Ah, Eric, you are joking with me!'

'No!'

'But you must be, or how else will you pay me?'

'With our swords.'

Ragnar laughed out loud, and the men in the hall laughed with him. 'But I cannot eat swords, Eric. And as you see,' he waved his hand 'I have many swords already.' He drank deeply from his cup. Each man followed his example.

'Well?'

Eric shrugged, 'The ship—' he began.

'The ship is mine,' Ragnar said. He rose and went to the back of the hall. There was a platform and on it was a big wooden chair. He snapped his fingers, and a servant ran to him and filled his cup. Then he settled in the chair. Now he was looking down instead of up. The game was over. The Sea-King was on his throne and judgement was to be given. 'Well?'

Eric rubbed his face and looked around. The men were leaning forward eagerly, their faces alight with cruel humour. 'Well?'

Eric straightened suddenly and strode forward. 'We have a great thing for you, Ragnar.'

'Ah! I knew it! I knew the great Eric would not come to my Hall with empty hands. Tell me—' Ragnar leaned forward confidentially. His voice was warm. '—Tell me what this great thing is.'

'A Wizard!' There was a stunned silence as Eric roared the word. 'A Wizard from the Western Isles. Here!' Eric seized Madaah and threw him before the platform. 'Take him, Ragnar. He is one of the old people who know the mysteries of this world. He changed the wind with his song. I saw it. Then Olaf struck him, and Olaf died, that night. Is it not true?' Eric turned to the crew.

There was a burst of excited noise in the Hall, then Ragnar raised his hand and the noise died away. Madaah stood before the platform looking up at Ragnar. He felt very small and solitary. Ragnar leaned forward in his chair and spoke softly. 'Are you a Wizard, boy?'

From the Hall Eric's harsh voice bellowed something, and Ragnar smiled, a patient tired smile. 'The boy, the boy, this great wonder, let him speak for himself.' He stared at Madaah, and again the smile crept across his face. 'Tell us, boy.'

Madaah avoided Ragnar's eye. Being a Wizard with Eric and Thorold was one thing, being one here, in the great Hall, before the patiently smiling Ragnar, was quite another. He looked at his feet. 'Yes,' he whispered.

Ragnar cupped his hand to his ear, 'Eh?'

There was a ripple of laughter round the hall, like the first patter of rain before a storm.

'Yes.' Madaah forced his voice up a little.

Ragnar leaned back and drank again. 'Yes,' he announced. 'The answer is yes.' Again there was the ripple of laughter round the Hall. Madaah had never before realised how unpleasant laughter could sound.

'And did you kill Olaf? Did you witch him to death?'

'He struck me.'

'Ah, yes, Olaf was always violent.' Ragnar nodded. 'So Olaf struck you and you took away his life—my servant, Olaf's?'

'The Gods took away his life,' Madaah said. His voice had a little tremor in it, now.

Ragnar stood up abruptly. 'Well, Wizard, we shall see.' He moved to the edge of the dais and beckoned Madaah forward. Madaah caught a whiff of beer, and he noticed that Ragnar's eyes were vague and unfocused. He realised then that Ragnar was drunk. He realised too, that Ragnar was standing sideways on, and that his arm was outstretched behind him, and that there was something odd about the arm. Involuntarily he craned his head forward, and then he saw that Ragnar was holding a club.

'Now, Wizard!' said Ragnar.

Madaah's head shrank between his shoulders, and a patch on top of his head began to itch. He wanted to run away but his legs would not move. Then, as Ragnar threw back his arm, a wave of alarm spread round the Hall, and the Norsemen, instinctively, moved back. The sudden movement made Ragnar hesitate fractionally, and in that second's hesitation, a great voice boomed down the Hall.

'Ragnar! Don't strike!' Thorold staggered down the Hall. He stood beside Madaah. 'The boy sees all—past, present, and what is to come. He talks to the wind—I know.' He grabbed Madaah and shoved him forward. 'Touch him at your peril!' he bellowed.

Ragnar looked baffled. He stared groggily at Thorold. 'What do you know of this?'

'Yesterday, on the beach, the boy read the stones for me. He threw the stones and the wind blew through them and spoke. He told me all—all! Where I had been and what I had done. The wind told him and he told me. Beware!' Thorold ended with a loud hiccough.

Madaah looked at Thorold astounded. Surely, he thought, Thorold told me this first. He found it hard to remember. The Hall was echoing with noise. Men were shouting and beginning to jostle each other. Thorold jumped on a bench and began bellowing of the incredible things Madaah had told him; of how he had seen Thorold's brother fall, fighting Frisians, and how to cure his mother, sick in Oseberg of a Finnish spell, and how he had lifted the curse some evil-wisher had placed on him, Thorold.

'And I,' he cried, 'I, Thorold, place my sword between the

26

wizard and any man.' He gave a huge drunken whoop and shook
his fists in the air. Then, from the gloom, a stool smashed into

his chest and he crashed from the bench. Eric screamed suddenly,
picked up the bench and heaved it down the Hall. A man,
bleeding from the head, fell against the platform, where Ragnar,

seemingly overcome by events, had slumped into his chair and was mumbling incoherently.

A general fight broke out in the Hall and in the bedlam of noise, among men's curses and roars of rage, and the yelping of dogs, Madaah decided that the wisest thing to do was to go; and he slid, like a fox, through the crowd, and through the gates of Ragnar's Hall.

Chapter 4

Several weeks had passed and the Northern winter had wrapped Orkney in its dark mantle. Snow fell rarely, and there was little frost, but the wind screamed across the island, day and night, and from the shore came the never-ending boom of the waves.

The hardiest Norseman had left his tent. The huts of the settlement were full, and Ragnar's Hall was never empty. During the long nights the men sprawled on the benches, talking, laughing, boasting, watched from the dais by Ragnar, while always, by his side, sat Madaah.

After the riot in the Hall, Madaah had run back to the ship. Eric had found him there and returned him to Ragnar. Madaah had returned, though, in triumph. Thorold's strange story, and Eric's tale, had created about him a halo of wonder, and every man on the island was firmly convinced that Madaah had made himself invisible, that day. Now he lived at ease, and men cast down their eyes when he walked by.

Whether Ragnar believed in Madaah was another matter. As much as any other man on the isle he believed in the supernatural, and the Gods were living realities for him, but Madaah knew there was a cynical reserve in Ragnar's manner towards him. But Madaah had power over the minds of the men, and through him Ragnar could wield his own power more effectively. It was an arrangement that suited them both, and by tacit consent neither pressed the other too hard; Ragnar never demanding spectacular feats of magic, Madaah always prompt to buttress Ragnar's opinions.

Madaah grew to like the life in Ragnar's Hall. He learned to say little and to make that little sound much, and he learned to listen and to watch, and to learn from both.

Ragnar was rich because he was clever; Eric was poor because he was dull. So then, he Madaah, would be clever. Thorold was a great fool. He told lies and believed in them. Better to tell lies and not believe them. Eric sat by the door in a cold corner and gnawed on a bone like a dog, while Madaah, young as he was, weak as he was, sat on a carved chair by the fire and ate the freshest fish and the finest meat.

The men he looked down on were a strange people. No men on earth could sail the seas as they did, and the ocean was their element and home as much as a seal's, and yet land was what they desired above all. Any man who had cleared an acre or two of Orkney's desolate moor was as proud as Ragnar, with his great Hall and his slaves and ten fine ships. The Norsemen were generous too. No man starved that winter, although few ate well, and any man could walk into the Hall and take a salt fish from the lines strung across the roof.

Madaah looked and listened. He heard of the Norse gods; the great Odin and the mighty Thor, gentle Baldir and cunning Loki, and of the dead heroes who feasted in Odin's hall, Valhalla, as the Norsemen feasted on Orkney, and who would, at the ending of all things, fight a last fight against the monsters, the enemies of all men—and of all gods.

Madaah thought much of these things. At times he would wander away along the coast and hear, in the crying of the gulls, the voices of his ancestors, as if they were calling to him not to forget them and their gentle ways. But he felt in the power of the waves, as they smashed against the rocks, the power of these new gods—the gods of iron sword and iron hammer.

Madaah began to learn of the world beyond the seas: of Norway itself, bleak and hard, with its landless men, like Eric, pushing out to plunder the rich lands of Ireland and England; of the Swedes, strong under their King, driving down the endless plains of the Rus, harrying its cities along the mighty rivers; and of the teeming lands of Europe and of softer, warmer countries, as yet beyond the reach of the sea-wolves from the North.

Events broke the monotony of the winter. Weland, a freeman with land of his own killed a thrall in a fit of drunken rage. In itself that was nothing; what was the life of a slave? But the thrall's owner, Hakon, a ship-owner, demanded payment. Weland contemptuously refused and a feud broke out. For a time the whole community was divided; then Ragnar called a gathering of all the freemen to judge the case. Weland was called upon to pay. Still he refused and, casting his sword before Hakon, called, ' Make me pay.'

It was a challenge Hakon could not ignore. He nodded grimly. 'Pay you shall.'

The two men met before the Hall, Hakon the ship-owner, dressed finely in a white tunic and a coat of mail and a helmet of leather and iron; Weland, the peasant, in a rough sleeveless coat, his fair hair tied back by a circle of leather. But for all his coat of mail, for all his elegance and wealth, it was Hakon who fell in the dust, crushed beneath the brute power of the peasant. It was a memory, and a lesson. As Weland walked away, his dark sword darker now with blood, Madaah realised that power came from inside a man, from his confidence in himself, and that the trappings of wealth meant nothing unless the wearer was worthy of them.

Before the fight Hakon had called for a fire burial, if the Gods wished his death, and that he was given. His body was placed on his ship, his sword and his shield, his drinking cup of horn, the plunder of his years. His dogs were killed and thrown at his feet, and each man on the island threw a burning brand on board. The ship was unmoored, drifted idly on the tide, and, burning, fell into the sea-mist. It was a good farewell, Madaah thought. He who had lived by fire and iron had been consumed by it, and now his spirit rose with the flames and smoke who knew where? To Valhalla? Maybe; but wherever Hakon had gone, Weland was on his fields, hacking at the stubborn turf, alive.

The days began to grow longer. There was work on the land for those who wanted it, but the men began to turn to the sea again, and the talk in the Hall changed from boasts of things done, to boasts of what was to come. They began to form groups, each, perhaps, the nucleus of a crew, and those who owned their own ships were flattered and courted by those who did not. Then, in the early spring, in the teeth of a gale, a ship, the first of the year, fought its way into the harbour.

The arrival of the ship gave rise to a drunken feast which went on for days, and Madaah spent much of his time away from the Hall. Then, one day, he sauntered in to find the drinking over, and Ragnar sitting in his carved chair surrounded by a circle of grave men. Madaah lounged against the wall but Ragnar called him forward. He walked forward and sat on a stool at Ragnar's right hand. On his right were Ragnar's men, and those other ship-owners who loosely followed Ragnar's leadership; across from them were the newcomers. Madaah knew them, at least by sight. Their leader was Harald Stavanger, thin for a Norseman, with a scarred face from which blue eyes shone coldly. Stavanger was a man of power in Norway. From a base in a deep fjord he had built up wealth by attacking the trade route that ran up the coast to the North, and in the loose confederacy of tribes that was starting, as the Swedes had done in the past, to feel itself one people, he was beginning to make his mark.

'Now Madaah,' Ragnar said, 'give us wise words'.

'Do you listen to a stripling?' Harald's voice was contemptuous, sharp with the arrogance of power.

Ragnar shrugged his fat shoulders. 'In my Hall I listen to whom I wish. Madaah is one who sees beyond the world; I know his magic. With these eyes I have seen it.' He turned to Madaah. 'Harald is a great warrior. In Norway he has much land and many followers. He is a man to listen to, but his ideas are strange to me. Listen, and tell us what you see.'

In his turn, Harald shrugged, 'As you wish. Ragnar has a great Hall and many ships, but a boy is master.' There was an appreciative gurgle of laughter from Harald's men.

Madaah looked cooly across at them. 'A ship is a great thing, too, but a little tiller guides it.'

Ragnar gave a hearty laugh. 'Just so!' His laugh was echoed by his men.

Harald reddened. 'A man guides the tiller.'

'And the Gods guide me,' Madaah blithely answered.

The effrontery of this remark quelled Harald, and Ragnar waved his hand in a conciliatory way. 'Enough of this. We are here to listen to wise words, from all who speak. Tell us your idea again, Harald.'

Harald looked sour but nodded assent. 'So be it! Last summer many ships from Orkney and from Norway roamed the seas. Few came back rich. It has been a bad winter for us poor Norsemen.' Madaah agreed. Harold did not look poor, but it was true for most.

Harald continued. 'Where the land is weak, it is poor; where it is rich, it is strong.'

Again Madaah agreed. He had seen it himself with Eric and Olaf.

'Let us go together then,' said Harald. 'Fifty ships, a thousand men striking as one, who could withstand us?'

Madaah looked at Harald with respect.

'The lands to the south are full of wealth. The temples are rich. Gold and silver lie there like rushes on the floor of this Hall. Every man would come back an Earl.'

Those who did come back, Madaah thought, but kept silent.

Ragnar rubbed his fat cheek. 'So many ships, so many men, where will they come from?'

'There are many ships, and Norway is full of men.'

'Men and rocks, yes, that is Norway,' Ragnar said. 'But who will rule so great a number, so many ships, so many men?'

Harald spat. 'Who rules the gulls on a dead whale? No one, yet all eat their fill. So will it be with us. Our interest will be the same, so all will do what is required. True, little wizard?'

Madaah did not like the sneer in Harald's voice, but what he said made sense.

'Harald Stavanger speaks well,' he said ambiguously, 'but where there is disagreement, let him who has the most ships decide.'

Ragnar beamed with delight. 'Good, good.' He smacked his knee. 'The wizard says the thoughts that are in my head,' he confided. 'I have ten ships. How many ships will the great Harald bring?'

'Five!' Harald glanced sourly at Madaah who smiled sweetly and waved his hand airily.

'The spirits!' he said.

Stavanger nodded. 'It seems the spirits can count—but I accept. Do we go?'

Ragnar nodded back, 'It is not a small thing of which we speak, but yes—we go.'

Chapter 5

Spring came late that year. March and April were a time of freezing fogs when land and sea were wrapped in a grey shroud, and the flat cries of the sea-birds came eerily from the mist. But the men worked on their ships every day and the beach was full of the sound of the thudding of their hammers.

It was a time for superstitious fears, and more than one crew, seeing evil omens in everything, withdrew from the idea of the great raid. Ragnar needed all his cunning, and Madaah all his prestige, to keep the spirits of the others lively.

In May the mists went, blown away by gales which carved enormous waves from the sea, and, day after day, the beach trembled as the water pounded it, and men's ears grew tired of the endless scream of the wind and the grating roar of the shingle. Harald, eager for the great raid, said that though the year was a month late, the autumn would be kind and they would have easy sailing back. Ragnar counted the lines of stock-fish in the Hall and wondered whether to start rationing. But Madaah, often now alone on the platform of the Hall, heard in the noise of the storm the clash of weapons, and the cries of men in battle.

Once, the gale lulled, and a crew who had withdrawn from the raid, set out for Norway against Ragnar's advice and Madaah's grave warning of disaster. The whole island watched them go, and Madaah felt amongst the men a great longing to follow them and leave the bleak land. The raid was in danger then, but the wind blew again, stronger than before, and after a day or so, the wreckage of the ship was washed back. Ragnar and Harald were triumphant, and Madaah knew that his place was more secure than ever.

On the dais a long discussion took place through the stormy months. Ragnar wanted to raid Ireland, that soft, fertile land to the South-West where there was land for the taking, and men

34

might plough all day, and never find a stone or a snake. Harald, too, wanted a quick raid, but he was not simply greedy. He looked to the future. This year a big raid as an experiment, to blood the men and the ships and test the organisation, to get wealth, but wealth to be used, next year, for an invasion. But not of Ireland.

'Times are changing,' he said. 'There are greater men in Norway than we, and they, too, think of Ireland. Better that we go elsewhere.'

Ragnar was angry at this. 'Let them go elsewhere! The land is for any man's picking, and the ocean belongs to no-one. I sail where I will.'

'It is not so. There are those in Norway who could crush us like beetles if they willed. You have been away too long. Let us go to England instead. There are temples there richer than those of Ireland, and they are on the coast, unguarded. It is a deeper land than Ireland. I have spoken to men who have been there. The kingdoms are falling apart, each Earl's hand is raised against the others. There could be kingdoms there for us, if we are bold. And there will be no-one in Norway to say no.'

Ragnar stared moodily at the fire. 'What do I know of great men in Norway?' he demanded.

'Nothing maybe, but they know of you.'

'And what do I know of England?'

'What I have told you. And it is on good report. My word on it.'

'I will think on it, and take counsel.'

'Very well,' Harald rose with his men. 'Listen to the words of your wizard.' He eyed Madaah harshly. 'See the truth, boy.'

When they had left, Ragnar faced his men. 'The world is becoming full of new things,' he grunted. 'First the Great Raid, now England. This Harald disturbs me. Now, let every man give counsel.'

'England or Ireland, what matter if the prize is good?' The speaker was a man called Thorgil. 'But if what Harald says is true—if there are those in Norway who would be angry if we go to Ireland—then let us take England.'

Ragnar's face set hard, 'No man tells me where I may go.'

'It is not that,' Thorgill said. 'The hawk is as brave as the eagle, but when the eagle comes, the hawk flies away. Why fight our own folk? And there are those of us with families in

Norway. What will become of them if we make enemies of those who live there? I will follow you, Ragnar. Where you go, I will go, but I say England. Those are my words.'

Wise words too, thought Madaah. Not all men were content, as Ragnar was, to live for ever on Orkney. He was not himself. What he had heard during the winter of the lands of the world had wetted his curiosity. His horizon had widened, and if going to Ireland meant narrowing them again, he, too, was for England. Man after man rose and spoke; some for Harald, some for Ragnar. As they spoke, Madaah considered them carefully. Those for the Irish raid were like Thorold, bold, dangerous, proud, but not necessarily the wisest men on the island, whereas those who wanted to go to England were men, he thought, worthy of respect. As valiant as any, they had that hard common sense he noticed amongst many of the Norsemen. A feeling for practicality that came from their burdensome life of toil, whether on their stony fields, or on the harsh sea.

The last man had spoken. Now Ragnar turned to Madaah. 'We have heard the words of men. Now let us hear the words of the spirits.'

Madaah's face was impassive. 'I see two things. Two things, Ragnar.'

Ragnar leaned forward eagerly. His fat face was creased with curiosity. 'Two things are better than one,' he cried, 'unless both are bad!'

Madaah chose his words with care. Much depended on his answer. His alliance with Ragnar was a delicate balance of interest, each using the other and each aware of it. Now, for the first time, their interests were opposed, and Ragnar was dangerous when that happened. His ten ships had not sailed to him as a gift from the ocean. 'I see Ragnar in his Hall,' he said. 'He has twenty—thirty ships. His arms are rich with Irish gold, he has so many slaves the dogs grow fat on them!' Ragnar chuckled and rubbed his hands together. Tell men what they wish to hear, thought Madaah, and you would never displease them. 'And then I see another thing,' he let his voice fall away and made his eyes grow vacant.

'What, what is this?' Ragnar was urgent.

Madaah waited, let minutes slide by, then raised his hands. 'I see Ragnar in a Hall. A greater one than this. He sits in a chair with twelve men to serve him. He speaks, and tens of hundreds run to do his bidding. He drinks from a cup of silver and on his head he wears a hat of gold. Those are the two things I see.'

'A golden hat; what can that mean?' someone asked.

'It is a crown!' Ragnar rose triumphantly. 'And only kings wear crowns. The Wizard has seen a great thing. What did Harald say? We could be kings in England! I bless the mother who bore me that I should know this day. Bring drink, drink for a king!'

The thralls ran to the dais with cups of horn, and the men drank. Madaah joined the toasts but he smiled secretly into his beer. King or no king, he drank to England.

Within a month they went. Fair winds blew, ships made the fast voyage to Norway, and came back with more ships, and more men, until one morning all was ready, and at dawn the fleet rowed from the still harbour, caught the wind, and like a black and poisoned arrow, headed south.

Chapter 6

As the ships pulled out of the bay and met the long ocean rollers, Madaah's heart leaped with excitement. He sat in the serpent prow of Ragnar's great ship, his sword across his knees, and stared, all day, at the mysterious South. He did not look back at Orkney. Somewhere ahead was a new land, new men, new ways of living, and, he guessed, new knowledge, although what that might be, he had no way of telling.

The fleet sailed on through a night made brilliant with stars, and when morning came, they saw to the South-West, and far away, a long line of snow-capped hills, glittering, pure, and remote. The ships behaved as Harald had prophesied. Like a migratory flock of birds they wheeled across the ocean, always changing places but remaining the same body. They sailed in closer to the land which lay to the west. Now and then, attracted by the glimpse of a few huts along the shore, a ship would swoop in, like a gull to a piece of offal. Once, a small boat appeared from behind a headland, near enough for Madaah to see its crew frantically try to gain the land when they saw the Norse host. They were snapped up by a ship and the three men on her taken prisoner. Ragnar and his men laughed heartily at their puny efforts, and so, too, did Madaah.

As evening drew in, Ragnar hoisted a long white banner, the signal for a landing, and made for shore. The fleet moved in with him, and they spent the night camped in a long sandy bay. Before a huge fire Ragnar spoke to the Norsemen. It was a scene that stayed in Madaah's memory: the crackling fire, the graceful silhouettes of the ships against the evening sky, the pressed crowd of men, shoulder to shoulder, listening intently to Ragnar while the sea whispered against the shore.

'The sheep are waiting,' Ragnar cried. 'But it is not the shepherd who comes!' There was a roar of laughter. 'From now, no ship leaves the fleet. These English do not know that guests are coming. Let it be a pleasant surprise.' The men laughed again, Madaah with them. It was a good joke! Ragnar stood by the fire, a look of hearty enjoyment on his face. He waved his hand for silence. 'Tomorrow we sail east, away from land. We will ride out the night at sea. Then, the next morning we will come in at dawn, out of the rising sun. Let no man be late for the feast!'

There was a shout of applause at this. A voice called from the crowd. 'I have heard they have a strange god in this England. Once a year they eat him.'

Harald stepped forward into the firelight. He leaned on his battle-axe. 'I have heard this too. These English feast on gods. Soon our dogs will feast on them. They will find out Odin's power.' He shook his axe high. 'And they will find out the power of Thor!' The men whooped wildly at Thor's name. Then Harald lowered his axe. 'Let every man sleep well!'

The speechmaking was over, and the men huddled on the ground around the fire. Madaah was long in sleeping. He looked at the clear stars above and thought of the coming days. It was a good plan, he thought, very like the Norsemen. Simple and direct, easy to understand, but cunning too. Finally he fell asleep and dreamed of woolly black magicians running blindly, this way and that, while he rampaged among them, bloodied to the thighs.

He woke, shivering, at dawn. A sea mist covered the shore and a light drizzle was falling. The Norsemen seemed subdued after their high spirits of the previous evening, but before the light had lengthened, they were away at sea, and Madaah sensed the power that flowed from their direct mindlessness.

There was no wind and the men took to the oars. The slow creeping of the boat was irksome, but a wind came off the land, a light air which filled the sails, black, or striped black and white, which dotted the ocean. At noon the three prisoners were dragged forward and lashed to the prow. While Ragnar leaned over them with a knife, Madaah stood high by the serpent's head and called a prayer. 'Oh Odin,' he cried, 'Take these lives as a gift and give us victory. Oh Thor, hear us call on you and give us strength. Oh Loki, give us cunning that we may deceive our enemies. Let those who die feast in Valhalla, and give riches and power to those who live.'

39

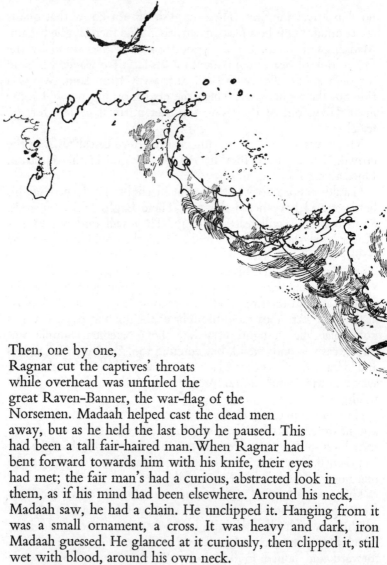

Then, one by one,
Ragnar cut the captives' throats
while overhead was unfurled the
great Raven-Banner, the war-flag of the
Norsemen. Madaah helped cast the dead men
away, but as he held the last body he paused. This
had been a tall fair-haired man. When Ragnar had
bent forward towards him with his knife, their eyes
had met; the fair man's had a curious, abstracted look in
them, as if his mind had been elsewhere. Around his neck,
Madaah saw, he had a chain. He unclipped it. Hanging from it
was a small ornament, a cross. It was heavy and dark, iron
Madaah guessed. He glanced at it curiously, then clipped it, still
wet with blood, around his own neck.

It occurred to him then that his own rewards for being a
Wizard were not very great, and he breathed a prayer in his own,
old, tongue that his prizes might be greater, before he helped
tumble the body overboard.

Towards evening Ragnar altered course a little towards the
South. The wind was shifting to the East and the men exulted.

'A good wind for the land, Wizard,' they cried. 'A fair wind for tomorrow.'

'The gods fill our sails,' Madaah shouted back, and half believed in what he said.

Bare-masted, the ships faced the wind which blew steadily during the night. Madaah lay on a bench, wrapped in a cloak, and saw racks of cloud blotting out the stars. He dozed at intervals, and when he was awake, he felt the sea moving in a long sickening surge. As the night wore on, the wind blew stronger and spats of foam began to slop over the ship's side. All the men were awake and Madaah saw Ragnar at the helm, and felt the first pricking of fear. The crew were fighting to get their oars out and the ship was a wild confusion of cursing men and long unwieldy poles.

41

Madaah stood up, and gobs of salt spray lashed across his lips. The sea was churning in vast tormented waves. He saw a ship, seemingly high in the sky, a black shape riding overhead, then it fell away as his own ship rose on a huge white crest. The oars were out now, and Madaah knew well enough what was happening. The wind, blasting from the East, was driving the ship due West, to the shore, and, in that gale, to disaster. The Norsemen's only hope lay in keeping the ship's head to the wind, and the only way to do that was to drive her forward faster than the wind blew her back. It was a hard task. The wild seas made it impossible to keep any rhythm in the rowing. Sometimes the oars snatched at water, sometimes at the empty air as the ship veered wildly. But somehow the men did it. Even in the fearful darkness Madaah admired their hardihood and endurance.

Ragnar, with five men was at the helm. He beckoned urgently to Madaah who strained forward to hear him. He caught a few broken words, 'Storm!—land!—sea!', understood and scrambled forward to the prow. The ship tilted, and he fell sideways into a jumble of men and oars and weapons. He was cursed and struck, but fought his way clear and clung to the prow. Above him the serpent's head carved in it shuddered and trembled as the sea struck them. 'Father of the Sea!' he called, but his words were whipped away by the wind which slashed at him as hard and cold as a sword. Drenched and blinded he clung to the serpent, and then he had a strange thought. It occurred to him that out there, on the dark coast of England, other men might be praying to their Gods for his destruction—and that their Gods might be listening.

A sickly glimmer shone on the surface of the sea, and though the ship still shook as the waves hammered her, the steady howl of the wind died a little. The waves were still enormous, vast and inevitable, but they were smooth now, and, although the ship looked tiny among them, the men at the oars were keeping a steadier rhythm, enough to keep the ship moving and to give the men at the helm a chance to keep the prow into the wind. Apart from themselves the sea was empty.

The false dawn glimmered and died. Darkness came again, and with it the wind returned. This time it came in gusts, smashing at the monstrous waves which broke now as they raised their crests. The oarsmen were becoming exhausted, and the ship began to swing crazily at each battering blast. There were six men at the tiller, but the ship, usually so gracefully obedient, was fighting them like a wild animal. Time and again she swung round, parallel to the waves, and began a long sideways slide to destruction, but each time the crew drove her forward a little, and the helmsmen brought her back. The intervals between the gusts became fewer. The Raven-Banner, streaming against the sky, cracked into shreds. The mast began to whip round in a circle. Then Ragnar went. One moment he was at the helm looking, for all his fatness, strangely heroic, and then a wave like a waterfall smashed into the boat, and when the ship rose again he was gone. Madaah, who was numbed by the cold and dazed by the hammering of the gale, gave a futile cry, inaudible even to himself, but another man scrabbled forward and flung himself on the slender piece of wood and the ship was brought back into the wind, inch by inch. Then, as she rose again, one of the men at the helm waved his arm in a gesture, part warning, part defiance, part despair. Madaah felt the ship halt dead and shudder. Above even the gale he heard the scream of timbers, and then the sky tilted as the ship heaved over, and the snake's head of the prow, black and twisted, smashed down on them. As the waves took them, he saw Ragnar's great ship, its back broken, go beneath a wave, locked in a last embrace with the serpent.

For a few seconds the force of the waves kept him afloat. A shape dragged against him, and he grabbed despairingly but the drowning man jerked away. Then he slammed against a balk of wood. He grabbed again, tearing his hands, but he held on like a wolf. The waves pounded him but he hung on. Only death could have loosened his hold and he had a vitality of spirit, a stubborn adherence to life, which kept death away, always on the next wave.

The wind drove him to shore. As the waves broke on the shingle, they took Madaah with him and cast him, casually and at last, on the coast of Northumbria—and then it was darkness for him.

Towards noon the gale died away, and small groups of men began to come out of the woods that fringed the shore. They carried clubs and sickles, rarely a sword, although one or two might have a spear. They moved up the beaches and through the rocks, looking among the litter of timber for men, who might, somehow, have survived the storm. When they found one, exhausted and barely conscious, they surrounded him cautiously, silently, pricking him with a spear, or slicing with their sickles, until they could rush without fear and club him to death. But they did not find many, and that day they did not find Madaah.

He awoke the next morning. Only the heavy swell beating at the shore reminded him of the gale. He stared at the sea for a time, in a dazed way, and then he was sick, a long heaving surge of nausea. His head ached and his hands and face and knees were raw where the shingle had skinned him. Flies buzzed around him and he waved them away, then grunted with pain. His ribs hurt. Under his tunic were great discoloured patches of blue and green. He looked stiffly round. He was in a small cove enclosed by steep sandy cliffs. A stream trickled through it and Madaah went and drank, mouthful after mouthful.

For a while he sat, vacant and confused, and then clambered out of the cove. He found himself on a spur of land. Below him, and to his right, was another small bay. A group of men were standing there in a circle, gazing intently down. Quite instinctively he opened his mouth to call to them, but then he caught the sound of a shout of laughter, and one of the men jumped back suddenly, as if he had just realised that he was standing on something unpleasant. It was quite funny, and Madaah grinned in a vacuous sort of way. He sank on the turf and lay with his head in his hands, looking down curiously. Something seemed to jerk out of the circle of men who quickly surrounded it again, still laughing. First one, then another, struck at whatever it was down there, with quick, careful jabs. They reminded Madaah of gulls pecking at a crippled crab, caught out of its element. Then the thing twitched clear of the circle. He caught a flash of red hair, and as it turned over in agony, he recognised the body of Eric.

His stomach heaved again and he felt sour bile rise into his throat. He gave a sob in which anger and fear were mixed. The bile spewed onto his chin, then he rose and fled.

Like an animal he ran instinctively for cover. Inland was the dark fringe of a wood, and he slipped under its mantle like a fox, and like a fox he ran until he could run no longer. Then, against the bole of a great tree, he turned at bay. There was no sound of men. He crouched in the gloom and listened; no cries, no calls, no baying of dogs. Madaah lay for hours, waiting, but there was still no sound of humans. But as the night crept in, the wood seemed to wake and begin speaking, as if to itself. A wind blew and the huge limbs of the trees creaked slowly, and their branches tapped and clattered. Above them, the canopy of young leaves whispered and rustled in the darkness. Things called through the night. There were sudden sharp screams, howls and whoops, and, from far away, long wavering calls like the keening of the dead. Madaah had never seen a wood before, had hardly seen a tree, only dwarfed stunted things on his stormy islands. He was afraid of the huge shapes around him, afraid of their mysterious movements, fearful of the cries and of the rank, rotten smells the wood gave forth, as though it were an animal breathing. He was unable to separate the noises, to differentiate the harmful from the harmless. At each sound his body jerked in a helpless nervous spasm, but at last he slept, to dream of ships manned by dead men towering above him, sailing across endless black seas.

The forest was silent when he woke. It was just before dawn. He was feverish and trembling, hardly aware of where he was. He rose and stumbled through the trees. All day he wandered. The forest floor was thick with fallen timber, rotting slowly into other long dead trees, and covered with a dense layer of fallen leaves, feet thick. He fell between the logs, scraping his legs raw, and walked blindly into tangled masses of bramble and briar. He had hallucinations and thought that Ragnar was with him, and he shouted loudly, in the Norse way, of what they would do to the English. Sometimes he had fits of laughter, and then he would find himself weeping. He found himself, once, gnawing on a branch, his mouth full of rotten bark, and was sick again. The forest was full of flies. They buzzed around his head in a black cluster until he tired of brushing them away, and all day birds sang in the leafy canopy, and a cuckoo cried maddeningly, cuckoo, cuckoo, cuckoo, cuckoo. Then, as dusk was falling, he came out of the forest, and saw a fire glowing in the twilight.

PART TWO

Chapter 7

Madaah stared at the fire for a long time as if hypnotised by its light, and then, involuntarily, he moved towards it. As he moved near, a dog barked and a voice cried out in alarm. The dark shapes of men leaped from the greater darkness of the night. Madaah lurched forward and dropped to his knees. He opened his mouth to speak but some last warning nerve tingled inside him and he closed it again. Then the fire shrank to a tiny spark and he fell towards it, onto his face.

When he had collapsed a man's voice spoke, ugly with hatred. 'A pirate pup! God has delivered him to us.'

Other voices answered.

'Tie a rock round his neck and drown him.'

'Peg him on the shore for the tide.'

'Burn him on the fire.'

There was a growl of agreement, broken by one voice. 'Is he Norse? He does not look like one.'

A fierce yelp cut him off. 'Look at those clothes! A pirate from head to toe.'

'Wait, listen!'

Madaah had moved and in his delirium he called for his father, and he called in his father's tongue.

'That is not the language of the raiders!' Then, 'Look!'

As Madaah turned, the cross on his neck which he had taken from the prisoner caught the firelight.

'Look, he is one of us, a Christian soul. Place him by the fire.'

Madaah was lifted and placed on a warm fleece and covered. 'A Christian,' the voice said. 'Maybe taken as a slave. Pray God he lives!'

The men sat gravely around and looked with some awe at the figure which had escaped the sea and the crueller Norsemen, while Madaah's cross, as he moved restlessly in his fever, winked ironically in the light of the flames.

A cock crowing woke Madaah. He found himself gazing at a thatch of corn-stalks. He slowly turned his head and saw a woman sitting in a corner. She bobbed her head a little and spoke, hesitantly, but what she said was meaningless to Madaah. He stared at her coldly and she rose and left the room. Madaah looked about him. He was in a hut, a poor place, he thought contemptuously, a slave's den. And the woman was like a slave too, with her sickly friendly smile and her nervous uncertainty.

He heard the woman call outside, and then she returned, ducking under the low door. The little room filled with people—women, old men, children. They were poorly dressed in tunics and dresses of undyed wool. They grinned at Madaah who stared back at them coldly. A woman brought him milk in a clay bowl and he took it and drank. As he did so, there was a little ripple of talk, like wondrous applause, but as he drank, he looked at them with care over the rim of the bowl. It was strangely reminiscent of something, some other experience, but what it was he could not remember.

When he had drunk an old man came forward. 'Wulfred,' he said, and pointed to himself with a dirty finger. 'Wulfred!' Madaah remained expressionless, and when the old man tried again, he closed his eyes and the woman ushered the crowd out. Madaah spent most of the day sleeping. He woke only to drink more milk, and to eat a soft, heavy cheese the woman brought. Each time he woke there was a face at the door, always grinning and nodding. He slept on through the night, and when he woke again, his head was clear and he felt strong, although his body was tender and painful. He lay on the rough bed and thought carefully. Why had he not been slaughtered, he wondered. It seemed to him that Harald had been right, these English were soft and foolish; but he was alone, and they were many, so he would be ready to strike if need be. Until then he would be still and silent like a snake. Cunning would be his weapon, Loki his guide, not Thor.

The milk-woman came in again and this time Madaah smiled at her and half rose. She clapped her hands in delight and her mouth opened in a wide grin, revealing a few blackened stumps of teeth. She ran out and Madaah heard her hoarse call. When she returned, she had more milk and cheese and a chunk of dark, coarse bread, and behind her was a man.

Madaah stiffened instantly. The man was better dressed than anyone he had seen so far; he was big, burly, and he had a sword. It was, Madaah noted malevolently, a Norse sword. The man spoke, slowly and carefully, but Madaah shook his head. The man gave an embarrassed smile, shrugged, and waved encouragingly. Madaah understood the gesture. He threw off the sheepskin which covered him and got up stiffly. He followed the man out of the hut. What seemed to be the whole village was gathered in a muddy space surrounded by miserable hovels. The man shouldered his way through the people and led Madaah to a bony and decrepit horse. Madaah knew what it was. He had never seen one before but he had heard tell of them, and seen carvings of them, and on Orkney, Ragnar had bemoaned not having one to sacrifice and eat at the feast of Midwinter.

He was obviously intended to climb on it and he did so with some assistance. The man took the rope bridle and the crowd drew back a little. The horse was docile beneath him and its head hung down, but Madaah, high on the animal, and looking down on the people, felt a sudden surge of pride and authority, and understood why the villagers had stepped back. The old man, Wulfred, stepped forward and began to speak in a high quavering voice, but Madaah kicked the horse into motion and shouted harshly. In an instinctive reflex to authority the man at the bridle moved forward too. The old man stumbled backwards and the villagers made way. They moved through the dirty square to a path which led out to the fields. There Madaah glanced over his shoulder. The last of the village he saw was a ring of faces, servile, obedient and kind. He spat at them.

Madaah and his guide and the old horse plodded along a rough path that jumped nervously from squalid village to squalid village, clearing to clearing. Once, through the trees, they caught sight of a Hall like Ragnar's, but smaller, raising its sharp gables above a cluster of huts. There were people in the fields, ploughing the land with teams of oxen, six to a plough. They stared at Madaah and his guide as dumbly as the oxen they drove. At a ford, where a stream ran thinly over green pebbles, they met a band of soldiers, big solid men, well clad and well armed. The guide talked to them. They were obviously interested and gathered round Madaah, but after mutual shrugs of incomprehension

they were waved on. Madaah guessed that the Norse raid had
caused a flutter of alarm far back somewhere, wherever the ruler
of this land lived—perhaps in the hills whose smudged line of
purple was always on their right as they rode south. The guide
was friendly and persistent, and Madaah finally understood his
name, Edgar. 'Edgar,' he said, and smiled, although his eyes
remained cold. At length they turned to the East and Madaah
began to smell the sea. His spirits rose a little. He felt trapped and
soggy inland, and the size of the country, the numbers of its
people and what, to his eyes, was its rank fertility, depressed him.

But the sea lay ahead, and when, in the late afternoon, they
broke from the cover of a straggly copse and onto the shore, he
dismounted and ran down the sand into the water. The tide was
going out and he ran, following it until the waves were at his
thighs. There he stopped looking at the low horizon with a
whimper at the back of his throat. Edgar called him, and he
walked back across the rippled sand and scrambled onto the
horse.

The beach ran in a long curve. Edgar stopped and pointed. 'Church,' he cried. Madaah stared, following Edgar's finger. A mile or so away, a jumble of rock rose above the sand-dunes. On the rocks he could just see what might be a building.

Edgar grinned up at Madaah and made an odd gesture across his breast. Madaah's stomach tightened. What did church mean, and what was the meaning of that curious sign? For a moment he thought of leaping off the horse and running, but where to? The sea was empty, and the forest only too full. Edgar tugged at the head of the tired horse, and they moved slowly down the sands. They came to a track which curved back inland a little, and then merged into a path wide enough to be a road. The road itself wound back, towards the rocks which ran out to a head-land, crested with buildings, solid and formidable.

They crept up the rise in the warmth of the long afternoon sun. The wind which had ruffled their hair all day had fallen and left the day quiet. There were no people, no birds called, even the sea was muffled into silence, and as they moved higher, the buildings seemed to slip furtively away behind the crest of the headland, as if hiding from them. Then, as they topped the hill before a high blank wall, a great bell began to toll deep inside the silent buildings. Madaah had no notion what could cause such a sound. He would have run then but he was seized by the paralysis of overwhelming fear. They came to a door and Edgar leaned forward and pulled on a rope.

Somewhere inside the walls a little bell jangled sharply, as if answering the terrible call of the great bell, which trembled in the hot, still air. Nothing happened, nothing moved. Edgar pulled again, again the sharp jangle. Madaah sat very still on the patient horse, but his breast jerked with each beat of his heart; and then the gate began to creak open. A slit of light shone brilliant against the deep shadow of the wall, and, as the door opened, the slip widened, and a figure was standing, blackly, against the arc of light.

Edgar spoke a few words and the figure retreated slowly, Edgar advancing, drawing the horse forwards. Then the figure stepped from the shadow into the light and Madaah's heart jerked within him as he saw at last, the sight so familiar in his dreams—a black wizard!

The gowned and hooded figure drew close to the horse. A nerve jumped in Madaah's cheek, and sweat prickled in his

50

eyebrows. The horse sensed its rider's fear and stepped nervously sideways, twisting its head. The black figure placed a calm hand on its neck. He spoke to Madaah who stared down. From under his hood the man looked back thoughtfully, then said a few words to Edgar. When he addressed Madaah again, he spoke in Madaah's own language. 'Come down,' he said.

Madaah climbed clumsily off the horse and the man took his arm. He led him into the sunlight, while behind them the door slammed shut. They were in a square lined on two sides by small stone cells. At one end of the square was a hall, surrounded by a jumble of small buildings. Facing it, at the other end, was another hall, taller and more slender. The man tugged on Madaah's sleeve and they walked across the square, through the hot sunlight, to the elegant hall. The man looked down at Madaah, 'I am Winfred' he said. 'God has shown great mercy to you, my son; although you need cleaning and food, it is right that first you give thanks to Him whose Almighty Hand has delivered you.'

He opened the doors of the hall and entered; Madaah followed him tentatively into the dimness. 'Give thanks!' Winfred said, and smiled. Madaah smiled back, slyly, and nodded. Then Winfred bowed, rose again, and left. Madaah looked around. To his astonishment the hall was empty. Where was he to whom he was to give thanks? He walked down the hall, there was nothing there, no tables or benches. And then, as his eyes grew used to the dim light, he saw that one end of the floor was raised in a dais, and that there was a table there. He walked towards it. That would be the table of the lord of this hall. It was covered with a cloth of fine material, and he ran his fingers over it, admiring the texture. Above him rose a cross. He craned his neck to see it more clearly. A man hung there, nailed through the hands and feet. Madaah looked at it carefully. The carving was fine. That was how men looked when they died, with spears grating at their ribs, the body gathered up for its last convulsive protest. But what did it mean? And who was the man nailed there with his curious crown? Was he a slave or a king? A captive taken in battle? A sacrifice? He remembered then the brooch Thorold had given him on the beach at Orkney. Surely that, too, had been carved with a man hanging, like this. Around the cross were pictures cut in the wall. From a tree, a snake looked at a man and a woman, a curious boat sailed across a stone sea, a man was being swallowed by a fish, and a man with wrappings falling from him climbed from a hole in the ground.

Madaah shook his head. What stories did the carvings tell? On the table candlesticks and plates glowed. He picked up a plate. It was gold! So Harald had been right. His hand tightened avariciously. Then he put the plate down. There would be a time for that.

The heavy flagstone on which he stood was carved and he knelt to see it more clearly. Curious marks ran across it, hard and angular. Then the door clashed open and he turned, fear prickling again over his body.

'Good!' A voice echoed down the hall. 'It is good to see you kneel at the altar of the Lord. True piety in one so young. But now you must come with me.'

Madaah walked down the hall and out into the square. The man was the same one who had met him at the gate. He had thrown back his hood revealing a thin pale face. 'What is your name?' he asked.

'Madaah.'

'Madaah? That is a strange name. What does it mean?'

Madaah did not know how to answer. His name meant himself. What else could it mean?

'It is probably a corruption,' Winfred said, 'But now we must feed you. That is a holy obligation. Then we will tend your scratches and clean you. You are to meet our Lord Abbot, and,' Winfred dropped his voice a little, 'the Lord Cedric himself—in here'.

He turned abruptly into a small doorway. They were in a kitchen. 'Sit,' Winfred commanded. 'Bread, cheese, milk.' At each word a dish clattered before Madaah. 'A spoon, a plate. And I too will eat.' He sat opposite Madaah who waited for him to start, but to his surprise Winfred closed his eyes and began talking. Madaah looked around the empty room in bewilderment, but at a sharp 'Amen' Winfred rapped the table with his spoon 'Eat!'

They ate and then crossed the square again and entered another small room. It was pungent with the smell of herbs, sharp and yet sweet. A man sat at a bench mixing a paste in a little pot. 'Here is our guest,' Winfred said. 'His name is Madaah, he says, but I have never heard such a word given to a person. He speaks the Celtic.'

The other man peered at Madaah. 'It is probably a corruption—'
'Yes, yes, that is what I said,' Winfred sounded testy.
'A corruption of . . . let me think.'
'Treat his face, Godwin, he has to see the Abbot.'
Godwin began smearing ointment on Madaah's face and arms.
'Madaah? it could be. . . . I *have* heard that word. It means fox.
Have you given thanks to the Almighty, Fox?'
'I found him on his knees before the altar,' said Winfred. 'He
is a very pious fox.' The two men tittered and Madaah felt a
surge of anger. 'Is he done
now?' Winfred asked.

Godwin nodded and Win-
fred leaned close to him.
'Will he live?'

'He will live, but watch the
hens!' The two men laughed
again and Madaah flushed red.
Winfred took his shoulder.

'Come, Fox, I mean
Madaah.' Madaah twitched
his shoulder angrily and
Winfred laughed again and
left the room. Madaah
following sulkily behind.

The square was cool now,
and a few figures were
ambling round. As they
passed the small cells, men
popped out shaven heads,
stared at them, then pulled
them in again. 'Like rabbits,'
Madaah thought contempt-
uously, and his fear ebbed
away a little.

'It is the hour of rest,'
Winfred said. 'But now we
must see the Abbot, our Holy
Father, Leofric, and the great
Lord Cedric. Be quiet unless
you are spoken to, then
answer clearly; be modest!'

By the gate there were horses, and armed men lounged against the wall. Winfred clucked in a distressed way, 'This kingdom has seen terrible things these past twenty years, Northumbria has wept for her sins, but never before have I seen soldiers in our monastery. What evil times are on us.'

They stood before a cell, the smallest of them all. 'Remember,' Winfred said, 'Be modest! You are as nothing beside the Lord Cedric and our Holy Father—although it is true that our souls are all equal before God,' he added, in a meditative sort of way.

Winfred went in the cell. Madaah stood outside in the cool evening air. He felt tired now after the long day and his eyelids drooped. The ointment on his face felt hot and sticky and his face throbbed. He was roused by Winfred's plucking at his sleeve. 'Now,' Winfred said, and pushed Madaah forward. As he stepped under the door, he felt a warning poke in the back.

The room was dark. A tiny candle hardly lightened it. He could make out the figure of a man against one wall, and a dark bundle in a corner. Winfred leaned over the bundle in the corner and whispered. He stepped back, and then a voice drifted from the bundle. It was an old voice, old and dry, like dead leaves.

'Welcome, Madaah!'

Madaah nodded, as though acknowledging the greeting of an old friend. Winfred's hand found him, and led him forward and pressed him onto a stool. The bundle stirred and a hand, dry and withered, ran over his face as lightly as a spider.

'You have eaten?'

'Yes!'

'And given thanks for your deliverance?'

'Yes!' It seemed wise to agree.

The old hand grasped his arm and pulled him forward. Madaah could see a face now, seamed with many wrinkles and with scanty white hair. Leofric's eyes were opaque and milky, and Madaah realised that the old man was blind. 'You are from the Western Isles. I, too have been there, in Holy Iona, many years ago. How goes the Church in the West, well or ill?'

The question was meaningless to Madaah, but he answered automatically, acting on his usual principle of agreement, when in doubt. 'Well' he said, slurring the words a little.

Winfred spoke sharply. 'Speak clearly!'

'Well!' Madaah shouted. Winfred tutted disapprovingly, while from the third man came a short sardonic laugh. There was silence for a while, and then the third man spoke. Madaah did not understand but Winfred translated.

'The Lord Cedric asks where did the fleet come from?'

'From Orkney,' Madaah answered. There was more talk.

'How many ships? How many men?'

Madaah tried to remember. It seemed a long time ago, and he was confused with tiredness. 'At first fifty, but some would not come. At the end, I think, thirty ships.'

'So many! And how many men?'

It was hard to say but Madaah thought about six or seven hundred. Winfred gasped and spoke urgently to Cedric. Then he addressed Madaah again. 'And were these all from Orkney?'

Madaah shook his head. 'No, many came from Norway.'

From the corner Cedric spoke again. 'Who was their leader?' Winfred asked.

It was hard to say, hard to remember. Madaah fumbled for words. 'There was no leader, all were equal, but Ragnar was the greatest, and then Harald of Norway.'

'What brought them here?'

'Harald said there was much gold and land, and no-one to defend it except—' Madaah halted abruptly.

'Except who?' The question was sharp.

'The—they said . . . Harald said—the wizards.'

'Who are they?' Winfred sounded bewildered.

'He meant . . . I think he meant—' Madaah opened his arms, disclaiming responsibility, 'I think he meant you.'

'Fiends from hell!' Winfred's voice was thick with rage. He spoke to Cedric and turned again to Madaah.

'And are there more of these devils in Orkney?'

There would not be many left in Orkney, Madaah thought, 'No, but I think there are many in Norway. Many men, and many ships.'

'God save us,' said Winfred. There was silence for a while; then Leofric stirred on the bed and whispered something. Winfred tapped Madaah on the shoulder.

'Come!' he ordered. 'The Abbot is tired.' Madaah rose from the stool, and again the old man held his arm.

'Pray for me, Madaah,' he said. 'Pray for the Church.'

Then the old man's grip tightened. 'You have no need to feel fear, my son.' The milky eyes looked blankly at him. 'Maybe you have been saved for some great purpose. The blessed Patrick too was cast on strange shores . . .' Leofric's voice died away and the grip on his arm relaxed. Madaah yielded to Winfred's pull and went outside. As he left the room, he realised that a little memory had been flickering in his mind: Leofric was like old Brin. For the first time in months he thought of the warm autumn day when the Norsemen had come to the island, and he had become one of them. What now, he wondered, in what strange world did his future lie? The night was calm and languorous. Lights shone from the hall and soft white moths fluttered aimlessly through the darkness. Madaah felt the gentleness of the night, and his body relaxed as his mind wandered in memories, as aimlessly as the moths. Then Winfred nudged him.

'The Lord Cedric is leaving. Bid him goodnight.'

Madaah looked up. Cedric was on a horse, high above him. Cedric held down his hand, and Madaah touched it timidly. He felt the coldness of rings, and stooped, quite involuntarily, to look at them closer and gauge their value. Cedric murmured something, then pulled his horse's head away and clattered through the gateway with his men. Winfred chuckled and rubbed his hands together.

'Good, good! You showed proper respect, Madaah. It brings honour to our house.'

'Who is Cedric?' Madaah asked drowsily.

'Who is the Lord Cedric?' Winfred sounded indignant. 'But of course you would not know. He is a great man in this land, one of our rulers—under the king, of course.' He added the last phrase a little thoughtfully, as though there might be a doubt there somewhere. 'But now you are to stay with us. We will see what we can make of you.'

As he spoke, the great bell began to call brazenly through the night. 'It is time for our devotions. A pity Lord Cedric could not stay for them. Come!'

They walked across the square to the hall of the cross. Other figures, gowned and hooded, were making their way to it. There was no sound but the tolling of the bell and the clatter of wooden shoes, as the monks filed into the church. Winfred pushed Madaah against the wall and joined the other monks who stood in rows in the centre. The bell fell silent and there was a deep silence, broken only by someone in the throng coughing harshly.

Then a figure glided in from the back of the church and stood before the altar. He was illuminated by huge candles which threw off a smoky light, and flickered in the draught, and he seemed to sway with them. To Madaah's tired eyes the man seemed huge, oppressive. Then he spoke, and Madaah recognised Godwin, the herbalist—but a Godwin utterly changed from the foolish old man who had made jokes at him. This Godwin seemed grave and aloof, remote from the changeable world, timeless and powerful, but possessed of a power new to Madaah, an authority that seemed to spring not from himself alone, but from the presence of those around him. Madaah could not grasp the idea, but that there was one there, and a strange one, he knew.

Godwin began to speak. He made the gesture Edgar had made that afternoon, bowed low and broke into a chant, plaintive to Madaah's ears and monotonous, but in a queerly satisfying way, and full of queer dying cadences. Then the monks broke into the same chant.

To the end of his life Madaah remembered that sound. Never before in his life had he heard controlled choral singing. The only music he had heard had been the wry bird-like calls of his own people, or the anarchic drunken howling of the Norsemen. Now he sagged against the wall, lost in wonder as the music welled over him. 'Deo,' the voices cried. 'Deo gratias, Agnus Dei Qui solvat peccata mundi, Salva me!' The candles flickered and glowed, and the monks raised their heads and the sound soared and filled the lofty roof. 'Deo, Deo Gratias.' More than anything he had ever wanted, Madaah wished to join the monks in their song, although its meaning and purpose was utterly beyond his comprehension, and more than once he opened his mouth, and his breath gathered in his throat, but then he fell back, defeated by the newness, the complexity, of the sound.

The service went on; the monks chanted and fell silent, and then fell silent again. They knelt and rose, knelt and rose, their quivering shadows chasing across the walls, while Godwin, solemn and mysterious, stood controlling them, leading and yet remaining a follower. The sound rose and ebbed on Madaah's tired ears and the figures dwindled and expanded before his tired eyes. He felt himself before a mystery deeper than any he had yet encountered, and when, at last, the service ended and he was led to a cell and lay on a rough bed, he fell into a deep sleep and dream, in which bells rang, men sang, the people of his island, led by Brin, danced in the church, and Ragnar drowned again in the cold sea. And from that night, the robe of the Norseman, the mantle of the magician, began to slip from his shoulders.

Chapter 8

The next morning Madaah was put to work. Winfred woke him at dawn and took him to the kitchen, one of the small buildings which huddled around the dining hall. 'This is a good place to start,' Winfred said. 'With food. The blessed gift of God, the fruit of His bounteous goodness.' He led Madaah to a trough full of dirty wooden plates and gave him a cloth. Madaah stared sullenly at the floor.

'You are not tired, Madaah?'

Madaah did not answer, and Winfred went on blithely. 'No? Good! Although it is good to work when one is tired, too. It is a discipline, and the body needs discipline, as does the mind. Clean the plates and you may eat.'

Madaah threw down the cloth angrily. 'This is slaves' work,' he spat.

'Slaves' work! We are all slaves here, slaves of God, and our work is blessed because of it. Take up the cloth.'

Madaah shook his head stubbornly. After Orkney it was inconceivable that he should do the work of a slave, a thrall. To do so meant becoming one, taking a slave's mentality. Better death!

Winfred frowned at Madaah. A cold, menacing note crept into his voice. 'Discipline is what you need, I think.' Quite suddenly he cracked Madaah across the face. Madaah was amazed. A little growl rumbled at the back of his throat, and instinctively his hand went to his side, to where he had kept his knife. Winfred missed neither the growl nor the gesture. He stepped firmly forward and hit Madaah again. Hating himself for doing so, Madaah stepped back. It was a retreat and Winfred nodded as if satisfied.

'No barbarian tricks here,' he snapped. 'Pick up the cloth.'

Madaah stooped and picked it up.

'Now, work.'

His face flushed, Madaah bent over the trough and began, slowly, to clean the plates. Winfred prodded him. 'Make haste.' Madaah rubbed a little faster and Winfred went to the door. 'When you have finished, you eat.'

The door closed and Madaah carried on with his task. Hooded figures came in and began preparing a frugal meal, bread and soft sour cheese.

The monks worked in silence, broken only by the sharp remarks of the cook, Ceolwulf, who harried Madaah whenever he paused. Madaah brooded over the trough. He had comforting fantasies of what he would do to the monks. Winfred he reserved for a knife in the ribs, but he found satisfactory rewards for them all. When he had finished the dishes, he was turned into server, and scurried backward and forward into the Hall with dishes. He took a great bowl of milk in and furtively spat in it. He despised himself, afterwards, for doing it; it was the action of a slave.

Throughout the interminable day he was harassed and prodded into work, menial and dirty; five times he was taken into the church, but the ceremonies were dry and boring, a long incomprehensible harangue. Madaah's spirit sank beneath the weight of tedium and fatigue. There were other youths, doing the same work, but none of them spoke his language, and he despised them anyway. They worked diligently and looked smugly contented. Occasionally they smiled at him, but he answered their smiles with a look of vicious hostility, and soon he was ignored.

The next weeks were a hard time for Madaah. For the first time in his life he was under discipline. He had to learn obedience to the ordered calm of the monk's life, to rules and regulations. He fought against his environment, not openly, but covertly, doing his work badly and slowly, always with an obstinate scowl. As he behaved stupidly, he began to be treated stupidly. The other youths played sly stricks on him, muddying plates he had cleaned, kicking dirt onto floors he had laboriously scoured, mocking his speech on the few occasions when he uttered the words of English he had acquired.

He thought, often, of running away, but knew in his heart it was pointless. There was nowhere he could run to, only the forest, and he had been there already and learned his lesson. His one hope lay in the return of the Norsemen, and he spent long hours dreaming of a day when the great bell would ring, not for

E

service, but in alarm at the coming of the long black ships of the Norse horde; there would be a reckoning!

The monks had a library and the librarian, Ceadda, was responsible for teaching the novices to read and write. Only the brightest were chosen, and Madaah's reputation was such that he had no chance of being picked. But one day when Madaah was in the kitchen, he looked up to see Ceadda. He was looking for Winfred and he asked Madaah, in his own tongue, where he might be. Madaah muttered that he did not know and bent over the dishes. Ceadda did not leave but leaned against the door watching Madaah. 'You speak the language of the Norse pirates?' he said.

Madaah, his back to Ceadda, nodded reluctantly.

'And you speak the Celtic tongue?'

Again Madaah nodded, a sullen acknowledgement.

'And the English? Do you know any of that?'

Madaah nodded again. 'Little bit,' he said, in English.

Ceadda walked into the room. On the table was a bowl of butter. He picked up a knife and scratched some marks on its smooth surface. 'Look!' he commanded. Madaah gave a cursory glance, then turned back to his dishes.

'Look again, properly.'

Madaah dropped his rag and stared at the marks. He had an expression of stupid insolence. One thing he had learned in the monastery, that expression annoyed the monks; it was his sole weapon against them.

Ceadda pointed to the marks. 'Madaah,' he said, 'your name!'

Despite himself Madaah was interested. It was writing, that much he had learned, but what writing was he had no real idea.

Ceadda took the knife again, and drew a fox. It was a good drawing, and Madaah half smiled. Ceadda pointed to the fox, then to the marks. 'Madaah,' he said.

Madaah rapped the table suddenly. The marks and the sound and the picture had a connection, but what?

Ceadda watch Madaah shrewdly. He wrote again. 'Ceadda,' he said, and pointed to himself.

Madaah clicked his fingers. He had it, the marks and the sound were the same, but how did the two fit together? He looked at Ceadda half-imploringly. Ceadda smiled and handed Madaah the knife. He took it, frowned in concentration, then crudely copied the marks. 'Madaah!' he cried, 'Me!' and looked triumphantly at the Librarian who smiled slowly.

60

'Yes, you,' he said.

The next morning Madaah went to the library to learn his letters.

It was work with point and purpose, and Madaah did not find it hard.

At first Ceadda had used a willow wand across Madaah's knuckles to quicken the learning:

'This is the letter A, Madaah.' Crack!

'A.' Madaah would answer.

'And this is the letter B, Madaah.' Crack!

'B.'

'A and B make the sound ab.' Crack!

'Ab.'

But the rod was soon laid aside as Madaah forged ahead. He understood quickly how the letters hung together, each supporting the other; each on its own meaning little, but together making words, and the words making ideas which liberated the mind from pots and pans, and transcended the narrow boundaries of Madaah's little world of resentment, boredom and animal torpor. As he learned to read, he began to understand the width of the world, to realise that it had a history, going far back into time. And as he felt the pressure of the past, he began to have a paradoxical sense of freedom from the present. For the past pointed to the future, and past and future gave meaning and purpose to the present. He began to be a scholar.

Now the A.B.C. was long past. Now it was 'Read the passage, Madaah!'

A little cough to clear the throat: 'After they had entered the lodging, they began to express the very apostolic order of living of the primitive church, serving God in continual prayer, watching and fasting, and preaching the word of Life to as many as they could, despising the commodities of the world as things none of their own.'

'Yes, Madaah, the great Augustine came to this dark land and lived as a saint should, and we also. And the Venerable Bede it is who tells us so, and we trust his word.'

As well as learning to read, Madaah still had humble tasks to do. He had to prepare the parchment on which the letters were written, scraping the bristle from the calf-skin, making it supple and smooth, pricking the lines along which the monks would paint, stroke by elegant stroke, letter after elegant letter. As the

61

months wore on, and Madaah with his flair for language advanced in English and even began a little Latin, he was turned to writing. Ceadda was a great illuminator of the parchments; his heart was rather in the decoration than the words themselves, but he made both words and book beautiful. The letters were firm and elegant, and round them crept curving tendrils of briar and woodbine, red and gold and green, as if the profusion of nature was invading the abstractions the books contained. Down the margins crept strange beasts, and birds and angels spread their wings over the words of the apostles.

Madaah tried to write as the monks did and listened and watched carefully as Ceadda instructed him: 'Hold the brush so, Madaah, full but not overflowing. Turn the brush, not your hand, so—then the curve is full of grace, that it might reflect the grace of God. Make your upright thus, use all the brush; it is strong and upright and firm, showing the strength of God and his firm purpose in our salvation. So—the letter 'D'. 'D' for Deus, the Lord God who laboured to create us, and for whose purposes we labour here, even as Augustine and Columba and Patrick laboured before us.'

Madaah squinted at his letters. Try as he might, they never came out as Ceadda's did; the same height, the same width, straight on the line—but he was less interested in the letters than in the ideas they carried. Ideas that were like chinks in the vast doors of time, through which he could see, although as yet only in tantalising glimpses, a world of sunlight, lucidity and reason.

At night he would lie awake thinking of this new religion, with its ideas of self-sacrifice and humility. His world had always been full of the supernatural, and he had believed in the Norse gods as easily as he had believed in the magical spirits of his own people. There was nothing strange in that. That men should differ in their gods was natural, for every man's spirit, going out on his breath into the formless universe, gave that universe shape and meaning, unique to that person; and the spirits of that universe were his, although any man might share them. Madaah himself had a spirit, though, which only he knew of. It had spoken to him once from a fish in a stream, and the fish was his secret sign.

But the monks' religion with but one God, invisible and remote, dwelling high in the heavens, was very strange. Madaah hardly knew what he believed in any more. The one bright spot was the devils. They at least were present, not perhaps under stones, but behind men's words and deeds, although sometimes they might come out in visible shape—an old monk had seen them several times—and they were a tangible connection between nature and the supernatural, between Madaah and the mysterious forces which governed the great tides of the universe.

Absorbed in his task of learning, Madaah rarely left the Abbey. But during the harvest he was called from the library to work in the fields. Every hand was needed then; Winfred and Godwin, Ceadda and Ceolwulf, all worked and sweated next to Madaah. Prayer and knowledge came second to the vital task of gathering food for the long winter months ahead and the seed for the next spring sowing.

The Abbey's land was bounded, partly by ground belonging to the free peasants of a village which lay inland, partly by land belonging to Cedric, the Aetheling of the district. The peasants and Cedric's serfs laboured in the fields next to the monks, but Madaah noticed that the Abbey's harvest was greater than either. He mentioned this to the Monks. Godwin piously gave the credit for it to God, but Ceadda was more practical. 'We work the land better, Madaah. Our ploughs are better, our land is one unit, not scattered among many. The freemen are idle because the land belongs to the village, and no one knows which land he will have next year so they will not work it properly. Cedric's men work for him, so they take no care of their work. Why should they? It is someone else who will benefit. But we hold our land for the community, and for God, so all benefit. Therefore all work well, and we work well because we are free; it is our choice that we do it. Look!' He pointed to the dark wall of forest that bordered the fields. 'When Leofric came here, fifty years ago, all this land was forest. It was we, the children of God who led the way here; the peasants, and Lord Cedric, came later. Those who did live here were heathen, worshipping idols. The monks had a hard time in those days. And now the heathen dogs from the North threaten us again.' He shook his head sadly. 'In those days a strong King ruled a strong land. They were the days of Bede and Caedmon; now the kingdom is weak and the throne is like a bone between hungry dogs. Six kings in thirty years!'

Madaah was interested. Working in the Library, immersed in the calm routine of the Abbey, he had half forgotten the world

63

outside, half forgotten even the Norsemen. 'Why have there been so many kings?' he asked.

Ceadda sighed. 'It is a long story. We had a good king, Eadberht, but he tired of this world and entered a cloister, to spend his days in meditation and prayer. Oswulf, his son, ruled us then, but the thegns of his own household slew him. Then Aethelwald Moll took the throne but he was driven out by one Alhred. Since then, those two Houses have torn the Kingdom apart. The Aethelings and the Ealdormen tire first of one, then the other, and so the throne sways to wishes. Only the Church remains, the Church and those—' he nodded at Cedric's bondsmen, toiling by the forest edge—'And they are always with us, as the Gospels tell us.'

'And who are the Aethelings and Ealdormen?' Madaah asked.

Ceadda grinned wryly. 'That is a story of its own. The Aethelings are royal, or claim to be. They hold their land and their power because their fathers held it, and so no King can depose them—although King Aethelred seems not to know that. The Ealdormen are rich men and strong, but they are the King's own choice—those he calls upon for wisdom in the Council and arms in the battlefield. Lord Cedric is an Aetheling, and a strong one. He rules his lands like a King, I fear much that one day the King will think that Cedric is a little too strong, and then—' he shrugged. 'But leave that to those who must concern themselves with such matters. I thank God that they are not my concern.'

The harvest was gathered in. There was a feast in the dining-hall and a great service in the church. The altar was swathed with golden corn-sheaves and scarlet poppies. The monks sang to the glory of God, whose hand had raised the crops from the decayed seed. Priests rode from the Abbey to the little churches in the villages, to hold services of thanks-giving and to ensure that the villagers did not slip back into heathen practices and thank the wrong gods for the miracle of the harvest. Madaah went back to the Library, became absorbed in his studies, and forgot, again, the outside world and its woes.

News of the world filtered in, though; news which sent ripples of terror through the Abbey. Aethelred, the King, had sent for Osred, the King before him, who had taken shelter on the Isle of Man, and, after promises of safe conduct, had slaughtered him. Osred's two children, in sanctuary at York, had been lured out and killed, too. This horrified the monks.

'They were safe in the hand of the Church,' said Ceadda, 'and the King broke his oath. What will become of the land?'

It was a question no-one could answer. The winter drew in and the monks suffered the ills it brought: toothache and gumboils, chilblains and heavy drenching colds that turned to bronchitis and pneumonia. The services in the church were full of racking coughs, and the old among the monks began to die. The Lord Cedric came to the Abbey for the Christmas services. He came with a heavy escort of armed men, who clanked about the quiet square and who got drunk at the Feast of the Twelfth Night. He brought with him, too, his son, Oswald, little older than Madaah, but full of pride and scorn, and contempt for those who prayed and worked in the Abbey. In the services he and his father sat on heavy carved chairs, and Oswald made no attempt to hide his boredom. Madaah, standing at the back of the church felt a prickle of contempt and anger at this, and realised that he had changed, that the church, or the Abbey, was claiming his being in some way, that he was becoming a part of it.

The winter faded, the snow began to melt before the lengthening sun, and the great services of Easter were held. The God, long stricken down, raised himself again and the long fast of Lent ended with another feast. Again Cedric and his men came into the Abbey, bringing with them a breath of the warlike world outside its quiet walls.

Then, one day, Madaah was sent for by Leofric. It was a year since Madaah had crouched in the little cell and listened to the dry old voice. He walked across the square, familiar now, with confidence, but, although he did not this time expect to be tortured, or eaten, thoughts which had crossed his mind in the darkness of that evening, he felt a ghostly breath of fear as he stooped under the low door.

Once again he felt the old hand run over his face, and again the old voice drifted from the bed. 'My son.'

'Father?'

'I have good reports of you. Although I lie here in darkness, I know of your progress.'

Madaah mumbled an embarrassed acknowledgement.

'It seems you have a gift for languages. You speak Celtic, Norse, English, and even Latin you understand. That is a great gift; God gave the Apostles the gift of tongues.'

There was a long pause. Madaah thought the old man had

65

drifted into sleep, then unexpectedly there was a creaky laugh from the dark corner. 'But it seems your singing leaves something to be desired.'

Madaah flushed. It was true. Although the music of the services was a great joy to him, perhaps the greatest in his life, he could not sing, his ear could never quite follow the subtle harmonies of the monks chanting. 'It is my voice,' he said, and felt foolish for saying it. What else could it be?

'God gives us all gifts, but not all gifts.'

Another silence. Outside a voice called across the square: Godwin reprimanding a novice.

Then, 'There is a deep mystery behind you, Madaah.'

Madaah nodded, automatically obedient; it was true, there was a mystery, but was it any more than the mystery every man had behind him, and before him too?

'There is a mystery behind you, my son. You came from the sea. I have heard of such a one as you, he too came from the sea and became a great hero to his people, and he warred against darkness. There is a song about him which I heard long ago. Beowulf was his name. When you came from the sea, you wore a cross about your neck and knelt at the altar. But little you knew about the sacraments.'

Madaah looked dreamily at the Abbot. How much did he know? And how?

'But what of that?' Leofric went on. 'In my youth I lived worse than the wolves of the forest. I was an animal and worse than an animal, for I rejected God's gifts to me while knowing them. And yet the word came to me. And when it came, I heard.'

Madaah leaned forward. He felt a profound obscure prompting to do something for Leofric. Perhaps it sprang from hearing the old man's voice which fluttered as feebly as a dying bird. 'Father, I must tell you. The Norsemen, they will come again.'

'I believe you, my son.'

'Then we, you, Father, should do something.'

Leofric stirred on his bed. 'We cannot stop them coming, my son.'

'No, but we could prepare, be ready for them.' As he spoke Madaah was surprised at himself; he had begun to see the Norsemen as his enemies. There was hatred in his throat when he spoke of them.

'That is for the King to do, and Lord Cedric.'

'Yes!' Madaah agreed with that, although he had seen little sign of preparation, and from the gossip brought in from the outside world it seemed that the strong men of the Kingdom were more concerned with their own struggles against each other, rather than with an outside threat. He fumbled for words. 'I mean we should do what we can, move the treasures, the gold plate. That is what the raiders want.'

'Yes. Many men seek such toys, but we have a treasure here which none can take away, although any man can have it for the asking.'

'I agree, Father.' Madaah was almost perfunctory in his answer. 'But if they find nothing here, then they will go away, raid elsewhere. They will go to Ireland!'

'And destroy the churches there? No, Madaah, you have learned much, but there is much you have to learn.' Leofric groped for Madaah's arm. 'My son, I will tell you a secret.'

Madaah bent forward, interested, flattered. 'Yes, Father?'

'It is good that the Norsemen come here!'

'What!'

Leofric's voice altered; a subtle note of humour entered into it, a sense of irony beyond Madaah's understanding.

'Yes, it saves us going to them.'

Madaah was exasperated at the Abbot's unworldliness. 'They will not come to hear sermons, Father.'

Outside, the great bell of the Abbey began to toll; 'Compline', Madaah thought. Another day gone in the life of the Abbey!

'Yes, Madaah, they will come to kill, but what of that? No man lives forever, and the Kingdom of Heaven calls always. God will not suffer his church to live without witnesses, kill they as many as they might.'

'No, Father.' Madaah was not convinced. It was easier for the Abbot, with one foot in the gate of heaven, to talk like that than for him, Madaah, to accept it.

'But I did not send for you to talk of these matters Madaah. You are to leave us.'

'Father?' Madaah was startled.

'Yes, we are not scholars, here, or teachers. We are a community of work and prayer. You must go where your gifts can be nourished. I am sending you where there are books and learned men. I am sending you to the Holy Isle of Lindisfarne.'

Chapter 9

Edgar saw the smoke first. He turned to Madaah and said, casually, 'What might that be?' No fear in his voice, or apprehension. But Madaah knew. He had seen smoke like that before, rising in a column, then billowing as the wind caught it, drifting along the beach, making one's eyes smart, making one cough.

'Norsemen!' he cried. 'Pirates!' He slipped off his horse and into the wood. He crouched there and listened. Edgar stayed on the path and gaped at him.

'Come on!' Madaah shouted. Edgar, slow to move, slower to think, walked towards him a little.

'Pirates? What do you mean?' His heavy face was creased with the effort of thinking.

Madaah spat with frustration. 'Those are buildings burning!' He edged further into the wood, Edgar lumbering after him.

'There are no buildings there, Madaah,' Edgar cried.

Madaah frowned. 'But . . .'

'No Madaah, only the Holy Isle, only the Monastery.'

'Then that is what is burning.' Madaah cocked his head and listened, hard.

'But that is impossible. The Holy Isle! Cuthbert himself has it under his protection. He lies under the altar.'

Madaah laughed in Edgar's face. What would Harald and Ragnar have cared if a hundred Saints were buried under the altar, and a thousand more looked down from Heaven. He thought hard, then made his decision and struck through the wood towards the shore. They were a mile from the smoke, and he doubted if the Norsemen would have come so far inland. At the edge of the wood he halted and crouched in the undergrowth. Edgar squatted beside him, his face full of doubt. A grassy slope ran down to the beach, and beyond that, across an arm of sea, lay the island, smoke rising to the sky like a black finger. A line of dunes rose from the water, blocking the rest of the island from sight. Madaah wondered what was going on over there. He shivered with excitement at the thought of the long black ships rocking in the shallows, while the raiders feasted by the fire. They did it, he thought—not Harald—or Ragnar—but Norsemen just the same.

He stood up. 'I am going over. Wait here.'

Edgar shivered. 'Alone?' He shook his head. 'Let us go to the village, Madaah; we will get help.'

In his turn Madaah shook his head. There would be no village left, ashes and dead men, nothing else. 'I am going over,' he said. 'Stay or come with me, it is as you wish.'

He stepped from the wood. The sands ran north and south, quiet, empty, peaceful. Well out to sea there was a flicker of white. Madaah thought at first they were sails, then realised that they were islands with the sea breaking against them. There was nothing else in sight. He ran, bent double, across the sands, down to the sea. A line of stakes ran into the water, disappeared, then rose again at the further shore. Things bobbed in the water, but he couldn't tell what they were. He stripped off his robe and tied it round his neck, and waded in. He went from one stake to the next, the water rising from his ankles to his knees, his knees to his waist, his shoulders, his mouth. He had reached one of the dark shapes now. It was the body of a man, his head gashed open with a huge wound. He pushed past it, and then, as the salt water broke over his mouth, he plunged forward, felt muddy ground beneath him, and he splashed onto the shore of Lindisfarne.

A line of low dunes lay ahead of him and he ran lightly forward and crouched under them. He listened. Nothing! The evening was quiet. He rose and inched up the dune, through the wiry grass, and under its sandy cornice he crouched, listening again. He glanced back across the water and to his rage saw Edgar on the shore, waving his arms. He froze again, like a hare in its form. The dusk began to gather on the coast, among the trees and round the dunes. He began, very cautiously, to pull himself up over the top of the dune. Then, from the dusk, a white shape rushed at him and caught him in the face.

He jumped sideways and ducked in a paroxysm of fear, and slithered half way down the dune. As he went, he grabbed at the shape and felt it crumple in his grasp. It was a piece of parchment. The edges were charred and brittle, but from the brown frame colours glowed, red and green and gold. Madaah stared gravely down and from the dusk a face looked gravely back at him. Madaah knew who it was. It was Cuthbert, greatest of all the Saints of the kingdom of Northumbria, founder of the Abbey of the Holy Isle, centre of learning and saintliness, holiest place in all the North. A few pieces flaked from the parchment as Madaah rose to his feet, crested the dune, and looked down on the burning Abbey and library of Lindisfarne.

In the orange flicker of the flames Madaah walked from the dunes. The meadow through which he went was covered with leaves of parchment, each the labour of weeks, and they moved through the dusk like moths. A 'Whoof!' from the buildings made him jump. A sudden burst of flame leapt from the darkness. In its light he saw his second body. It was a monk lying face down. A huge jagged wound grinned in his head. Madaah stooped over

him helplessly. He gently turned him over and saw something in the dead man's hand. He pulled it free. It was a Gospel, St. Mark's, and he held it pressed against his face as he wandered through the meadow. He came to more bodies, monk and peasant, and he moved through them like a child lost in a dark wood.

He came to a little wall and leaned on it and stared, almost dreamily at the burning Abbey. The little tingle of excitement had quite gone. This was the reality. Dead men and burned books.

Then Edgar's voice trembled at his side. 'Mother of God, it cannot be! It cannot be!'

Madaah stared blankly at him. There was nothing strange in it; he had seen it all before, seen the flames, smelled the smoke, tasted the acrid soot, and chased terrified figures across small fields before sending them into everlasting darkness. And now— this! A wall collapsed with a crash, and Edgar fell on his knees and sobbed. Madaah started to walk forward. 'We must help,' he said, and then stopped, inert. There would be no one to help. No one left alive, no man, no beast. And this is what his dreams had been. He thought of his visions he had had in the past: of the silly monks running before him and his sword. He looked at the crumpled bodies around him and remembered Leofric's innocent talk. It is good they come, he had said. It saves us going to them. Well, they had come, and gone too, without waiting for a sermon. The Norsemen sat in their long ships and feasted in their halls, while the monasteries burned on the coast of England.

Behind him Edgar shouted through the darkness. 'We must pray, pray!' but Madaah stayed on his feet. Just then there seemed nothing to pray to.

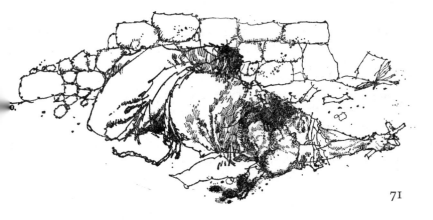

They slept eventually, and woke, stiff with the morning dew. The buildings still burned, and the morning air was foul and tainted with smoke—and worse than that. They walked to the buildings and stood idly, watching the flames, like peasants round an autumn bonfire. Then they heard the sound of horses through the mist. Edgar ran forward foolishly, but Madaah stayed where he was, taut and ready for flight. A horse and rider loomed through the mist and Madaah recognised Oswald, the Lord Cedric's son. Oswald stared at the fire, then down at Madaah. 'Is there anyone left?' he asked.

Madaah shook his head. 'No, my Lord.'

'Not one?'

'Not one, my Lord.'

Oswald slumped on his big grey horse. 'Who would have believed this? The greatest Church in the Kingdom. . . .' He looked at Madaah's smudged face. 'I know you, Monk, somewhere . . .' His voice died away again. 'They would not have soldiers, though my father—' He dismounted, the damp leather of his saddle squeaking. 'Kings have lived here, Saints and holy men. Where are they now?' His voice was high pitched, and it began to rise in a hysterical way and Madaah felt uneasy.

'Where are they now, the Saints and their prayers?'

Madaah plucked at his sleeve. 'My Lord, my lord!'

Oswald looked round, almost vacantly.

'The pages, the pages of the manuscripts, we must collect them.'

Oswald stared at him heavily. 'And we must bury the dead,' he said, and then, for no reason Madaah could understand, he broke into laughter.

During the morning, the dead were gathered together and the precious pages collected. More soldiers arrived, a priest or two, and peasants began to drift in from the woods. It was a dead and heavy day. The sea mist hung over the island and clung to the woollen clothing of the men, covering them with a membrane of gleaming bubbles. There was little talk, and that was dull and muffled, and the men loomed greyly through the mist, stooping and gathering the harvest of men and books.

At evening they managed to break into the church. It was full of charred and mutilated bodies, and they were thickest around the altar. They hauled out the bodies, while a priest intoned a prayer, long and mournful. Under the last few bodies was a huge slab of stone, cracked across the middle, and tilted. The

72

men stared at it nervously, and Madaah shoved through them and peered down. Letters were carved across the stone and Madaah read them out. 'Cuthbert,' he said.

He looked up at the circle of faces. 'It is the grave of Cuthbert.' In the dusk, someone made a little noise, a nervous involuntary cry. Madaah licked his dry lips. 'The stone must have moved when the roof fell in.' There was a half-hearted mutter from the men, and they drew back a little, Madaah with them. He had a sudden disturbing vision of the body underneath the stone, in its narrow cell, narrower still than any it had known in its life, hearing the Norsemen scream and whoop, and hearing the cries of his monks, seizing the stone in its withered hands and . . . Madaah was not the last person out of the Abbey when their work was done. That night all slept uneasily, every man aware of that tilted stone, and not one convinced that a falling beam had moved it.

Cedric himself came the next day. He shrugged helplessly at the devastation. On his big dappled horse he rode through the ruins, crossing himself piously at the charred altar, then he cantered to the shore and for a long hour stared out at the empty sea. When he returned, he called to Madaah, who ran obediently over to him.

'What are you doing here, little monk?' he asked.

Madaah explained and Cedric nodded heavily. 'This news will travel the world,' he said. 'And we must be the first bearers of it.'

Madaah raised his hand. 'Should I return to St. Wilfred's, my Lord?'

Cedric looked at him thoughtfully, then shook his head. 'No! I think it best that you come with me. The King is at York. It may be that he will want to hear you. No man I know in this kingdom has seen these Norsemen, save you.'

He kicked his heels against the side of the horse and moved away. Oswald remained for a moment. He gazed down at Madaah through pale blue eyes. Madaah stared steadily back through his warm brown ones. Before Lord Cedric Madaah was prepared to be modest and humble, but not before his son, one no older than he himself, no older, no stronger, and certainly more ignorant. Oswald had a curious face, round and vacant with a loose mouth, a little blurred round the lips. We could be enemies, Madaah thought.

'You came with these Norse dogs, did you not?' Oswald asked.

73

'That is so, your Lordship.'

'And they come again, and you are here.' It was not a question. Madaah nodded coolly. 'In that order, your Lordship.'

'What?' Oswald frowned, puzzled by the form of Madaah's reply.

'They came, then I came! I did not bring them.'

'Better for you that you had never been born if you had.' Oswald bent forward. 'I will remember you, Monk.' He tugged the reins viciously and twisted his horse away.

And I, you, Madaah said to himself. He jerked his head with contempt.

At noon, when the tide was out, Cedric, Oswald, their soldiers and Madaah splashed across the shallow arm of sea and struck South, for York and the King.

Chapter 10

The long journey began solemnly. Cedric rode at the head of the column, followed by Oswald, hawk on wrist; then came Cedric's own priest, then a solid group of soldiers, twenty in all, and last, on a battered dun horse, came Madaah.

At first they rode in a brooding silence, but as they moved south, away from Lindisfarne, the troops began to relax. There were snatches of chatter, coarse jokes, and, from Oswald, bursts of high-pitched laughter. Cedric kept a heavy brooding expression, but it seemed to Madaah somehow forced and artificial, an act of public piety rather than the expression of real grief. Madaah's own emotions were mixed. Behind him lay the ruins of Lindisfarne, and his thoughts were clouded by memories of charred bodies and books. The burning of the books moved him more than the killing of the men. What, after all, was a man? A finite creature, born to die, moving from darkness to darkness, obscure, unnoticed, flickering a little in the light of life like the sparrow in the poem Caedmon had made at the Abbey of Whitby long ago. The sparrow which had fluttered into a hall, into the light from the darkness outside, and then gone back into the night. But the books were different. They remained; stable and enduring, from century to century. Brief the life of man, long the life of books. Madaah, who had laboured through a long winter, copying with frozen fingers the wisdom of the past, hated the witless destruction of the manuscripts.

But though Lindisfarne lay behind, York was ahead. That was something. York was where the Bishop held his court; learned and watchful, close to knowledge, close to the King, and close to God. And the King, too, was there. Aethelred, overthrown once but now, after twelve years, back on his throne, and holding his kingdom in an iron and oppressive hand. And York was, too, even more than Lindisfarne would have been, a window on the world. Alcuin, the greatest scholar in the land had taught there, had seen blood dripping from the roof of his great church and now, in the half-legendary lands across the sea, at the court of Charlemagne, ruler of half the world, warned and admonished of worse horrors if Aethelred and his nobles would not make peace.

Towards the end of the first day, Oswald left them, but not before a strange incident occurred. They had come to a ford across a shallow stream. For some reason Oswald had lagged behind, and as Madaah splashed through the water, he found himself riding side by side with the young noble. Oswald's horse stumbled, and he was thrown forward across its neck. Madaah grabbed Oswald's arm and shouldered him back onto the saddle. It was nothing. Oswald had been saved from a ducking perhaps, at worst from a few bruises, but his face went white and the corner of his mouth jerked and little flecks of spittle streaked his chin. He rose in his stirrups and raised his arm to strike. At that Madaah, too, rose and stared grimly at the jerking face. Oswald held his fist raised for a second, then dropped it and kicked his horse forward. It occurred to Madaah, then, that perhaps Oswald was insane, and when the young man left with a dozen men, to ride to Cedric's hall, he felt a profound sense of relief.

Cedric's troop jogged on south. At first they kept to the coast, following the line of great abbeys; Bamburgh, Jarrow, Hartlepool. Madaah was stunned by their wealth and magnificence. The Abbots ruled like princes, and princes they in fact were. They ruled not only over men's minds and consciences, but over vast tracts of land; and the Abbots, and Abbesses—for women ruled over some of the abbeys—spoke to Cedric, great noble though he was, as equals.

As they went South and carried with them the tale of the destruction of Lindisfarne, a ripple of terror and incredulity eddied before them. When they had told their story, messengers rode on to the next Abbey, and they would be met there by fearful monks. Madaah was the chief centre of interest. As the one person who had lived with the Norsemen, he was endlessly questioned. Who were they? Where did they come from? Were they men or strange beings—devils? How did they come? Did they fly through the air? The further south they went, the wilder were the beliefs. Monks had seen dragons flying across skies streaked with blood. Were these the raiders? Huge serpents breathing fire had been seen along the coast. Was it they who had destroyed the Holy Isle? To all the questions Madaah gave the same answer. No! They were men, no matter how many dragons had been seen. The monks were always reluctant to accept the fact. That men could have burned Lindisfarne was incomprehensible to them, and yet Madaah stood before them as living proof of the fact that the men from the North were—men. Strange were the ways of men, and stranger still the ways of God, and each Abbey held solemn services to the end that God might, in his mysterious way, change the ways of men. Madaah, in the services, sang and chanted too, but more in hope than expectation.

Each Abbey wished them to stay, but Cedric would have no delay. When, at the crossing of the river Tees, they turned inland, he speeded up the pace of the journey, and Madaah, no horseman, found the going hard. His back and buttocks ached and the inside of his legs were rubbed raw. They rose across waste-land and heath, and now, when they stopped, it was not to enter the splendours of an Abbey, but dirty villages, ruled by petty nobles from dirtier halls. And the stops were short. His tale was half-listened to and then he was dismissed. Cedric had changed too. His air of shocked piety had faded. They would come to some rough stockade, a thegn would stand at Cedric's stirrup, and Cedric, leaning down, would talk earnestly with him. But it was not of the church he spoke. The talk was furtive, secretive, as if each man was probing the other's mind, but reluctant to reveal his own. But Madaah heard enough to know that the talk was not of the threat from the North but of the King, of Aethelred, of changes that might take place in the kingdom if . . . if what was never revealed, as Thegn and Aetheling raised their drinking horns and drank to each other, but Madaah had the feeling that Cedric was like a man sowing seed in strange fields, and ready to wait for it to grow, but into what he could not, as yet, tell.

The weather broke as they rounded the dark bulk of the moors to the South East and they entered the vale of Cleveland in driving rain. Cedric drove them hard down the shallow valley, and on the sixth day of their journey, mud-spattered and weary, they came at last to the town of York.

They entered the town by huge fragments of ruined wall and forced their weary horses through the mud of a narrow street lined with houses, most of them hovels of twigs daubed with clay and crudely thatched, but with more substantial buildings

77

of wood among them. At the end of the street they came to a
stockade pierced by a gate. The gate was open but they were
challenged by a soldier, a hard looking man dressed in leather
which glistened with the rain. A word from Cedric took them
through, but there was none of the respectful attention they had
received on the way South. These were the King's men. Anyone
less than he would be of small account to them, great though he
may be in his own lands. But one of the troopers held out his
hand and touched Madaah's wet gown as he passed. That gave
Madaah a tingle of satisfaction. Although it was the Church the
man paid homage to in that rough gesture, he, Madaah, was a part
of it and shared in its power.

Two buildings dominated the square inside the stockade. On
one side was a Hall. It was massive, bigger than Ragnar's, and the
gable was finely carved with oak leaves and tendrils of briar.
Antlers were nailed above the doors and, in front of it, hanging

damply in the rain, was a white banner on a high mast, a sign
that the King was in his city. The other building was a church,
but such a one as Madaah had never seen before. It rose majesti-
cally from the muddy square, its roof overtopping the King's
Hall, and its fine proportions giving grace and significance to its
bulk. Though the King's Hall was splendid, it was made of wood,
but the church, Madaah saw and appreciated, was made of stone.
And so the two buildings faced each other, King and Church,
the temporal and the eternal, the changing and the timeless.

Armed men in plenty stood before the Hall, but as they dismounted, servants ran out and took their horses. A man followed
them from the Hall, a tall man well dressed in blue and white
linen. He raised his hand ceremoniously.

Cedric raised his gloved hand in return. 'I see you, Wulfstan.'

'I bid you welcome in the King's name,' Wulfstan said.
'Although you bear evil news, yet you are welcome.'

Cedric nodded. 'Although the news is none of my making, tell it I must.' He paused significantly, 'And in the King's ear first.'

'That is as it should be,' Wulfstan agreed. 'But the King is in church with his great men. He does penance for the sins of this kingdom which has brought down God's wrath upon it.'

'Then I shall join him and the other great men of this land.' Cedric turned and strode across the square. Wulfstan half stepped forward, 'Will you not eat first?' he cried. Cedric ignored him, and Madaah, after a moment's hesitation, trotted at his heels. There had been sly undertones in Wulfstan's voice, and a grimness in Cedric's replies that made Madaah feel uneasy, but it was none of his business he thought. His place, as newsbearer, was with Cedric.

The Spring evening had gathered now, and light glowed from the church door. There were armed men there, too, lounging carelessly against the walls, and there were more inside the porch. Cedric thrust through them, and Madaah slid behind him, and found himself in Alcuin's great church.

The church was crowded. A body of monks, drab in their grey gowns, filled the nave. From the front of the church came the sound of chanted prayer, muffled and yet echoing, and, as the monks knelt, Madaah saw the high altar and before it, kneeling, a man in green and scarlet with a thin gold circlet around his tawny hair; Aethelred, King of all Northumbria, offering his prayers and his penance to God.

The monks rose and fell in response to the liturgy, steady and orderly, and Aethelred knelt, rock still, before the altar, but by the porch Aethelred's retainers gathered in groups and moved and talked in barely muted voices. Cedric himself walked from group to group talking easily, and once, to Madaah's amazement he heard a burst of muffled laughter from a dark corner. The service came to its appointed close. Then all kneeled; monk, Bishop, Aetheling, thegn and soldier, as Aethelred, in his green and scarlet, strode down the aisle. Madaah saw his face as he passed and was surprised. There was no softness in it, and yet no savagery either; it was quite an ordinary face. And yet this was the slayer of children, the breaker of oaths, the man of blood and iron and terror. It was a frightening face though, but in a strange way; in the way that one might find frightening, not a snake, but reaching for a stick and finding it a snake, or seeing a friend who had turned, inexplicably, into a foe.

80

As the King reached the door, his thegns rising behind him, Cedric rose and saluted. Aethelred paused. 'Your message reached us, as you see.' He waved his hand at the crowded church. 'Now, as the wisdom of the Heavens will surely guide us, we will hold our Council and think of worldly things—tomorrow.' And then he was gone, surrounded by his men, and Madaah caught sight of Cedric's face, gripped with anger. Then he, too, swept through the door and into the night.

Madaah slept in the Abbey that night, in the dormitory the monks kept for travellers. When Cedric left the church, a friendly monk took Madaah in charge, whisked him down a long corridor, fed him hastily, and, ignoring his cries that he was the bearer of important news, placed him firmly in a hard and narrow bed, threw him a rough blanket, and left him. But the next morning was different. He was woken brusquely, washed and brushed, and, as the Abbey bells rang for Matins, he was led across the square, from the church to the Hall of the King.

The Hall, inside, was sumptuous. The roof was finely carved—Northumbria was famous for its craftsmanship—and banners of crimson streamed down the walls. Madaah was led up the Hall and pushed onto a bench. 'Be still and silent!' the monk hissed. Madaah needed no telling. He stared intently at the dais. A long table ran across it. On the right of the table sat the clergy: the Bishop, Madaah guessed, and the Abbot, and their chaplains and secretaries. On the left were a line of thegns, the warriors of the King's own household. They were dressed in heavy robes of blue, clasped at their throats with silver brooches. Beyond them sat Cedric, and in the middle of the table, in a high carved chair, still in green and scarlet, still with his tawny hair bound with a gold ring, sat Aethelred. On the table before him was an unsheathed sword.

It was a moment of high excitement for Madaah. He had spent a year now in this vast country, still mysterious to him, and now he was here, at the very heart of its mystery and power, sitting before its Bishop, its nobles, and its King. Disregarded, a slight dark figure in a drab gown, he leaned forward intently. The Bishop had been speaking as he had entered the hall, and Madaah leaned forward to hear what he was saying. He picked up the remarks in the middle of a sentence. 'The wrath of Charlemagne, which has been made known to us by our brother in Christ, Alcuin.'

Aethelred nodded gravely. 'We are indeed grateful to our servant Alcuin for his services to us with the King of the Franks, and we will be glad at his return. Whether we shall ever see Charlemagne I much doubt.'

There were amused smiles round the table at this. Madaah followed the joke; that the great King of the Franks was full of anger at Aethelred was well known to every monk in the kingdom. But whether Charlemagne's anger could ever be turned into action—that was another matter.

The King spoke again. 'But let me hear no more of Charlemagne. He rules his lands, I mine.'

The Bishop splendid in a purple robe, half rose. 'The Pope—'.

Aethelred cut him off abruptly. He made a chopping movement with his hand.

'The Pope rules the church, I rule Northumbria.' He looked round the table and raised his voice, 'As my father did and his before him.'

Madaah understood the point of that remark too. Aethelred was stating, before all there, his right to the throne as hereditary King, and not usurper.

'It is as your Lordship says.' The Bishop bowed and sat down.

Madaah stirred on his seat. What had the council been discussing, he wondered. Some complaint by the church about the slaying of Osred and his children? Very likely. The Bishop as guardian of morality had spoken, and had his answer.

'And now we will hear from our Aetheling, Cedric. He has journeyed far to join us.' Aethelred turned and looked down the table, past the line of his thegns. 'The Church tells us to look for good in the worst evil. This terrible happening in the holiest of Islands has brought you to our council table, there is that much good in it. It is long since we have seen you.'

Cedric bent his head, stiffly. 'It is long since you called a council my Lord, else we should have met sooner, but it is as you say; from evil can come good.'

The Abbot coughed sharply. 'That is not the teaching of the Church.'

'We are not here to talk of theology,' Aethelred tapped the table impatiently. 'We wish to know of these attacks on our Kingdom.'

'As your Lordship knows, last year a fleet of these heathen dogs came down from the North, but they were destroyed—'.

82

'By God's hand,' the Abbot cried.

Cedric agreed. 'As the Abbot says, by God's hand they were destroyed. This year they have come again, although God, it would seem, has stayed his hand. For what reason is not clear to me.'

The Abbot solemnly made the sign of the cross, 'As a punishment for our sins.'

'It is good to have with us holy men who can tell us of God's ways,' the King said, 'but we would hear more of the ways of these men from the North. Say on, Cedric.'

'There is little more to tell. This year they came again and struck at Lindisfarne and now they are gone. They burned the buildings, stole the treasures, and drowned the Monks. When I arrived, there was nothing.'

'This much we already know,' the King said. 'But tell me, why were there not soldiers at Lindisfarne? And why was there not a warning? Are the coasts of our kingdom unguarded now?' Aethelred's voice was polite, the tone was of a man asking a casual question, but the very lightness of his manner was more sinister than any anger. Aethelred had the easy control of a man who knew he held power, and how to hold it. Now, in the light contempt with which he spoke to Cedric, he was making his power felt.

Cedric answered the King's question. 'The Abbot would not have soldiers, my Lord. I cannot guard all the northern coast. As for warnings, these pirates strike from the sea. I have no ships. They may land where they wish. What am I to do, or any man?'

'Put your men in the Abbeys, whether the Church will or not. These sea-wolves will not raid at nothing, but where treasure is. Guard the Abbeys!' It was a thegn who spoke. A massive man with a dark face.

Cedric frowned. 'I spoke to the King.'

'It is our answer,' Aethelred spoke harshly. 'No matter to you who it comes from.' He snapped his fingers. 'Now we will hear this monk who has seen the pirates.'

The monk with Madaah leapt to his feet and pulled him forward. He led the way to the dais and bowed deeply, once to the King, once to the Bishop. Madaah followed his example. When he raised his head, it was to meet the King's eyes. They were pale blue, but there was nothing vacant in them as there had been in Oswald's eyes. They were hard and cold, although the mouth beneath smiled. 'You are the one?'

'Yes, my Lord,' Madaah bowed again.

'You are young to have seen such things.'

'Yes my Lord.' Another bow.

'We had expected someone older.' Aethelred looked at the Bishop, who looked at the Abbot.

'He is but a novice, my Lord. He must have been taken by these savages when only a boy.'

'Tell us about these raiders,' the King commanded.

Madaah bowed yet again, and there was a burst of laughter from the table. When he looked up all the men before him were amused, except Cedric.

'Bow much more and your head will fall off,' Aethelred said. There was more laughter from the thegns, and Madaah felt his face flush.

'Yes, my Lord,' he said. He nervously cleared his throat, and launched into his tale, carefully keeping his early years vague. When he had finished, there was no laughter at the table.

Aethelred stared at him. 'This one from Norway, this Harald, he talked of taking land?'

'That is so, my Lord. He said there were many in Norway to follow who wished land of their own.'

'And they have many ships?'

'Yes my Lord, many.'

'And this is the land they seek?'

'So Harald said, my Lord. This and Ireland, but they talk of many places. They will go wherever the land is weak.'

There was an angry mutter from the thegns and the one who had spoken bluntly to Cedric banged his fist on the table. 'They will feel our strength,' he shouted, 'as Osred felt it when he was driven from his throne.'

The thegns growled again, but the King stilled them with a wave of his hand.

'This land of Norway, where is it?'

Madaah shook his head. 'That I do not know. To the North, one, two days' sail from Orkney.'

'And Orkney?'

The Bishop coughed loudly. 'It is an island, my Lord. Beyond the land of the Picts. It was known to the ancients—Ultima Thule, the furthest—.'

He was cut off by Aethelred. 'Beyond the Pictish lands—then it is beyond our reach. That I do not like. It has ever been my way

84

to seek out my enemies, wherever they may be.' He stared grimly down the table at Cedric. Madaah stepped back a pace as he saw that look. It was not a conscious move but he was dissociating himself from those whom Aethelred might regard as his enemies.

'We will call a great council of all in the Kingdom—when it pleases us,' the King said. 'Until then let those here look to their defences. It might be that I shall place my thegns along the coast that my kingdom be well guarded.' He put his hand on the hilt of his sword as a signal that the council was over, but Cedric burst out angrily.

'You need put no thegn on the Tweed! I will hold that land as my father did, and his before him!' It was a conscious echo of Aethelred's own words, and a reminder that the Aethelings also were of noble descent, and held their land by right of birth, and not at the will of the King.

Aethelred extended his hand towards Cedric, palm upwards. 'In these days men hold what they have by holding it.' He closed his fingers and turned the open hand of friendship into a fist. 'Hold your land on the Tweed and you will see no thegn. But twice these Norsemen have attacked. Once they were destroyed, by none of your doing, the second time they landed and ruined our Abbey of Lindisfarne. Maybe, as this monk says, there will be a third coming, and what then? This is one kingdom under one king. What any one man loses, I lose as the King. But I say now, nothing shall be lost from Northumbria because any man, be he peasant or Aetheling is too weak to hold it. The council is finished.'

He rose, and all rose with him. Cedric stepped down from the dais, gave a cursory bow to the King and strode from the hall. The clergy, too, stepped down and made respectful obeisances. Aethelred bowed back, the two powers of the land acknowledging each other. The Bishop and the Abbot moved down the Hall, with their attendants falling naturally behind them in a ceremonial procession. At its tail lingered Madaah. By the door he paused and looked back. Aethelred and his thegns were sitting immobile. In their bright colours they looked like paintings on a church wall, but, as he passed through the doorway, he heard a deep cry from the thegns. What it was he did not know, but it was ominous, like the baying of dogs and he skipped forward to the line of priests, as if eager to lose himself in their anonymity.

That afternoon Madaah was placed in the care of the Master of the novices, one Sigulf, who turned him over to a monk, Brother Colman. Colman walked Madaah round the Abbey. Its size took him aback. Mentally he had been prepared for a larger St. Wilfred's, a church with cells for the monks, and a dormitory for travellers, and a library. But the Abbey of York was more than this. The hall was greater than the king's, the kitchens bigger than the church of St. Wilfred's, there were rooms beyond rooms where monks bustled back and forth with scrolls of parchment, busy with the affairs of the Church's land and possessions. As they went through the huge rambling buildings, down long cold corridors which echoed with the clatter of wooden sandals, Madaah began to realise that he was, now, and however strangely, part of a vast organisation, the greatest and most enduring in the land.

The next morning he was sent for by the Abbot. Sigulf was there also. He knew well enough now the ritual of behaviour, and in the Abbot's room he knelt and touched Edwin's fingers, felt the gentle pressure of the Abbot's hand upon his head, then rose. He stood, humbly enough, but from under his lowered brows he looked keenly at the Abbot. Edwin was a lank man with deep lines running from his nose to his lips, which were thin and turned down at the corners, and when he spoke, he revealed toothless gums. Not a pious face, Madaah thought, nor, when he spoke, had he a pious voice. It was harsh and grating, and with sour undertones, though what he said was pleasant enough.

'We are pleased to see you, my son. We have heard of you from the saintly Leofric, and of your miraculous deliverance. You spoke well before the King, where many would have faltered. Who received you into the Church?'

It was a question that by now Madaah was well prepared for. 'A holy man,' he said, 'one who came to our island and lived there quietly.'

'The North and the Western seas are full of such saints. I would that we could emulate them and pass our days in quiet holiness!' The Abbot's voice was wistful, but Madaah was not convinced. Who would exchange the life of York for a windswept isle in the western seas?

'And now we must find a place for you. We are told that you have a talent for learning. You can write?'

'A little, my Lord,' Madaah answered, modestly.

86

'The story of his adventures would be of interest. It may be that he can write them here,' Sigulf said.

Edwin pursed his lips. 'Perhaps! It seems you have a talent for survival, my son. It may be that talent is one of service to the Church. We shall see. In the meantime those talents God has given you must be nurtured. We shall put you in the library. You have done such work?'

Madaah nodded. 'Yes, Father.'

'Our standards may be different,' Edwin gave a superior smile. 'But then we are a little closer to the world, although the holy Leofric and his brothers are, no doubt, nearer to God. Remember it is Him whom we serve.'

Madaah gave an obedient assent to this.

'Good. Then you shall go to our library and work under the learned Ealdred. He was himself a scholar under Alcuin; do you know that name?'

'Yes, my Lord.'

'St. Wilfred's then is not so remote.'

'No, my Lord,' Madaah wondered why Sigulf was smiling, 'he is talked of much there.'

'And elsewhere.' Edwin raised a finger. 'Go then. We shall think of you again.' Madaah bobbed his head and backed through the door. As he closed it behind him, he heard soft laughter, and wondered what had amused the Abbot. He looked too severe to be easily moved to levity.

A monk was waiting for him who led Madaah through the long corridors, across the cloisters, up a flight of stone steps, and opened a massive door. He stood politely aside and Madaah stepped through, into the library of York.

Chapter 11

It was a long narrow room, with a pointed ceiling. Light filtered in from small windows set high in the walls. Along the walls were tiny cubicles, each with a desk. In the centre of the room was a table, littered with parchment. A few figures moved about the room, but there was no clattering of feet. The atmosphere was hushed. Only from the cubicles came a soft drone, as some monk there muttered to himself the words of a manuscript he was copying. The walls of the room were lined with shelves, which were full of roll after roll of parchment, and the costlier vellum. Madaah looked about him nervously. The apparently endless rolls of manuscript, containing the knowledge and wisdom of the world, seemed physically oppressive. It was as if the shelves and the building and the shoulders of those who worked in it were bowed down by the burden of the past.

At the end of the table a man was looking at a piece of parchment. He held it up and crumpled it in his hands, testing it for suppleness. He caught sight of Madaah.

'Yes?'

His voice echoed down the library. Madaah stepped forward a little. 'I am Madaah,' he said.

'Come here,' the man beckoned, and Madaah walked down the long room, acutely conscious of his wooden soles clacking on the stone floor. He caught a disapproving 'Tut' from the cubicles as he made his way to the head of the table, and went a little red in the face.

'I am Madaah,' he repeated. 'I was told to come and work here.'

'Ah, the novice from the North, St. Wilfred's?'

'Yes,' Madaah was uncertain how to address the man. He contented himself with a bow.

'And I am Ealdred. Under God this library is in my care. Do you know what this is?' He thrust the parchment at Madaah.

'Yes—' Madaah was still uncertain how to address Ealdred.

He decided that there was nothing to be lost by using a high title.

'Yes my Lord.'

'Yes, my Lord! Save that title for those who wish it. We are brothers in Christ; Brother Ealdred is my name. And this is parchment?'

'Yes Brother Ealdred.'

'Is it good parchment?'

Madaah ran his fingers over the skin. It was not flexible enough, and there was still the feel of bristle where the skin had not been shaved carefully.

'Not very good, Brother. The work has been skimped.'

Ealdred looked thoughtfully at Madaah. He had a pale face, paler than the parchment, but wrinkled, as parchment was before it was treated. But his eyes were bright and shone from the pale face like illuminations on a page.

'And this?' he handed Madaah another piece of material.

Madaah took it. It fell softly over hand like good cloth. He shook his head.

'It is vellum, I think, Brother Ealdred.'

'And is it well worked?'

'I do not know. I think so but—' Madaah shrugged. 'I have not seen such workmanship before. At St. Wilfred's we rarely used vellum, it was too costly. I would say it is very good but I have no way of telling.'

'You are honest,' Ealdred said. 'That is good. You speak English well, and you speak the language of the barbarians?'

'Yes, but I have forgotten some of it.'

'That is natural. And you speak Celtic, too?'

'It is my own tongue.'

'And Latin?'

'A little, Brother. I was taught at St. Wilfreds.'

'It would seem that you have a talent for language.'

It was true, Madaah thought. He had little trouble in learning. He found it easy to grasp the patterns that lay beneath sounds, and easy to remember words—what more was there to knowing another tongue? 'Father Leofric said it was a gift of God,' he exclaimed. 'He said it was given to the apostles.'

'That was well said. But a raven can be taught to speak. It is not the speaking or even the knowing, but the understanding. Well, we will put you to school. We will test your knowing. Is that your wish, little Madaah?'

Madaah thought carefully. Was it his wish? Did he desire to become a scholar, to master this knowing of which Ealdred spoke. It depended on what the knowing meant. He met Ealdred's steady eyes, gleaming from the pallor of his face. The librarian was curiously impressive, Madaah liked his quiet, even voice, and his refusal to be called Lord. Many men desired that; many men—Madaah had known them—had killed to gain that title, and yet Ealdred had spurned it. Brothers in Christ he had said, and in saying that had raised himself, Madaah, to Ealdred's own level. It was new to Madaah and the newness interested him. If knowing meant being like Ealdred, if the means led to a wise end, then he wished to be a scholar.

'Yes,' he said.

'You thought before you answered. You are wise beyond your years. Maybe we have another Alcuin or Bede in our library?' Ealdred smiled, but not mockingly. He called to a monk and told him to take Madaah to the Master of Novices. 'Tell him he has our approval,' he said. 'He will commence to learn tomorrow.'

Madaah walked with the monk down the hall. Halfway down Ealdred called to him.

'Madaah.' The librarian moved towards him. He stood by a monk who was working at the table. 'Do you see what this brother is doing?'

Madaah peered at the monk, who was sorting pieces of parchment. The parchment was charred and flaking. He looked up sharply and gazed at Ealdred.

'Yes, it is from Lindisfarne,' Ealdred said. 'You saved some wisdom there and it will not be forgotten, not though a thousand years pass.'

Madaah was one of many novices, for York was more than a stronghold of the King, more than a great church, more, even, than a great Abbey. It was a centre of learning for the whole kingdom, and it was known beyond the bounds of that. Scholars from all Europe could be found in the great library, or in the lecture halls; and courtiers from the Pope and from Charlemagne crossed the square between the Abbey and the King's Hall.

It was agreeable to Madaah. Those lands to the South, of which he had heard vague allusions in Ragnar's Hall and which had so stirred his imagination there, became realities as he ran about the library carrying books and manuscripts for men to whom Rome and Aachen and Rheims were as familiar as the shelves of the library were to himself. Bright lands they seemed too. Warm and lighted, not merely by the sun, but with a clear luminosity of the spirit as if there the limpid skies irradiated not only men's bodies, but their minds also.

In turn he was an object of interest to them. Often he was called for by Ealdred and before some traveller, black haired and with a skin of a clear pearly tint, he would tell of the Norsemen and their ferocity and strength, and of their Gods. Madaah was often struck by their manner as he told them of his experiences. Always there was shock, but it seemed to him the reaction, rather, of one who has seen a breach of good manners, like seeing a noble tear at his meat with his fingers instead of using a knife, rather than the horror and terror of men faced with a real and monstrous danger.

They were too secure, Madaah thought. Their books may have led them to knowledge, but his knowledge had led him to books, and that would take him beyond the scholars—to wisdom.

But the road to wisdom led through discipline, although Madaah was prepared for that by his experience at St. Wilfred's, and Ealdred was a great teacher. When, on the hard benches of the schoolroom, Madaah began to slide into day-dreams of his free life on his island, or on Orkney, it was the Librarian who seemed to know what was going through his mind and who could recall him to an understanding of the process of learning, could relate the learning to knowledge, and the knowledge to wisdom.

'What does it avail us,' he would say in his even voice, 'that we know the words of the Fathers if they are only sounds that we croak forth as a raven might. Many a man has died for another, and thought the dying glorious, as do the thegns of the lord our King, as even did our Lord, the Saviour of the World, but these Fathers often died for an idea. It becomes us then to think of those ideas, for although we shall pass away, as all things pass, as the world itself shall pass, yet these ideas will remain, and so, in thinking of them, we share in eternity while yet we live.'

Many of the scholars found these ideas incomprehensible and were content to learn to read a little, write a little, count a little—enough to equip themselves for a career as a Parish priest or a clerk on some great estate, a life better than they could hope for doing anything else. Indeed there was nothing else to do. Without land there was only one choice in Northumbria—to fight or to learn.

But a handful of novices grasped what Ealdred taught and they became a special privileged group. Not for them the laborious scraping of hides to make parchment, or the dusty work of cleaning the shelves, but even in this group Madaah remained on his own. He knew well enough why. It was his strangeness; his accent was different, he looked different, but most of all, his experience was different. The oldest and cleverest of the novices was childish compared to him.

So he lived in the great Abbey; solitary but not lonely, and learning to accept under the benign influence of Ealdred not only knowledge, not only the doctrines of the Church, but also the supremacy of those doctrines over all others. It was a hard task for him. The other novices had known no other beliefs. They had been born into the Church and had lived, always, under its shadow. But Madaah had known other beliefs and other ways of life. He was the only novice with a standard of comparison; he could place God against Odin, Christ against Thor, the Apostles against Baldir, and the world of angels and devils against those old beliefs with which he had grown up; that world where there had been no distinction between the natural and the supernatural, between 'them' and 'us', between 'then' and 'now'.

Then, one day when the mild early autumn sun gleamed through the high windows of the library, Sigulf, the Master of the Novices sent for him.

Madaah went, not nervously, but not confidently either.

When Sigulf sent for a novice, it was not usually a pleasant experience—for the novice. So when he had entered Sigulf's room, he stood before the Master tentatively. Sigulf was sitting

in a chair with a piece of parchment in his hand. He gave Madaah a thoughtful look through his pouched eyes, then peered again at the parchment. He looked at it for what seemed to Madaah a long time, and then he spoke. 'What is this?' he asked, coldly.

Madaah craned his neck to see more clearly. He recognised it. It was a piece of work he had done himself—a translation into English of a Latin prayer.

'It is a prayer for forgiveness, Father,' he said.

93

'Is the work good?' Sigulf asked.

Madaah was modest. 'It is the best I could do, Father.'

'Yes,' Sigulf's voice had lost none of its coldness but it became reflective. 'The work is good. Not many would have found the words you have found to translate this prayer, this holy thought. Without you there would have been no writing here, and what would we have had? A piece of skin—maybe one that would have been made into a shield, that men might slay each other the better.' Sigulf waved the parchment slowly. 'Where does the parchment come from, Madaah?'

'From the skins of calves, Father.'

Sigulf nodded. 'That is so! From the skins of calves. Without calves there would be no parchment, and without parchment there would be no writing, and without writing there would be no learning and darkness would come again on the face of the Earth. Is that not so?'

Madaah agreed. It was so.

'Yes,' Sigulf said. 'The Church has turned the skin to its own use. A better one than it might otherwise have been. Where did the calf come from?'

Madaah was surprised by the question but he answered dutifully. 'From the farm, Father. From the Abbey's land.'

'That is so. It came from our land.' Sigulf fell silent for a while. 'From toil and labour came this parchment. Elijah in the wilderness was fed by the ravens, but the Church must not depend on miracles for its survival. It must have parchment. It must have food and drink for its scholars. And for those things it must have land. Although we look beyond this world we are bound by its laws. Should we ignore them, then the Church might perish and there would be darkness again on the face of the Earth. It was the Church that brought light to that darkness and we must keep its flame burning. You are a scholar and you will appreciate that.'

'Yes, Father.'

Sigulf place the parchment down and looked gravely at Madaah. 'Do you love the Church, Madaah?'

'With my body and soul.' Madaah surprised himself with the force of his answer. Once he would have spoken glibly, deceitfully. But now? He had told the truth without thinking.

'What friends have you among the novices?'

'I have none, Father.'

'No. Nor have you brothers or sisters, father or mother—so

you think—but the Church is your father and mother, and brothers and sisters you have in thousands, tens of thousands. Remember that, my son.'

He would, Madaah promised, and indeed he felt that it was so, and the idea was not strange to him. The tribe, on that far island of his birth, had been, each one, a member of the same community, brother and sister each to the other.

'Very well!' Sigulf gazed at Madaah, as though he were in judgement over him.

'I will tell you a story Madaah. Listen well. Ten years ago I went on a pilgrimage to Rome. The journey there is long and goes through mountains—such mountains! I had not thought their like existed upon this earth. So high they are their peaks are covered with snow and ice that never melts. I saw the sun shine on them and they reflected its light in haloes of gold. They were crowned in glory, like the saints in heaven, and yet they rested on fearsome rocks so barren and unfruitful they made my heart sore to see them. Nothing grew there; no grass, no trees, no flowers; nothing lived there but wolves, and bears, and evil men, and maybe things worse than those. And yet those crowns of glory shone because of that grim desert of rock. The Church is like those mountains, Madaah. It too is crowned with glory, and yet its crown rests upon the sorrows and evils of this world.

'To keep one's eyes on heaven and one's feet on this muddy earth and not overbalance is a gift, a rare one, but some possess it, and those who do must be ready to use it.'

The Master fixed his eyes on Madaah in an unspoken question. Madaah understood the question and knew the answer: 'If I be such a one, then I am ready.'

'Good!' There was no warmth in Sigulf's voice, no hint of pleasure; he spoke as one accepting a neutral fact. 'Now you will go back to Ealdred, to the crown of glory, but you will also spend time with me, among the rocks. Now go.'

For a day or so, it was as Sigulf had said. Madaah spent his time in study, among the pure peaks of scholarship, undisturbed by the events of the world. But, one afternoon, as he sat with Ealdred, working on a Testament which was to be the greatest work of art and scholarship the Abbey had ever produced, he was sent for by Sigulf and set to work in the Abbey's office, under Benedict, the Steward.

Ealdred was disturbed by this. When Madaah was first sent

for, he gave him leave to go, but when Madaah told him that he was to go every day, he frowned and rose from the table. 'I will see into this,' he said, and strode from the Library. But, when he came back, he had nothing to say, although he looked withdrawn and thoughtful.

Madaah did not dislike the altered rhythm of his days. It was interesting to have work which had a connection with the outside world, and the contact, he soon saw, was a tangible one. Sigulf had said that the Church lived from the land, and the evidence was here in the great yellow Tax Rolls of the Abbey; so much flour left, so many mouths to feed, so much salt, so much ale, so much seed, so many sheep, so many cows, so many oxen—and so much fodder. How many animals to slaughter before the coming winter, when there would be no grazing,—and which? It became clear to Madaah that Sigulf had said no more than the truth when he had claimed that the splendours of the Church came not from miracles, but from labour, from the toil of the land.

In the evenings he had his third lesson, and that was the most interesting of all. One night, after finishing his work in the office Sigulf took him to the Hall and placed him on the dais. 'You will be here tonight, and every night,' he said. 'Not as a guest,' he added hastily, 'but as a servant—a servant of the servants of God. And while there you will be as one who is deaf. Away from it as one who is dumb.'

During the next weeks, when Madaah stood discreetly at the end of the long table he understood Sigulf's choice. He heard much; those who sat at the table were men of rank, worldly or spiritual, and their talk was not merely of light trifling affairs, but of power—how it was gained, and how it was held. And one thing Madaah learned; it was not gained or held by prayer, but by ruthless and iron hands, not least in Northumbria, nor it seemed in other places either.

But another thing he learned. Power was not gained by prayer, but it was rarely held for long without it, for the Church had its own way of influencing the world. God moved through it to influence the World, and brief could be the reign of a King who thought otherwise, for though there were many Kings, and more men who wished for a throne, there was but one Church and that oneness gave it strength, richness, and power too.

It was a contrast Madaah did not grow tired of. On the one

96

hand, the Church, source of all morality and spiritual power, on the other, the King, the fountain head of all strength—as long as his hand was strong, and Aethelred's seemed that still, as he once showed.

There was a feast in the Hall. For nine years Aethelred had held the throne, and it was in celebration that King and Ealdormen, cleric and thegn, gathered in the lofty room, swathed in its banners of scarlet and gold and hung with spears and shields. Although there were many great men there, Madaah noticed that there were many who were not, the Aethelings for instance. But Aethelred seemed unmoved by that and the feast went on in all its splendour.

Although the Abbot was present, the feast became a drunken one. That was not remarkable. What were ale and mead for if not to be swilled? and there was much drunken boasting by the thegns. That too was traditional, but one thegn became a little too drunk. He was a local man, a petty landowner from Cleveland, one hardly regarded, sitting alone in a dark corner, last to be served, last to be fed.

One of the King's warriors stood in the centre of the Hall before Aethelred, and told of his valour in battle.

'Thus I struck—and thus!' he swung an imaginary battle-axe around. 'And thus the men of Osred fell when we overthrew him and brought the noble Aethelred to the throne. Thus they fell, I say—those who did not run!'

There was a burst of laughter from the listeners but the man from Cleveland did not laugh. He leaped angrily to his feet and paced to the centre of the Hall. 'Not all ran. Many stood and fought until they waded in the blood of their enemies. My axe swept down many; Godwin and Uhtred and Waltheof.' And then his voice faded away. Aethelred was looking at him.

'It seems to me I recall those names,' the King said. 'One Godwin bore my banner before me when I rode again into this Kingdom.' His voice was as quiet as ever, but the Hall was quieter still.

The thegn looked around, but there was no help for him in the faces of those who listened.

'You bore a sword for Osred?' Aethelred asked.

'That is so my Lord,' the thegn muttered.

'It was sworn to him?'

'Yes, my Lord.'

'It is well that a man should keep his word,' Aethelred nodded, as one well satisfied. He nodded and waved his hand and the feast went on. The next day the thegn from Cleveland was found hacked to death in a ditch.

Madaah brooded over this. He went to Ealdred and asked him his opinion. The librarian shook his head impatiently. 'It is nothing to us,' he said. 'Among such as those, blood demands blood. They live in a mire of deceit. What good can come from such a bog? Does it not say in the Gospels—they who live by the sword shall perish by it? Think instead of the blessed Augustine and live in the City of God.'

Sigulf was more sympathetic. 'It is evil that such things should happen. Who has condemned them more than the Church? But that one, that thegn from Cleveland, he was foolish. Foolish to drink and talk so, to let himself be provoked by such idle boasting. Foolish, too, not to have sworn himself before now to Aethelred's service. But I tell you now Madaah, better that one man should die than many. Better that one hand, however harsh it be, should rule the land than that many such should seek it. And that thegn, he was not a godly man, that is sure. Had it been one of the Church treated thus—but it was not. There is a lesson there for us—and for you. Remember it.'

Madaah remembered it. He went on with his studies and his lessons. Now in the church, now in the Library, now in the King's Hall; a slight dark figure, quick, adept, good with figures, clever with words, anticipating wants before they were told him, growing and maturing, but for ever keeping a veil of reserve between himself and all others—except Ealdred.

For some time he had been working on a psalter. It was his own translation and a good one. Over the words of the psalms he had drawn King David with his harp, and over that, in a sky of the most delicate blue, God Himself in all His majesty. Unusually for Madaah, no great artist with a brush, the illumination was good and there was one thing that pleased Ealdred. David's hair was bound with a thin gold ring, and he was dressed in scarlet and green, Aethelred's own colours.

Ealdred smiled when he saw it. 'This surely is the way to see these holy words,' he said. 'Not as mere mutterings from long ago, but related to those we see and know. The King will be leaving York soon. It may be that this will be a fitting gift for him. I shall see.'

He consulted with the Abbot and with Sigulf. Both agreed. The psalter was bound with the finest calf and Ealdred took Madaah across to the King, bearing the gift.

Aethelred took the book and looked for long at the picture. 'Who did this work?' he asked.

Ealdred placed his white hand on Madaah's shoulder. 'This one, my Lord. It is a present from the lowest in the Church to the highest in the land.'

The King showed neither pleasure nor displeasure. 'Music we have ever loved. You shall stay for a while.' He raised his hand. 'It is our wish to hear our minstrel.'

The King's harpist came before them, bowed low, and swept his fingers across the strings of his harp, but it was not a song of David he sung.

'Then was shattered the linden shield by the spear of ash,
Like hail fell the arrows, like snow the seax.
Eagle and wolf watched the dying men
While over them walked the warriors, mighty thegns,
Boar-crested were their helmets, sharp their swords,
In the service of their King, great giver of gifts,
Bearer of bracelets.'

He finished his song and Aethelred waved his dismissal. 'Such songs I like,' he said. 'We will keep your book and look at it for our pleasure.'

Ealdred and Madaah left the Hall silently and thoughtfully. 'We will go into Church,' Ealdred said. 'There is other music.'

There was. It was the time of Vespers, and, as they entered the Church, the voices of the monks were raised in song. They stood quietly at the back of the church. Before them, facing the altar, the monks raised their voices in that chant which had so moved Madaah when he had first heard it, bewildered then, stranger on a strange shore. It was a psalm of David the monks were singing, that David Madaah had dressed in the robes of the King.

'Fret not thyself because of evil-doers.'

Madaah knew the words. Had he not himself made them over into English? Rest patiently in the Lord, for He would bring righteousness and justice. He would bring it to pass. The powers of the Earth might be brought against them, but the meek would inherit the Earth. Although the wicked might flourish for a while, they would be cut down like grass. Their time would be short and the Lord would laugh at them.

'I have seen the wicked in great power, and spreading himself like a green bay tree.'

And I too, thought Madaah, and every man in the kingdom. When would they wither away, and how? The psalm came to its moving close;

'The salvation of the righteous is of the Lord:
He is their strength in the time of trouble.
And the Lord shall help them, and deliver them:
He shall deliver them from the wicked, and save
them, because they trust in Him.'

Madaah looked sideways at Ealdred. His face was tranquil, luminous with belief and trust. Was his own the same? he wondered, or would it ever be?

The summer wore away, and Madaah worked steadily on, gaining the approval of Ealdred, and of Sigulf also. Although nothing was ever said openly, Madaah felt that there was a subtle struggle taking place between the Librarian and the Master, and that he was in some way the prize. He thought about it often; was he to be a scholar, like Ealdred? Or a man of power, like Sigulf? He thought, too, of the world in which he found himself. There was the realm of the King, the ruthless despotic world where a wrong word could mean death in a ditch, and there was the world of Ealdred, those pure glittering peaks of scholarship where a wrong word could gain a reproof, often as sharp as any spear, and there was the world of Sigulf, where men laboured and toiled to ward off the wolves of the kingdom and keep in peace and safety the learning of a thousand years.

As Madaah struggled with these ideas, the summer ended. The King left York to collect his dues from his subjects on the river Don in the South. The Abbey turned out to give him homage at his departure. Madaah stood by the gate and watched the King's messengers on their grey horses pound out of the town to give warning that Aethelred was coming. He saw the huge wagons, pulled by eight oxen each, drag through the dust of the road, and then the horsemen and the spearmen, thegn and chaplain, and then the Royal Standard, and at last the King himself. With all others Madaah bowed low, and with the others, as he straightened himself, felt a sense of profound relief as the last of the long procession wound through the broken walls. Then he turned to Ealdred, who had bowed as deeply as any before the Oath-breaker.

'Why do we do homage to one such as he?' he asked.

Ealdred clapped him on the shoulder. 'Render unto Caesar what is Caesar's. And what is his is what he can enforce. Now we will render unto God what is His, and no rough hand will bend us to our task before Him.'

The answer was not unsatisfactory to Madaah, but he felt within himself vague dissatisfactions. The memory of the King's departure, with its air of splendour, began to haunt him, and with that memory came others; of the baying of the thegns at the Council, and the deep battle cries of the Norsemen in Ragnar's Hall, as some warrior told of his deeds against foes as cruel and ruthless as himself, and he would think of the days when he held mastery, not only over books, but over men, and he had wielded not a brush, although that might hold in its full bristles the mastery of the ages, but a sword.

And then, one day, in the Library he found a poem. It was a strange work. A tree spoke, a tree hewn from the forest by unthinking men and carved into a cross and planted again into the ground. Onto it stepped a young hero who was pierced with nails and died there. Then darkness covered the face of the Earth and the young hero was taken down by his thegns, his faithful followers. All this the tree told, and of its own agony as the nails which pierced the hero gouged into itself.

He mentioned it to Ealdred. 'I know that poem,' he said. 'It is called "The Dream of the Rood." How far we can accept it I am not sure. That trees should talk—even that tree which bore our Saviour—I do not know.' He shook his head thoughtfully. 'When the words of the Apostles was first brought to this land, men prayed to trees and stones, indeed they still do, the shadow of those days has not yet passed, and that poem—does it look back to those days, or forward to new ones? If it looks forward, good—if it looks back, then it has its dangers. Once, in this land, an infant could be strangled at birth, a man could be killed at the whim of another, and that man was counted the most glorious who could slay most others. We have altered that. We and these!'

He waved his hand at the shelves of manuscript. 'These, dusty as they are! It may be there are such things as talking trees, but we must be careful what they tell us.'

He went away and left Madaah at the table, uncertain of the truth of what he had been told. How far had the Church altered men? The thegns who rode with Aethelred still thought battle glorious, and the King himself could break his word, sworn before the high altar of the Minister, kill two children, and still rule.

But the poem was profoundly satisfying to Madaah. Those desires which welled in him below the order of the Church were answered by it—the desire for a hero, the wish to share in the warrior's heroism, the longing for a universe which lived and felt as he did, and in which he could share, and his feeling for a time which came before *his* time and which would go on after it—a past and a future, as well as a now.

The first chill of autumn began to creep about the Abbey's stones, and with it came stories of the outside world. An Ealdorman, ruler of the lands of Lindsey, where the King was wintering, had risen and attempted to seize the throne. Aethelred had crushed the rebellion and killed the Ealdorman and his family, and the rebel thegns and their families, down to the last babe. The whole of Lindsey was a waste land.

The monks shuddered at the tales, and there was endless talk of them in the Abbey. But Ealdred was firm. He would allow no gossip, no tales of terror in the Library. 'Woe unto the world, for offences must come.' He quoted. 'But woe unto those who add to them by idle chatter,' he added meaningfully.

But still the Abbey was full of whispers, echoes of the terrors of the Kingdom. Throughout the bitter weather travellers came, messengers from other Abbeys who spent long hours with the Abbot. Madaah was close to the tales and heard much. The Aethelings, those princes who had overthrown Osred and recalled Aethelred, were stirring in his terrible grip, and those furthest from his hand stirred the most. Madaah began to understand the problems of ruling Northumbria. The Kingdom was so vast that, if the King was in the South, he was powerless in the North, and, if he was in the North, the South was in the hands of any man strong enough, and bold enough to rule. Only by the exercise of terror could the King keep his Kingdom.

And there were threats from beyond the Kingdom too.

Madaah became aware of a new name, Eardwulf. He was one whose claim to the throne was good, for his line of descent ran through the last King, Osred, and Osred's father Alchred, back to the great Ida, half legendary founder of the Kingdom. He was one with strong allies in the kingdom, ealdormen and aetheling, and he was cousin to the Aetheling Cedric, the most powerful man in the North. There was little doubt that, if he were to return, he would be welcome, and there was less doubt that he would—and then there would be again the horrors of civil war. Madaah recalled Sigulf's words. Better one harsh hand than many such; better one tyrant, such as Aethelred, than many!

Much Madaah heard, but little he told. Those monks who spoke to him of what he may have heard were met with a cold look, or even, as Madaah grew bolder in his knowledge of his own position, with a stinging reproof—none of which was lost on Sigulf.

The winter came and the travellers grew fewer. The stories of the terror in the South died away. The iron weather imposed a peace on Northumbria no King seemed able to do. Madaah sat, day after day in the Library, night after night with Sigulf, learning to slide easily from the heights to the depths, and to become at last and truly, a man of the Church, and the Church's man.

It was a hard winter. The food grew worse as the weather grew harder: salted fish, salted meat, hard bread, and little of it. The monotony of the food dulled the taste buds, and, short of nourishment, the weak and sickly began to die. Everyone suffered and a community of misery grew up among the monks. Each had a tale of woe, but they survived—through December, through the great feast of Christmas, when a massive banquet raised their bodies and their morale, through the New Year when snow came and gave the Abbey a fresh and glittering beauty, and the novices played snowballs, and one or two monks, noted for their severity, found it repaid with a hard lump whizzing onto the back of their necks. But every day except Sunday found Madaah at his work, taking another step along the road to wisdom.

In Lent, during the long fast when necessity was made a virtue, Madaah was taken out of the Abbey and onto the Church lands. The nature of the land was carefully explained to him. This was arable, that pasture, next year this would be altered, that changed.

It was all carefully noted, woods and mills, beasts and men—
especially men. Their stooped backs supported the weight of the
Church, and the dirtiest and most ragged peasant, staring dumbly
at the monks, paid, in his labour, his unwitting tribute to the
thought of Alcuin, Ealdred, and Madaah.

Madaah was sometimes moved by the peasants. He admired
their strength and steady, slow persistence, but Sigulf, himself
habitually cold, discouraged any warmth in Madaah. 'Warm
hearts are for confessors,' he said, 'and we are not those. Our
task is to rule, and how can we do that if we bend at every sigh
of pain. The Church will give comfort enough to those whose
hearts are sore, but each man to his own anvil.'

In his own way Ealdred said the same thing. To be a scholar,
he told Madaah, was to be above the world, away from its woes,
for they did not last. From them both Madaah took his lesson,
and, yet, at the heart of the teaching of the Church lay a message
of compassion and hope, that message brought so long ago by the
son of the carpenter. Surely that had to lie somewhere, he
thought, and when he asked Ealdred he found his answer.

'It lies in the heart of every man,' the Librarian said, 'and waits
for its hour to be called forth. Your hour has not come yet. First
the learning, then the wisdom.' And then he said a surprising
thing, 'I pray your hour comes after the learning.' He would add
no more.

At the end of Lent the Abbey held a great feast. As usual
Madaah hovered behind the great men of the Abbey, but at the
end of the meal, instead of being dismissed, Sigulf took him to the
Abbot's room.

'You are going to talk to the Lord Abbot,' he said. 'Listen
carefully to what he has to say. There will be one with him. Of
him you will take no notice. Do you understand?'

Madaah murmured that he did, although the remark mystified
him, but he followed Sigulf obediently to Edwin's room. Sigulf
went inside and Madaah stood in the corridor wondering why
the Abbot should wish to see him, and who the mysterious person
would be whom he was not to notice. Then the door opened and
Sigulf waved him in.

He entered and bowed low before the Abbot. Although he
saw him often at the high table, Madaah had not spoken to the
Abbot since his arrival at York a year before. He knelt, felt the
Abbot's hand press lightly on his head, then rose. In a corner of

the room was another man. He wore a cloak which he held so high that little of his face was visible. Madaah let his eyes flicker once towards him, then looked squarely at the Abbot.

Edwin smiled, a mere cracking of his thin lips. 'I have reports of you, my son. You have given great satisfaction to our learned brother, Ealdred, and to our holy brother, Sigulf.'

Madaah bowed his appreciation.

'You have seen much since you came to us.'

'Yes, my Lord.'

'And learned much, too.'

'Yes, my Lord.'

'Has this work been of interest to you?'

'Yes, my Lord.'

Sigulf leaned over the Abbot's shoulder. 'He is one who says little, my Lord.'

'But listens much?'

'Just so!'

'Then he has wisdom already.' Edwin looked approvingly at Madaah who felt uneasy. Where was this talk leading? What had the silence of a novice to do with the Abbot? And who was the man in the corner with the hidden face? He had a feeling that there was something happening in the room of which he was unaware, a force that would affect him but in a secret way, as a still river might have hidden currents, unknown until one entered it.

Edwin folded his hands in his lap. They were old and wrinkled with blue veins running down them like mistletoe on an oak tree. He studied Madaah carefully. 'Sometimes there comes to the Church one who is above all others of his generation. Such a one was Bede, such a one is Alcuin. Who knows who will be the next, or from what dark mystery he will come?'

It was not a question Madaah thought required answering but he felt an agreeable prickle along his spine.

'The road to those heights is long,' Edwin continued, 'and can lead in strange ways. But the road must be followed!' Edwin paused and looked at the muffled man. From the corner of his eye Madaah saw him give a nod, the slightest jerk of his head.

Edwin raised his eyes to the ceiling. 'My son, we are going to send you on a journey. At the end of it is a task you must do. The church has mouths, many of them, that are open wide in praise, but it must have eyes and ears also. We have work to be done, and it is our belief that you can do it. It will call for humility and silence, watchfulness and—' The Abbot paused, choosing his word carefully, ' "discretionum," ' he used the Latin. 'Do you know that word?'

'Yes, my Lord. It means judgement.'

'Good, good. That will be your work. To hear much, see much, and say little. Except, of course, to us,' Edwin ended flatly, staring penetratingly at Madaah, 'do you understand?'

Madaah thought he did. 'I think so my Lord. I am to hear, to be silent, and to tell you what I hear.'

'That is sufficient for our purpose, although it is not in our service that you go, but in that of the Lord, our God. We are sending you to an Aetheling. You will keep his accounts and watch over his land, as you have here. But you must remain humble, as befits a man of God, and a servant of His Church. Then, in our time, we will recall you, and we shall not forget your services to us. Write to us in the Latin that we shall know you have not forgotten your learning. You will leave tomorrow. The King rides North to Catterick and we will send you to travel with him. That will be a great honour for one such as you.' Edwin gave his cracked smile again. 'Our prayers will be with you, remember us in yours.'

Madaah bowed reverently. 'Each night I shall, my Lord.' He hesitated, then spoke up boldly. 'This Aetheling, my Lord, I shall serve him well.'

'Indeed you shall, and us too.'

'He is at Catterick, my Lord?'

Edwin gave a little cough. 'Ah, we have not told you of him yet. You do not go among strangers, my son. You are going to the land of the Tweed, to the Hall of the Aetheling Cedric.' He extended his hand and Madaah bent and kissed it. Sigulf bustled around and led Madaah to the door. As they reached it, the silent man in the corner leaned forward toward Edwin and his cloak slipped a little. Madaah caught a glimpse of his face, and then he was out in the corridor. As Sigulf hurried him away Madaah realised that he had seen the face before, and wondered where. It was during the night that he remembered—it was the thegn who had spoken so brutally to Cedric at the King's council.

Chapter 12

The next day Madaah left the Abbey, but, before he went, he saw Ealdred, to make his farewell. Ealdred took him to the tiny cell which was his dwelling place. He gave Madaah a stool and himself sat on his hard bed and listened as Madaah told him what was to happen. When Madaah had finished, he nodded.

'Then that will be your work,' he said. 'Do it well!'

Madaah wanted more than that. 'I shall, Brother, but have I not worked well in the Library?'

Ealdred's face was impassive. 'Yes, none better.'

'Then why am I sent away?'

'Because the Church has need of you elsewhere. It is sufficient reason. Not for you, or I, to question it.'

'I do not question it in that way, Ealdred, but—' Madaah paused, 'there were things I did not fully understand. There was a man there, he—'

'Do not speak of that,' Ealdred said sharply. 'You have been told to hear much and say little. Remember that. Be obedient!' He sighed. 'The shadows deepen again over this Kingdom, and they fall on us, too. Go Madaah, do the bidding of the Church. It may be that what you will do will keep our light burning. Trust those who send you. It is not for their own ends they give you this work to do.'

'But why me?' Madaah pressed his question.

Ealdred's face, normally so calm, creased, almost as though in pain. 'You are young, Madaah, and yet you are old. I will say this; men will sometimes speak before a youth when they will be silent before a man. I can say no more.'

He stood up and placed his hand on Madaah's shoulder. 'It is none of my doing that you leave.' His voice was suddenly harsh, and he turned away. 'Now go!' he commanded.

At noon, with a guide, Madaah left York. He had a letter of

introduction, a box of brushes and inks and parchment, his gown, and a horse. Nothing else except the cross he had taken from the prisoner, slaughtered on Ragnar's ship, two long years ago.

They rode north, along the valley of the Swale, through the rough hamlets and villages that Cedric and Madaah had galloped through the previous year. The guide, a monk, wanted to talk, but finding no response fell into silence. Madaah was not inclined to chatter. He thought about his errand and about the talk with Edwin and with Ealdred. The remarks of both had been full of insinuations, of subtle hints. Madaah remembered his ride with Cedric and how they had stopped at the halls of the petty thegns and the talk that had gone on then. Edwin's talk had been like that. Little said, but much intended, and he, Madaah, was not sure what the intention was. Well, events might tell him that. In the meantime he would be obedient, say little and learn much, and write to the Abbey in the Latin tongue. But he wished in his heart that it was not Cedric's Hall to which he was going. Oswald would be there, and he had not forgotten him, nor the antagonism each seemed to bear for the other. A problem waited there. He shrugged. That, too, would have to wait.

They stayed overnight in the hut of a priest, rose early, and before Matins had reached Catterick and the King's camp. They were two of many entering the camp. The King's stay in Catterick was not for his pleasure, nor for the amusement of his subjects. He was there to collect his rents, and they could only be paid in kind so the road was choked with wagons bringing flour and meat, timber and cloth, metalwork of all kinds; for, of anything which the countryside could produce, so much was the King's. He was there too, as judge, and, when Madaah and his guide had fought their way through the crowds, they found him sitting in his high chair before a poor hall, his bodyguard flanking him, while in the crowd the suppliants and the criminals waited for his rough and abrupt justice. Aethelred looked unchanged. His face still had that deceptive ordinary look, and his tawny hair blew slightly in the wind. Behind his shoulder stood a monk, with a massive roll of parchment. They were the dues. Each Lord was down there with what he owed the King, and woe to him who could not pay. A man stood before the King speaking earnestly. Behind him was a group of villagers, sturdy men, freemen obviously. The man finished speaking and stepped back.

Aethelred addressed the villagers who raised their right hands. The King spoke over his shoulder to the monk, who whispered urgently back. Aethelred nodded as if satisfied and lifted his hand. Then the monk walked forward and shouted in a voice clear enough for all to hear.

'Let Ceolfrid of the Crooked Leg come forward.'

Whoever Ceolfrid was he did not appear. Twice more the monk repeated his commandment. No Ceolfrid. 'Then let the King's judgement be known, this Ceolfrid is cast from the folk. Let him wear the wolf's head!'

Madaah shivered a little as he heard the judgement. Ceolfrid had been cut off from mankind by those words. He had committed some crime and failed to appear for judgement. Now he was an outlaw and any man could kill him, as any man might kill a wolf. It was a terrible punishment, to be excluded from all normal life, condemned to wander in the forest like a wild beast. His crime must have been a bad one, the punishment death, for him not to take the justice of the land.

Madaah wandered away to find someone who could fit him into the King's retinue. He found a minor steward who peered suspiciously at the letter Madaah waved, then grudgingly gave him a place at the table where the King's officers were snatching a meal. All afternoon the King sat in judgement on his high chair, then, as night fell, he retired with his thegns into the miserable Hall. All others were left to fend for themselves. Madaah filched a blanket and found a place under one of the carts. As he dozed off, he comforted himself with the thought that the next move would be along the coast where they would stay at the great Abbeys. There at least they would find comfort and good food.

The next morning he was disabused of this idea. The King was going inland, to Hexham. It had been a long time since he had travelled there, and he had heard rumours of rebellion, or rebellious thoughts, along the wild borders of the Stainmore Forest. So the King would go there and grind whoever challenged him under his heel, while his minister Torhtmund was going to travel to the coast and look to its defences. Madaah asked with whom he should travel, and the steward shrugged. It was a matter of indifference to him. After some thought Madaah decided to stay with the King. The thought of the journey across the wild flanks of the Kingdom had no attractions for him, but the idea of moving with the King did. Besides that attraction there was another consideration. Madaah had seen the thegn who had been present at his meeting with Edwin in York. Cynwulf was his name. Madaah felt a profound curiosity about him. In some way Cynwulf was responsible for he, himself, being where he was. Madaah had not forgotten that slight nod which had implied approval of Edwin's choice.

So when, on the third day, the King broke his camp and moved, Madaah went with him. He was an unnoticed member of the throng, free to wander along the column as he chose, although if he came too near the King there was always a massive thegn to shoulder him back, and that not gently. Once it was Cynwulf who bore down on him. Madaah looked him straight in the face, but the thegn showed no flicker of recognition, and Madaah meekly turned away.

At the crossing of the Tees, Torhtmund broke away with a column of soldiers, but the King's band moved on. Now they were moving into wild country. To the East, grey hills shouldered their way through mists of fine, penetrating rain. Innumerable streams flowed down from them into wild valleys, tangled with forest. There were people living there, though few, and they came from their clearings to stare dumbly at the King's procession, kneeling as the banner went past them, and then at the King himself. Those too slow, or ignorant, were beaten to their knees by the soldiers.

It took two long days to reach the Wear, a journey of no more than twelve or fifteen miles. But once there, the King moved away, up the river, leaving the wagons and baggage behind. He took with him his thegns and soldiers and went at a hard run up the valley. When they returned, three days later, meeting the baggage train a few miles south of Hexham, Aethelred looked grim, but the warriors were boastful and drunken round a huge fire. Madaah stood at a distance and looked over the thegns and the fire at the line of hills behind them. Some lord up there, feeling over-secure in his fastness had spoken, perhaps a little too freely, of his views on Aethelred's Kingship. But the King had heard, and now, beyond the woodlands, there would be the smoking remnants of a Hall, dead men and crying women; Madaah shook his head. How had the King known? Perhaps some priest had mentioned it in a report to his Abbey . . . he felt a spasm of unease. Something stirred in the back of his mind, but with an effort of will he stilled it. Better a few men dead than many! Better that one quick brutal blow than a long drawn-out rebellion! Better one harsh man holding power than many such ravaging the land to seek it! Such, at any rate, was the teaching of the Church, or so he told himself firmly as they came to the great monastery of Hexham.

The King had his own fine Hall in Hexham, and though the land about looked bare, it was deceptively so. There was good land in plenty, enough to support the Abbey and the King.

Aethelred intended staying in the North for the summer. He had harried the South; now, Madaah wondered, did he intend harrying the North? But that was not Madaah's concern. He turned to the Abbey and was made welcome there, and was again the centre of attention. He told his tales and received gratifying gasps of horror. In turn he heard more of Lindisfarne. The Abbot had escaped—that had not been noticed at the time— and now he travelled about Northumbria with the body of Cuthbert, seeking to found a new Abbey. 'It will not be easy for him,' said the monk who told Madaah this. 'It is not as in the days of old when there was land to be had for the asking, when—' he dropped his voice to a whisper—'when there were pious Kings over us.'

Madaah spent a day or so in the Abbey. He admired the carving in the church, better than any he had seen before, although the library he thought was not as good as York's. But still he felt profound respect for the Abbey. After his journey with the King, with its air of savagery, the tranquillity of the Abbey was like a different world. Indeed it was a different world, and he prepared to leave it with regret. But before he left, an amazing thing happened. He was in the library, examining some fine illuminated manuscripts when a monk rushed in. 'Are you the one known as Madaah?' he asked, and when Madaah answered 'Yes,' he seized him by the arm.

'You are wanted by the King; come!' He tugged Madaah urgently, but Madaah needed no urging. When Aethelred crooked his finger, Aethelings came running, not just mere novices. He ran through the Abbey and across the square to the King's hall. Wulfstan, the steward was at the door.

'You are the monk from York?' he demanded, and when Madaah gasped he was, took him by the arm and led him in, to the King.

Aethelred was sitting, as usual, in his high chair, but before a flaring fire. His thegns were by him, on benches, and before them, their arms lashed cruelly behind their backs, were three men. Madaah took one look at them, and needed no telling as to

who they were—they were Norsemen.

Wulfstan ushered Madaah before the King. Madaah made a deep bow.

'We have seen you before,' Aethelred said.

'That is so, my Lord. At your council at York.' Madaah remembered not to bow again.

'We have not forgotten. Now these men—' Aethelred waved at the prisoners, 'These men have been brought to us from our burgh of Seaham. They were found on the shore. They speak no English, nor the Latin either, neither do they speak in the Frankish tongue. So it comes to us that maybe they are from the lands of the North of which you told us.'

'They are, my Lord. I have seen many like them.'

'We remember that you speak their language, it is so?'

'I do, my Lord.'

'Then you will speak for us, but let our words grow neither big nor small in the telling. Nor theirs, either.'

'I will do my best, my Lord,' Madaah said, but thought it wise

112

to put in a qualification. 'Some of the language I forget, it is a long time since I spoke it.'

'That we understand. If there is difficulty, tell us. We shall not be angry. Now, ask them from where they have come.'

Madaah turned to the prisoners. Two wore the Norsemen's dress of tunic and woollen trousers, though one was naked to the waist. His chest was marked with cuts and whip marks. The other two had bruised and swollen faces. One of the men was better dressed than the others, his tunic a little more elaborately worked. The man stared back fearlessly. Madaah pointed to Aethelred. 'This is the King of all this land.' He thought for a moment. He had used the Norse word, Jarl, but it meant less, somehow, than the English 'King'. 'He is, he is the Jarl of Jarls.' As the Norse words came from his tongue, he felt an odd stirring of sympathy for the men. That was strange, he thought. For a year he had hated the Norsemen, but, at his first meeting with them again, he saw them merely as men; cruelly pinioned, ill-treated, lost too in the darkness of paganism. The feeling prompted him into further words.

'He is a King who rules with an iron hand,' he tried to inflect his voice with a warning note. 'He wishes to know where you are from.'

The Norseman flicked his eyes at the King. 'Tell him we come from a land where we bend iron.'

It was not an answer Madaah could give. 'You are from Norway?'

The prisoner nodded. 'From Westfold.'

Madaah turned to the King. 'They are from Norway, from Westfold. I do not know of that place.'

'Nor I.' Aethelred rested his face on his hand. 'Ask them why they are in my Kingdom.'

Madaah translated, and again, under that little spur of sympathy, he added a rider of his own. 'Was your ship blown off course?' he asked.

The Norseman spat contemptuously. 'Tell your iron King that I, Nils Hallvard of Westfold, came here because it was my pleasure to do so.'

Madaah shrugged. He had done his best to give the Norseman an excuse and it had been scorned. It was as he might have expected. He gave the King Nils' answer. The thegns growled angrily, but Aethelred's face remained impassive. 'It is a man's answer,' he said. He brooded for a little in his high chair, then spoke again. What he said was unexpected.

'It is cold in here.' A servant sprang to his side but Aethelred waved him away. 'We are warm enough in our cloaks, but these—' he pointed at the prisoners, —'these have no cloaks. Put them nearer the fire.'

A soldier pushed the Norsemen closer to the fire.

'A little nearer,' Aethelred said.

The men were moved again. Now they were uncomfortably close to the flames. The fire glowed on their legs. The King nodded, as if satisfied.

'Ask them about this Westfold,' he commanded. 'How many men, how many ships?'

Nils looked grimly at Madaah as he heard the translation. 'More men in one ship than in the whole of this Kingdom—' he stressed the word 'men'— 'if these are the men of England.'

Madaah gazed, half imploringly at the other two men. They stared back implacably. 'Tell your King those words,' Nils shouted.

'What harm to tell the truth? Answer the question,' Madaah implored.

'It is the truth. Untie me and I will face your King of Iron bare-handed. My hands against his sword and shield. Tell him my words.'

'Very well,' Madaah faced the King and his thegns, and told them.

A thegn stood up, massive in his cloak. 'I take his challenge,' he cried, 'sword against sword.'

Aethelred shook his head. He alone seemed unmoved by the words, he merely waved his finger a little, and the soldier moved forward. 'Warm them a little!' Aethelred said.

The soldier seized Nils and thrust him at the fire. Now the Norseman was standing in the ashes, and the wool of his trousers was smouldering.

Madaah moved to intervene. 'They will not speak, my Lord, he cried, 'I have seen them before.'

'They will speak,' Aethelred's voice had a cold certainty. 'It is just that these men from the North need a little warming. Stir the fire.'

As the soldier moved to jab the fire with his spear, Madaah cried to the Norsemen. 'They are going to burn you—they will throw you on the fire!'

'It will be a slow way, but it is still the way to Valhalla,' Nils said. His face was firm, his voice as steady as the King's. There was no defiance in it, no braggart boastfulness, but he meant it. Then Madaah had a quick thought. The men would die, no question of it, but they could be saved the fire. He was the only one in the hall who understood both languages. He turned to Aethelred. 'They will talk my Lord, he says they will talk.'

The King smiled. 'How many times have men told me they will not talk, and how many have died silent? Tell them I will be merciful if they answer.'

'Yes my Lord.' Madaah addressed the Norsemen. 'The King says you are brave men. He admires your courage. He says . . . Madaah searched for words. 'He says that there is room in his army for such men as you.'

Nils looked contemptuously at Madaah. 'Tell your King I have a Jarl. I gave him my oath at Trondheim.'

'My Lord he says that in Norway there are many thousands of men, and hundreds of ships. He cannot tell how many exactly, but in Westfold more than—' Madaah took a wild guess—'more than seventy.'

'Now ask them why they are in my Kingdom.'

'The King says that a man who gives his word should keep it,' Madaah lied.

Nils looked directly at Aethelred. 'I have heard you are one who breaks it. Such as you I would tie beneath my ship when I launched it.'

'They were blown off course,' Madaah said. 'They were sailing for Orkney but the wind changed and they were blown here.' He thought for a moment. 'They are nothing, my Lord. Mere ceorls, almost slaves.'

'How so?' the King asked.

'No warrior would have talked because he was singed a little. These are ignorant men. They know nothing.'

'Who is their Lord?'

Madaah was relieved at having a question he could put, but was shaken by the answer he got.

'Harald Stavanger.'

'Stavanger!'

'You know that name?'

Madaah frowned at Nils. 'I have heard of a Harald Stavanger, but he was drowned in a raid on these shores, two years ago.'

Nils laughed scornfully. 'It is the same one. But he was not drowned. He is Jarl of Stavanger now.'

'What does he say?' The King spoke, sharply, impatiently.

Madaah was quick to answer. 'He tells me of his master, Harald Stavanger. I have told you of him, my Lord. He was at Orkney, but now he has grown into a great man in Norway.'

'Ask them if the men of Norway plan to come again this year to my Kingdom.'

This time, though, it was Nils who had the question. 'How is it that you speak our tongue?' He looked searchingly at Madaah. 'The Jarl Harald has spoken of one such as you. A wizard who made the wind blow foul two years ago, when Ragnar of Orkney was drowned.'

'It was not I,' Madaah said hastily, 'I am of the Church. In this land wizards are put to death.'

'It would be well for you if you were,' Nils said, 'Jarl Harald will come again to this land and he will sniff you out.'

'He is coming then?'

'He is coming.'

'This year?'

'When he comes, you will know without my telling. Now—' Nils looked contemptuously at Aethelred,—'tell your King to kill us.'

Killed they were. After Madaah had told the King Nils' last words, Aethelred had wrapped his cloak around him more closely. 'I said I would be merciful,' he said. 'Tie stones around their necks and cast them in the river. By water they live, by water let them die.'

It was done, but Madaah did not stay to see the doing. He went back to the Abbey, took a horse, and carried on with his journey. But before he left the King's presence, Aethelred spoke to him. 'You have been of service to us,' he said. 'It is our command that you stay with us.' Then, before Madaah could answer, the thegn, Cynwulf, stepped to the King and whispered in his ear. Aethelred gazed thoughtfully at Madaah, then gave him leave to go.

It was more food for Madaah's thoughts as he rode North-East to the coast. The Church wished him to go to Cedric's hall. Now, it seemed, so did the King. Madaah felt himself moved by powerful forces, invisible pressures, and it made him uneasy. His fears were stilled, though, by Ealdred's words; be obedient, trust those who send you. That he could do. Ahead of him, beyond the high rise of the hills of Cheviot and in the country of the Tweed, there lay his duty. It was a comforting thought. By obedience, by duty, he was freed from the perplexities of all doubt. And those who commanded his obedience were wise men, and good. It was in a lighter frame of mind that he rode then from village to village, church to church, until he came at last to Cedric's Hall, dark behind its stockade and looking down on the river Tweed.

Chapter 13

He was greeted well, respectfully but without undue reverence. A servant took his horse and waved Madaah into the Hall. A stout, jovial looking man was standing by the fire. He took Madaah's letter and read it, then beamed down.

'I am Guthrun, the Steward,' he said. 'You come at the right time. The accounts are behind. The last clerk the Church sent us was unfitted for his work.' He cocked his hand to his mouth and laughed.

Madaah did not laugh back. 'I am no drinker,' he said. He cast an enquiring eye at the dais.

'Lord Cedric is out hunting,' Guthrun said. 'He loves the hunt, none more so. You will be presented to him this evening, and to his son.' He led Madaah from the Hall and across the yard. 'There is our church,' he pointed to a small building. 'Father Tuda will be glad to see you also, but this is my kingdom.'

They entered a small hut. Madaah's heart sank when he saw it. The murky interior was littered with rolls of parchment and musty manuscript. Guthrun clapped Madaah heartily on the back. 'You can see that it needs a patient hand, but we will work together. You will attend to this—' he waved his hand at the depressing mass of documents—'and I will deal with the practical matters. That is how it should be, am I not right?'

Right or wrong that was how it would be, Madaah knew. 'But first I must see Father Tuda,' he said.

'Yes, you men of the cloth must stick together. Go and see him and then I will show you the Hall. There is time before we eat.' Guthrun laughed heartily, meaninglessly, and sent Madaah away.

Tuda was even more glad than Guthrun to see Madaah. 'We are short of priests,' he explained. 'The folk of the land need constant preaching. Their memories are short and even now they are likely to slip back into their old ways.'

Madaah was taken aback by this. He protested that he was unfitted for pastoral work. He was too young, merely a novice, and besides he said, he had come not as a priest but as a clerk.

Tuda curtly dismissed both objections. 'It is the cloth that counts,' he cried. 'And your Abbot assures me in this letter that you have great understanding.' He patted Madaah on the shoulder. 'Have no fear, the folk will be glad to hear you—and it is rewarding work, to preach, as our Saviour did, under God's own roof; many would be glad of the chance.'

'But the accounts—' Madaah said.

'Why!' Tuda was genuinely surprised. 'Why, you will do those during the week. It is on Sundays that you will work for God. It would not be proper for you to do the accounts on Sunday.'

Madaah left the little stone church thoughtfully. He knew, now, what his work would be in Cedric's Hall; it was to be the drudgery of doing the work Guthrun and Tuda found too tedious.

He met Guthrun again in the little shed and the Steward walked him round the Hall and its building. There was nothing new about it to Madaah, although of course, it was big, as suited an Aetheling's Hall. There was the hall itself, barns, with little in them now after the long winter, brew-houses, stables, odd sheds with tools, the smithy, but Guthrun had a great deal to say about them all. Whatever his merits as a steward might be, he was a great talker. Before the most insignificant hut he stood and pointed out to Madaah its merits—the cunning of its workmanship, its age, its fitness for a great Aetheling's Hall.

But before one building he did not pause, and that was a curious thing for Madaah to think about. He did not ask what the building was for, or what it contained, although he looked at it carefully and at its crude lock, but let himself be led meekly back to the office. There for an hour, he tidied up until he had room to move, for he had decided to use the shed to sleep in.

As dusk was falling, he brushed the dust from himself and went outside. It was quiet and peaceful although there were men about in plenty, lounging in the dust, talking idly, throwing dice, laughing among themselves. There were, Madaah thought, rather too many men, even for an estate as big as Cedric's, and these men were obviously not servants—too many of them had a hard, confident look,—but they were not thegns either, although they had the air of men more used to swinging swords than scythes. Then, from beyond the dark stockade, there came the shrill sound of a horn. The Hall sprang to life; Tuda waddled from the church, the lounging men stood, respectfully, and Guthrun ran to the gate. The Lord Cedric was returning from the hunt.

The Aetheling swept through the gate surrounded by his thegns and his servants, huntsmen and hounds, and his falconers with their hawks, hooded on wooden frames. And with them came Oswald. Madaah stood discreetly in the doorway of his hut as the horsemen trotted across the square and dismounted. Guthrun bowed them into the Hall and they entered, jesting and laughing.

Madaah waited for a while, then went to the Hall and slipped onto a bench by the door. Cedric sat at the high table and Madaah stared curiously at the man he had been sent to spy on. The last time he had seen Cedric had been at the King's council at York. Then the Aetheling had been alone—isolated and threatened, but here he sat in state, his son by his side, and flanked by his own thegns, men sworn to him and none other. He looked what he was—a man of power and pride, a fit enemy for a king, and one whom Aethelred might well wish dead.

Madaah himself received some curious glances from the men about him, but no-one spoke to him. It was of no concern to him. He was content to sit quietly in his dark corner, chewing on his meat, thinking of the building Guthrun had ignored and what might lie in it—and to listen and observe. He heard nothing that was revealing—the talk of the men was mere idle chatter—but he was interested in their voices. Many of them had the accent distinctive to the far North, a harsh guttural accent he had grown used to at St. Wilfred's, not so very far away, but there were other accents too; the lighter pattering rhythm of the land beyond Stainmore, and the deep drawl of the South. Those were all areas where Cedric held land, but although it was natural that men from Cedric's lands should be in his Hall, it was strange that there should be so many.

And there was another, stranger thing. Across the Hall from Madaah, in a compact group of their own, there was a band of men in blue cloaks who spoke not English, but the language of the Franks. Madaah recognised it, he had heard it many times on the lips of scholars at York, but, whatever these men might be, they were not seekers after truth. They were soldiers.

And then he heard his name called and he rose from his dark corner and walked across the Hall to the high table, and to Cedric.

The Aetheling was as Madaah remembered him, massive, heavy featured, with a look of slow endurance, in some way not unlike the land he ruled. Guthrun muttered something to Cedric who nodded impatiently.

'I know this monk,' he said. He beckoned Madaah forward and gave him a hard steady stare. 'So you have returned to this land which first knew you?'

Madaah gave a courtier's bow. 'Yes, my Lord.'

Cedric held a goblet in his hand, brim full of mead. He gazed into it for a while then spoke again. 'It seems a strange thing to me that I should send to Hexham for a servant and get one from York. Are there no clerks in the North in these days?'

It was a question Madaah had been prepared for. 'I was to be moved from York to Hexham my Lord.'

'Then why are you not there?'

'They have clerks enough of their own, my Lord. But I am good at figures, I know the land and how it is worked. It may be that the Abbot of Hexham wished to—' he was about to say 'please you' but Oswald broke in. He pushed his face forward. It was as large and white and empty as Madaah remembered.

'To get rid of you!' he shouted, and burst into laughter.

Madaah waited until the witless noise had died down, then turned to Cedric to finish his explanation. But Cedric was staring into his goblet.

'My Lord,' Madaah began.

Cedric looked up at that. His face had a curious expression, sad, half despairing.

'My Lord,' Madaah said again, but Cedric waved his hand in dismissal. It was an odd gesture, almost one of surrender. A few minutes later he left the Hall.

With Cedric gone Madaah was free to go. He went to his office, made up a rough bed, and lay for a while, listening to the drunken laughter from the Hall. That died away, finally, but he lay awake, thinking of the mysterious building. Finally he rose and went to the door. By the gate there was the sound of men's voices but then they too ceased.

He moved out of the shed, keeping in its shadow, waited a moment, and then slipped across the yard to the building Guthrun had been so careful not to mention. It was locked but

Madaah slipped his knife into the crude mechanism and the door swung open. He listened for a second, and then moved inside. He felt around cautiously and touched something cold and hard. He ran his hand along it. It was a bar, and heavy. There were many of them, stacked high. As far as he could tell, there was nothing else in the room, and he left as silently as he had come. Back in his little shed he lay and thought about the bars. They could be only one thing—iron. Every manor had a stock, and it was locked because it was valuable, but there had been a lot of iron in that building, far more than any normal requirement, even of the largest manor. There was enough to equip an army. It was something on which to ponder, and he did until he fell into a deep sleep.

The next morning he started work. The accounts were complicated. Cedric's tenants paid their rents in labour and produce. It was often difficult to measure one against the other, and the previous clerk had not tried very hard. Half-way through the morning, when he was deeply immersed in a dispute of the previous year a shadow fell across him. He looked up and saw Oswald in the doorway.

Madaah gave a perfunctory bow. There was a deep antipathy between the two young men. On the one side there was intellect and reason, on the other, mindless power, stupidity, cruelty.

'Do you wish something, my Lord?' Madaah asked.

Oswald giggled, that unnerving sound, and threw something soft and shapeless into Madaah's face.

'Wash this, monk,' he said.

Madaah picked up the object. It was a hunting tunic, old and torn, foul with blood and grease. 'To clean this is not my work,' he said. 'As you well know.'

'I know what I know,' Oswald spat. 'Wash it!' His voice rose to a squeak.

Despite himself Madaah smiled. He held out his hand reasonably, ready to point out the absurdity of the demand but Oswald's face was twisted with rage.

'You laugh at me, you dare laugh?' His hand went to his side and when it came up again it was holding a knife. He gave a bubbling cry and lunged forward. But Madaah knew as much about knives as he did about books. As Oswald came forward, Madaah slashed him across his eyes with the tunic, seized his wrist, and heaved. Oswald sailed across Madaah's hip and smashed into the wall. It crossed Madaah's mind, then, to break Oswald's wrist. Instead he picked up the knife and the tunic and walked out.

He went about the Hall until he found Cedric. The Aetheling was in the stables with his Horsemaster. Madaah waited patiently until Cedric had finished, then stepped in front of him.

'What is it?' Cedric asked.

Madaah held out the tunic. 'The Lord Oswald wishes this to be cleaned.'

Cedric frowned. 'Well?'

'He wished me to clean it,' Madaah said evenly. He held up the knife. 'When I refused, he tried to stab me.'

Cedric's heavy face did not change. He made no gesture but merely looked at the ground, the wind ruffling his hair. Then he raised his head.

'See my Hall, Monk? It is a great thing to own, is it not? I have hawk and hound, horse and man. I am a prince in my own kingdom. No man in Northumbria has more, save only the King. These are great things to have, Monk, great things. But a man might have all these things and yet have nothing.' He looked again at the tunic. 'This—it is fit only for a servant.' He paused, looking again at the ground. 'The knife, you took it from my son?'

Madaah nodded and Cedric nodded too, as if in agreement.

'Do as the Lord Oswald says, Monk. Clean this rag. I do not order it, and you will clean no more.'

He held out the tunic, and, after a fractional pause, Madaah took it. He went to the trough where the washing was done and washed the tunic. He was surrounded by a circle of spectators and endured a barrage of joking and comment, little of it pleasant, especially when Oswald's special cronies joined the crowd. But he carefully and scrupulously finished his task, washing the tunic twice, and three times, until it was spotless. Then he took it to Oswald who threw it to the ground and spat on it.

After that Madaah was free from interference, although he took care not to go too close to dark corners and he made sure his door was firmly locked at night. But a wave of malignant hatred lapped from Oswald and Madaah's only escape from that was on Sunday. Then he rode out to the remote hamlets, far up the Tweed, or on the moors, and preached to the peasants. He was glad then that Tuda was idle. For a few hours he was freed

I

from Oswald's petty tyranny—and that high-pitched snigger. To his surprise he began to like the work for its own sake.

Away, beyond the arable, he would find himself at some sheepfold on the bare foothills of the Cheviot, or in a squalid hamlet on the forest's edge and there, by a boulder, or under an ancient tree long ago consecrated to other Gods, he would stand and preach, as Tuda had said, the words of the Saviour, as handed down by the Church.

At first Madaah was reluctant to talk, and the peasants were reluctant to listen. But he did preach, it was his duty he supposed, and the peasants listened, at first from a fear of the consequences if they did not. His sermons were simple; be good to one another, do not fight, pity the helpless, respect the law, both of the Kingdom and the village. To his own surprise he found that he had a gift for preaching, and that the peasants were beginning to listen to him because they liked him, and he in turn began to like them. This surprised him. At first he regarded them with something like his old contempt for the underling, but as he began to know them he began to appreciate their qualities. They were simple and direct and warm, and they faced their life of endless labour with a stubborn courage that he admired.

As they began to listen more attentively to his message, he started to try and stretch their minds a little, as his own had been at York. He tried to show them that the past had not been just a series of bloody wars but that some men had worked and thought—and died—to make life better for those who came after them. Talking of the past led him to the future—but there he faltered. The world was moving to a great judgement, to the Doom of God; he could preach that and be understood. And that all souls would be judged equally then, Archbishop and outlaw, King and slave, thegn and peasant, that too he could make clear. But what lay between now and then? Would life go on for ever in its cycle of sowing and mowing, birth and death, generation to generation without change. He did not think so. He felt forces stirring in the world that would quicken the slow tread of the centuries—perhaps the Norsemen were a part of them—but what really lay between now and the Day of Judgement he could not say, except that, remembering the Doom which was to come, it behoved men to believe the Saviour's words, lest they be thrown into the fire that burned for ever.

After his sermon he would be given a meal in a small cottage,

124

deal sometimes with small affairs of justice, perhaps promise to look at a grievance about the village dues, and then it would be home, to Cedric's Hall—and Oswald.

Oswald kept up his torment of Madaah. Petty malicious attacks, but Madaah bore them without further complaint. They were irritating, like a thorn in a finger, but no more than that. And what was Oswald to him? Had Maddah been a mere clerk, condemned to a life time of drudgery, it would have been different, but as it was, as a spy secretly observing the movements in Cedric's vast lands and bringing about, however indirectly, Oswald's downfall, he could afford to shrug off Oswald's spite.

There was much to observe. As the days slipped away and the oats and barley turned green, and the great blue and silver salmon shone in the dark waters of the Tweed, more men came to the Hall; tall Franks with their long swords joining the group already there, thegns from Cedric's own lands and another group of men, blacksmiths, some from as far South as Lindsey. The shed was opened now and the long black ingots of iron were brought out and the air was full of the sounds of the smith's hammers clinking as they forged spearheads and metal strapping for armour.

Guthrun had a ready answer for Madaah when he asked about this. 'Lord Cedric will be ready for those heathen dogs from the North if they come again.'

It was a poor excuse, hardly worth giving. If Cedric was waiting for the Norsemen, he would have had his men in his strongholds on the coast, but Madaah wrote it down carefully and gave it to the priest who came every week from Hexham. In turn the priest brought news to Madaah. The King was still at Hexham, and he, too, was bringing in his troops. The country between the Hall and Hexham was full of patrols, Cedric's and the King's. There was no fighting, nothing open, but both sides were carefully watching the other. They were like two dogs, Madaah thought, baring their teeth but keeping their distance, each waiting for the other to make the first move.

Madaah wondered who would be the first to attack. Aethelred had a crafty patience that would enable him to wait, and wait, and by waiting force Cedric into action, the Aetheling could not keep his mercenaries for ever, and if he struck first, then the King could meet the challenge and claim moral justification. But Aethelred had other enemies and without doubt they would be stirring now, although he need not fear a revolt in the South. Not after the terrible blows he had dealt there the last year. But that was beyond Madaah's control. He waited and watched, as craftily patient in his way as Aethelred was in his.

The long days of summer began. The fields turned from green to yellow as the crops ripened. The long bars of iron were turned, under the magic of the smith's hammers, into weapons. More men came, the villages were full of them and their swords and axes. As the days grew longer and hotter the tension in the Hall grew. Cedric showed his power during those days. Although there were clashes, eruptions of temper, drunken brawls, the Aetheling held his men together.

Once he showed his real authority, and his courage. A Frank, tall and arrogant was in the yard, showing his skill with a sword— the Franks were legendary swordsmen. He turned and moved with the strength and grace of a fine horse, his sword a blur of light. Someone, a Northumbrian, made an insolent remark, the Frank's sword flashed once, and the soldier lay dead in the dust. For a few minutes there was a danger of open war in the Hall. A massive thegn from Stainmore moved forward swinging his axe, the Franks drew their swords, but before there was any more bloodshed Cedric had shouldered his way through the angry men. He clubbed the Frank down with his gauntleted fist and faced the mob. 'Who fights next, but not against my enemies, I will hang,' he said.

The action and the words were enough. There was no more taunting, no more fighting, but still Madaah was glad to escape from the Hall and ride the bare hillsides. Then, one Sunday, he rode North to the very edge of Cedric's lands. There was a settlement there with two freemen and a few theows—bondsmen —not quite slaves but men who had lost their land. It was a thing which could happen to a man. The Lord had a right to so much of his time, his labour, his produce, and if, for any reason, he failed to meet his dues he could slip down the society and cease to be free.

The hamlet lay across the Tweed. It was not just at the limit of Cedric's land but nearly at the border of Northumbria itself. Beyond it lay a vast stretch of forest and beyond that a no-man's-land of moor and wilderness, and then the Kingdom of Strathclyde. It was a desolate place. There was scanty pasture for a few thin cattle, and the usual herd of swine grunted outside the thorn hedge which surrounded the miserable cottages.

126

Madaah gave his simple message. The villagers listened to him and followed him in a prayer. Madaah suspected that they hardly understood the words they muttered and made a mental note to come more often. It was in isolated places like these that men slipped back into superstitions—began worshipping trees and stones—and that could lead to darker things: to ritual killing, infanticide, and things perhaps worse than those.

As he prepared to leave, he was approached by a man. The man was tall and strong looking, though gaunt. He came to Madaah nervously, but with the air of one who had made up his mind to do a daring thing.

Madaah looked at him encouragingly. 'Do you wish to speak?' he asked. The man nodded dumbly but looked over his shoulder at the others. Madaah understood. He led the man through the thorn fence. 'What is it?'

The man took a deep breath. 'I heard your words in there.'

'I hope they were of comfort,' Madaah said.

'Yes.' It was a half-hearted assent. Obviously the man had something else on his mind. Madaah was curious.

'My name is Aella. I am a theow,' Aella hesitated for a moment. 'Your words were kind.'

'They were not my words,' Madaah said. 'They were the words of Christ.'

'Yes.' Aella's agreement was perfunctory. He screwed up his gaunt face as he groped for words. 'You said them as though you believed them.'

'Pray God I do,' Madaah said.

'Then . . . then . . .' Aella straightened himself and looked squarely at Madaah. 'Then it may be that you will do a service for me.'

'If I can.'

'I am a theow now but it was not always so. I was born a free-man, and bred one too,' Aella's voice grew stronger as he spoke. 'Then I had hard times come upon me. It could happen to any man.'

'It could,' Madaah agreed. 'And what is this service I can do for you?'

Aella took hold of Madaah's arm. 'You are a minister of the Lord Cedric. Speak to him for me. At his pleasure I could become free again.' His voice shook with urgency. 'I lived too long as one of the folk to live like this. Speak to him.'

Madaah considered. It was not beyond possibility that what Aella wished could happen. There was nothing to stop Cedric giving the theow tools and land, and bringing him back into the community of free folk. Cedric could even gain by it. A free man could bear arms, and would bear them the more willingly if he was fighting for himself as well as his master. And he would work better. Madaah thought of Ceadda's words at St. Wilfred's. Free men work better than bondsmen.

He was grave as he looked at the bondsman. It was indeed a hard thing to slip from freedom. He had known its bitterness himself. It was, perhaps, a harder thing to ask for it back. It took courage for a theow to speak as Aella had done to one such as Madaah; one as high above him as the Bishop was above Madaah himself. He mounted his horse and looked down uncertainly. Aella, as if sensing Madaah's lack of decision stepped forward and pulled at his gown. 'It is not only for myself I ask. I have a family—a son and a daughter. See them. See my son, see if he is not worthy of freedom.'

Madaah moved restlessly. The talk of families disturbed him. What had he to do with the theow's family? He had a family of his own—the Church—and he had a task to do for it. Aella ran inside the village. Madaah heard him call and then he came out with a woman and two young people.

'This is my son.' Aella clapped his hand on the shoulder of a strong looking youth. 'His name is Stigmund. Is he not a fine boy?'

He was, Madaah agreed. Then he glanced over Aella's shoulder, at the woman. Aella noticed the glance. 'My wife Hilda, and the girl is my daughter, Anna.'

'You have a fine family,' Madaah said.

Aella's face lightened. He thrust the boy forward. 'Has he the look of a bondsman? He has the blood of free-men in him, see!'

Madaah nodded his agreement, but his eyes were not on the boy, but on the girl. Her eyes were cast down shyly, but he could see the fine oval of her face, and the full curve of her mouth. She was about his own age, he guessed, and about his height, but of course he was small.

'You will speak for us to Lord Cedric?' Aella's voice trembled with eagerness.

Madaah also trembled. He felt a strange surge of emotion, like nothing he had known before. He swung his horse away, as nervous now as Aella was. 'I can promise nothing,' he said.

'But you will not forget?'

No, Madaah would not forget, he could promise that. Embarrassed he pulled away and kicked his horse into a canter. He rode back across the moors, a small solitary figure, lost in thought. Once, far away in the distance, he saw a long line of mounted men, armour flashing in the late sunshine; but his thoughts were not on war, or rebellion, but on the girl in the hamlet; on the curve of her cheek and the long sweep of her flaxen hair.

The thought of Anna haunted Madaah during the next weeks. He moved about the Hall observant of every detail, writing careful letters to his masters in York, but his mind was as often on the remote hamlet high up the Tweed as on the events around him. And they were gathering speed.

The summer was fine, with long days of sunshine and the crops ripened early. The harvest began and the peasants worked as Madaah had never seen them work before. Harvesting was always toilsome—it was vital to reap when one could—but this summer the men were driven ferociously. From dawn until dusk they were in the fields, and if any man lagged, be he freeman or theow, there was a thegn on horseback to flog him on.

Madaah knew very well why this was. The drive for an early harvest was to free every man for the short period between the end of harvesting and the beginning of the winter—the time for war.

In the hall at night the talk was freer now. Men openly discussed the coming war, and a name began to circulate. Eardred—that name Madaah had heard of in York, Cedric's cousin and claimant to the throne. He was coming, it seemed, and when he came—Aethelred would die.

Madaah was less interested than he should have been; again and again, instead, he found his mind on Anna. He asked Guthrun about Aella's freedom, but the Steward was indifferent. 'It could be done,' he agreed. 'But now is not the time to talk of such a thing. Lord Cedric has other things on his mind. Why worry anyway, what matter to you if a theow be free or not?'

Madaah himself half-agreed with this. Although he felt a certain feeling for Aella, a sympathy with his desire for freedom that came from a growing sense of humanity in himself, he knew that what really prompted him was not Aella, but Anna.

It was a new and baffling emotion for him. He had spent all his life in male communities. At Orkney there had been few women and fewer girls, and he had thought them tiresome creatures. In

Northumbria the only women he had seen in the closed world of the Church had been nuns. He had seen them rarely and although he remembered the effect of their cool voices on him, they had been remote from his life. But Anna. . . .

He wished to do something great for her, to appear noble and radiant, but what gifts could he give her? One Sunday he rode to the hamlet and offered to teach Aella's children to read but the theow was scornful.

'No need for them to read. We are not clerks of the Church. Give us our freedom, give us that great gift.'

Madaah approached Guthrun again, but this time the Steward was impatient. 'Do not bother me with your theows. Sometimes I think it would be better if we had no freemen at all. What is their freedom? In the end all that they have belongs to their Lord.'

Tuda was equally unsympathetic. 'We are all servants,' he said in his unctuous voice. 'None more so than we. Why should this theow not be bound? It is God's will, I have no doubt.'

For the time Madaah thought of approaching Cedric, but, as Guthrun had said, it was clearly not the time for that. Cedric was never an easy man to approach, but now he strode about the Hall, his face set and grim. Clearly it would be useless to ask him. Madaah rode again to the hamlet. Aella was despondent and Madaah tried to cheer him. 'Perhaps after the harvest,' he said, but Aella looked glum and disbelieving, and Madaah himself knew that he was only offering scraps of comfort.

That night he stayed late at the hamlet. Deliberately he stayed until it was too late for him to leave. He was offered a bed, a mere heap of straw and took it gladly. It was near Anna, and the thought gave him deep happiness. For hours he lay awake, wondering about the new emotion which had seized him, and wondering, too, how it would affect his life. There were married priests—and he was not really a priest anyway. A few doubts flickered warningly across the back of his mind, doubts about the wisdom of seeing the girl, or becoming involved too deeply in other people, but he thrust them from his mind and warmed by the thought of the nearness of the girl, he gave up speculating and slept.

The next morning he rode down to St. Wilfred's. He had a wild idea that Leofric might help but he got there to find that the old Abbot was dead and so was Godwin. Ceadda was away. He had taken a manuscript to Jarrow. Winfred was the new Abbot and he was incredulous when Madaah suggested the Abbey might buy Aella's freedom. He clicked his teeth.

'Madaah, what has come over you to suggest such a thing! Buy a theow—and one belonging to Lord Cedric!'

Madaah murmured that he thought it would be a worthy act of charity but Winfred clicked his teeth the harder. 'Yes indeed, but we have nothing spare, and there are worthier causes. Our church could do with many things, a cross of gold for instance.'

Madaah gave up and rode back to the Hall determined after all to speak to Cedric, but when he arrived, he had no chance to speak to Cedric of anything. The Aetheling had gone. The Norsemen had struck again at the kingdom.

Chapter 14

So the words of Nils Halvard had come true. The Norsemen had come again, and the Kingdom knew without his telling them. This time they had struck south, at the mouth of the Wear, and had destroyed utterly the Abbeys of Jarrow and Wearmouth whose splendours had so impressed Madaah the previous year.

Madaah was stunned. He gaped at Guthrun who told him the news. 'Jarrow? Wearmouth?'

'That is so.'

'And Lord Cedric has gone there.'

'Ah!' Quite unexpectedly Guthrun gave a jovial smile. He leaned forward confidentially and Madaah caught a reek of beer. 'He has not gone to the coast, he has gone to Hexham! Yes—' He looked at Madaah's bewildered face and laughed delightedly.— 'The King has gone to Jarrow, he had to go to deal with these heathen dogs, and while he is there, our Lord Cedric has taken his stronghold! The whole land north of the Tyne is ours. Who knows what will come next?'

What would be next would be open war. While Aethelred was dealing with another foe, Cedric had taken the initiative and struck. And now Aethelred had been forced to abandon his stronghold and, instead of menacing, was himself menaced.

Madaah was taken aback by the speed with which the Aetheling had moved. He had not thought him capable of such swiftness, although the incident with the Frank had shown that he could deal with a crisis. But now, what of himself? Cedric had shown his hand, he was in rebellion, and Madaah's role in the Hall was over. His duty lay in going South, to his home in the great abbey, but, and he realised it with dismay, his instincts, his heart, and all his feelings were against that now.

His perplexity was plain on his face. Guthrun saw it but misinterpreted it. He clapped Madaah on the back. 'No need to worry. The Tyrant's days are numbered, and who knows what may not come from it for us? You have done good work for us, Madaah, and it shall not be forgotten. I have already remembered you!'

Madaah frowned a question and Guthrun beamed again, a beery, self-indulgent smile. 'I mean last night. The Lord Oswald was in a good humour and I asked him about this pet theow of yours. He said that he would speak to you about it. Is that not good news?'

It was not for Madaah. The last thing he wished was for Oswald to become involved in the affair. It would be in his character to try and degrade Aella yet further. He walked thoughtfully away from the Steward to the hut. He did no work but let the afternoon slip away. The Hall was quiet after the bustle of the past weeks. There were few soldiers left, and only a handful of thegns, Oswald's cronies—as deeply foolish and vicious as Oswald himself. Madaah could hear their voices, raucous and empty, breaking the quiet of the day, and he waited for one to call his name, but none did. Then, as dusk fell, a servant came to him and told him Oswald wanted him in the Hall.

Madaah rose from his stool, crossed the square, and stood in the doorway of the Hall. He waited a moment and then heard Oswald's voice.

'Here, Monk.'

Obediently Madaah walked across to the dais. Oswald crooked a finger and Madaah stepped up. Oswald was sitting with three thegns, the sons of better men who had ridden south with Cedric. As usual they were drunk. Oswald smiled at Madaah through his blurred lips.

'Preacher,' he said. His face was as vacant as ever. 'What did I want you for?'

'I do not know, your Lordship,' Madaah said.

Oswald frowned, and then his face cleared. 'I remember!' he cried, as if that was a great triumph of the intellect. 'You wish to free a theow!' He giggled. 'Guthrun told me. Is this true?'

Madaah was wary.

'It is nothing, my Lord', he said. 'A . . a mere fancy.'

'A fancy!' Oswald turned to the thegns at the table. 'In our kingdom now it seems that monks can have fancies!'

'I mean, your Lordship,—the man—he seems a good man,' Madaah fumbled for words. 'He wishes his freedom so that he can serve you better.' It was unconvincing even to Madaah's ears.

'A very noble theow,' Oswald sniggered and the thegns at the table laughed.

'It is a natural wish to be free,' Madaah said, and in saying regretted it. What would Oswald know about natural behaviour? He was eager to add more, to deflect Oswald from any personal probing. 'He will work the better and be your man.'

Oswald slammed the table with his fist. 'He is my man now. As for working—he will work as his master bids. Who is this theow?'

There was no escaping from that question. 'Aella.'

'Aella? I do not know that name. Where does he live, this noble theow?'

'At the far end of the manor, over the river by the forest.'

Oswald slumped in his chair. 'What is your interest in this, Monk?'

'Mine, my Lord?' Madaah tried to sound indifferent. 'None. It is the man's own wish.'

'A man with no interest. It seems to me such men are rare. What has he offered you?'

Madaah was shocked, and the shock showed in his voice. 'Nothing, my Lord!'

The tone of his voice had an effect. Even the thegns were silent and cast their eyes down. Oswald sensed that the game was turning the wrong way.

'Every man has his price. None too high for this theow. Let him remain as he is. Away!' he waved his hand contemptuously.

Madaah turned on his heel, glad to escape further questioning. But as he turned, a thin, sneering voice spoke behind him.

'I know this theow, my Lord.'

Madaah knew the speaker. It was one Cuthwine; a degenerate, trinket-clad, lisping, but clever. Madaah had a premonition of disaster. He stepped down from the dais of the high table, casually, and made to saunter off. But before he had gone a step, Cuthwine called to him to halt. He turned, his stomach heaving but his face impassive.

'This Aella,' Cuthwine drawled. 'He was a spear-thrower under my father. I learned to hunt boar with him when I was a boy. A big, stupid man. Big, stupid—and married.'

The hall fell very still. The word 'married' had caught the ears of every man there. Cuthwine leaned back on his bench and crooked a finger. A servant ran forward and filled his drinking horn. Cuthwine drank slowly, in no hurry to end the game.

'Yes, he married. He took a drab with a red mark on her face. Is that not so?'

He grinned at Madaah who shrugged. 'As your lordship says.'

'Yes!' Cuthwine drank again. 'As I say. And this drab had a litter. Is that not so? Monk, is that not so?'

'It may be so,' Madaah spoke casually, as if of matters indifferent to him.

'It is so. She spawned a dog—and a bitch.'

'A bitch?' Oswald leaned forward, snuffling a little.

'That is so, my Lord. A bitch with yellow hair. It is my manor, my Lord, under your father. I know the live-stock on it. As does this monk.' Cuthwine's voice was venomous. 'He goes there often enough.'

So he had been followed. Madaah's face tightened. 'I go to many villages,' he said. 'It is my duty.'

'It is your duty.' Cuthwine raised his hands in a mockery of prayer. Oswald giggled, his cronies snickered. In the hall men laughed, although not all.

'It is your duty to care for bitches with yellow hair. Yes. We know how monks care for bitches—when they are sixteen. She will be sixteen, will she not, Monk?'

Madaah shrugged. 'I do not know. It is Aella I speak for. His family is his own affair.'

'Is it now?' Cuthwine laughed. 'It is his lord's affair. This theow belongs to Lord Oswald, and his dogs and his swine—and his litter. And Lord Oswald will wish to see his property.'

Madaah made a last effort to avoid disaster. 'Why bother with a village girl? She is not worth the journey. She is a dirty, ignorant thing. It is the man who is of interest. I will bring him to the Hall.'

But it was hopeless, and Madaah knew it. He could only pray that by tomorrow Oswald would have forgotten about the girl. His mind was weak enough to do that. It was a slender hope, but one Madaah clung to as he stepped down from the dais. He spent an anguished night, clutching at his hope, but the next morning Oswald remembered and he went. Madaah saw him ride off, alone for once. He knew why that was. Oswald would not want anyone from the Hall to witness what could be a humiliation if what Madaah had said was true—if the girl was a mere dirty, ugly, village girl.

Madaah spent a tormented day. He imagined Oswald stupidly mocking Anna, and Anna herself, shy, humble before her Lord, frightened by his insinuations. . . . As evening drew in, he went to the gate of the stockade every few minutes and looked across the shining river for Oswald. At last he saw him, a hunched figure on horseback splashing across the ford. But when Oswald entered the Manor house, it was a changed figure from the swaggering young man who had ridden forth that morning. He was white with rage, and his face was swollen with a huge bruise. Aella had not stood by idly while his daughter was humiliated. He had dragged Oswald down and beaten him, and Oswald, coward that he was, had run away, back to the Hall, to gather his cronies.

That wasn't Oswald's tale, of course. As he told it he had been seized by Aella and his son by deceit and beaten savagely, without chance to defend himself. The thegns gave a servile assent to this thin story and though there were grave faces at the Hall that night, there was much furtive grinning at Oswald's expense. Madaah exulted at Oswald's defeat, but he was terrified and remorseful too. Aella had forfeited his life by his action, and it was he, Madaah, with his well-meaning attempts who had led to the situation. Aella would die, and what would become of the family? Nothing lay ahead of them but further degradation—his mind recoiled from the horrors of the future.

He spent the night in an agony of remorse. It was something he had never known before. All his life he had, as it were, been acted upon. He had done things in his life that were terrible—he had killed and thought nothing of it, then or after—for circumstances had led him to it, and he had felt indifferent as if he were a mere force of nature, like the wind. But for this he had a direct personal responsibility. It was the heaviest burden he had ever had to bear, and one no action, as far as he could see, could ever release him from.

One thing he did do. The next morning Oswald rode out with a thegn and two soldiers to bring Aella in, and Madaah followed them. He gave them an hour's start, then went to the stables and, overriding the protests of the ostler, took a fine horse and set out at a hard pounding gallop. When he caught sight of Oswald's party, he held back, but timed a last hard run so that he arrived at the hamlet with them. But Aella and his family had gone.

Oswald was insane with rage. 'Gone!' He towered above the

freeman who told him. 'Gone!' He was yours to hold. 'Where has he gone?' The freeman stepped back from Oswald's horse, his hand out in a placatory gesture.

'He went in the night, my Lord. We could not hold him. He had an axe and his son a spear.'

'A theow with arms?' Oswald spat the words out in a dribble of foam.

'He had been free, my Lord. He must have kept his arms, hidden them somewhere. We tried to stop him. He cut down Edda like a sapling.' He pointed to a crumpled body. 'He was a good warrior when he was free.'

Oswald drove his horse forward. He stared blankly round the squalid enclosure. 'You will regret this,' he screamed. 'He was your man to hold.'

The thegn grasped the bridle of Oswald's horse. 'He cannot be far, my Lord. We will get him,' he turned to the freeman. 'Get your dogs.' He jerked his head warningly.

The freeman waved his hand. 'Yes, my Lord. We have dogs.'

'We will have him in hours,' the thegn said. 'Come my Lord, it will be a good hunt.'

'Yes.' Oswald's face cleared. 'A good hunt. Better than deer. A man!' Then he caught sight of Madaah and his face darkened as suddenly as it had lightened. 'What are you doing here, Monk?' he demanded. 'Get back, get back', his voice cracked with rage and he raised his whip.

Madaah threw his arm up protectively but the thegn moved his horse between them. 'Time lags, my Lord. Deal with these matters later.'

'Yes.' Oswald's erratic mind was diverted. 'We will hunt this dog.' He swung his horse round and left the hamlet. The freeman was waiting with the other theows. The freeman had a spear, the theows, clubs, and the dogs were ready too, great brutes with iron collars and massive heads.

'This way, my Lord.' The freeman was eager to show his willingness. They followed him through the pasture and scrub, and came to the edge of the forest.

The peasants, who had been talking excitedly, fell silent as they came to the dark wall of foliage. Who knew what lay in there? What demons? What evil spirits? What ghosts? Madaah felt their fears too. This was not woodland, hunted over by the King or the Lord, known to the foresters and huntsmen, but the ancient forest of the old world. It had covered the land since the beginning of time—who knew what memories it held? Evil ones for sure. And in there, somewhere, was Aella and his family.

The men beat the forest's edge with their dogs, then one of them called sharply. They went to him and found a gap in the undergrowth. The bushes were beaten down and there were footprints in the damp mould of the soil. It was clear enough. This was where Aella had broken into the forest. The party crashed through the gap, the peasants first, clearing the way for the mounted men. It was hard going, the forest was a wild tangle of undergrowth and rotted timber. The thegn cursed and said, bluntly to Oswald that the task was hopeless. Then, after an hour's weary beating through the thorns, they came to a path. It had, probably, once been an animal track but it was well-marked. The freeman was excited. A year before there had been trouble with raiders from Strathclyde and some cattle had been lost. This must have been their track. The theows looked carefully at the ground and one of them whooped triumphantly. There were fresh marks of human feet—obviously Aella's and his family's.

Madaah's heart sank. He had hoped that the theow would have the sense to keep in the forest itself. If he was going to use the track, he lost his one advantage of mobility. The hunters moved on, fighting through the undergrowth and cantering across glades and clearings. All of the men, except Madaah, caught the savage spirit of the hunt. Oswald gave long piercing cries and the thegn answered them. The dogs bayed savagely and Madaah imagined the theow, hearing the howls, and hurrying his family on through the dimness of the forest. He wondered where Aella thought he was going to. Strathclyde lay to the North but what was there in that Kingdom for a runaway bondsman?

Then, as the long afternoon light glanced through the trees, the hunters came to a glade. The track ran across it, clearly marked in the long grass, and into the dark trees beyond. And there they met Aella.

Across the glade they saw a flash of white and a voice screamed at them, some hoarse, desperate, cry of defiance. Oswald's party stopped dead, and then, with an equally savage scream, the thegn whipped his horse forward, a soldier following him at a

138

gallop. The thegn entered the trees, leaning forward to slash down the figure in his path—and then Aella stepped from behind a tree and hacked the thegn from his horse with a terrible blow of his axe. It was an ambush, and well planned. As the thegn fell, the soldier following him crashed into him. His horse reared and as he tried to bring it under control Stigmund came from the trees and lanced him in the side with a spear. Then Aella and his son were gone—back into the forest.

In that one swift and terrible fight the odds had altered. Now it was Oswald and his remaining soldier, the freeman, and the theows, against Aella and his son. Instead of odds of five against one, it was three against two. Stigmund was obviously to be reckoned with, and the theows with Oswald would be of little use. The light was failing. Two more hours and it would be too dark for horsemen to move, but not for Aella. Madaah felt a surge of hope. If Aella could keep clear for a little longer, he had a chance to escape.

Madaah and the soldier dismounted and stooped over the men who had fallen. The thegn was dead and the soldier dying. Madaah and the soldier looked at each other. For a moment Madaah thought the man was going to give up, but he merely shrugged and turned to Oswald.

'What now, my Lord?'

'The dogs,' Oswald bellowed hoarsely. 'Loose the dogs.' He lashed at the theows with his whip. 'In!' he screamed, 'In!'

The theows reluctantly moved forward. Oswald lashed at them again. 'Hurry!' They moved into a slow jog-trot, followed by the soldier and then Oswald. The dogs ran ahead. They heard them howling in the gloom, and then there was a confused and terrible screaming. The dogs had caught up with Aella. It was almost dark now but there was enough light for them to see, when they, in turn, caught up with the dogs.

Aella was standing against a thicket. Around him two or three dogs slavered and barked. At his feet were the bloodied bodies of two or three more—and his son.

The end was inevitable although Aella stood them off for an hour. Stigmund who had been torn by the dogs staggered to his feet and guarded his father's flank with his spear. The dogs were not effective against an armed man holding his ground; the theows were timid, poking ineffectually with their clubs and Oswald held back—a coward to the last. It was the soldier and

the freeman who finished it. While the theows jabbed at
Stigmund, they rushed Aella. The freeman fell before the
bondsman's axe, but the soldier caught Aella with his sword and,
as he fell, finished him with one deep thrust. Oswald rushed
forward then. He was quivering with rage.

'I wished him alive,' he yelped. He hacked at Aella's body. 'He had a price to pay.'

The soldier looked grim. 'He has paid his price, my Lord, and he deserved this death. No man in Northumbria more.'

Madaah looked around the clearing. Two theows dead, the freeman was not going to live, Aella was dead, and back in the forest were two more men—the thegn and the other soldier, dead or dying. Six men dead for the satisfaction of a coward. Six men dead and another to die. Oswald made that clear. Stigmund was torn and slashed but alive.

'He shall pay,' Oswald cried viciously. He bent over the boy. 'Do you hear?'

'He cannot hear you, my Lord. He is unconscious. Leave him. He fought like a warrior.' There was a warning note in the soldier's voice and Oswald heeded it.

'But he will pay the price tomorrow.'

'Tomorrow, my Lord.'

They spent the night in the forest and the next day, for a few hours, looked for the women, but it was obviously hopeless. The soldier was openly mutinous and the theows were too frightened to go into the darkest recesses of the forest without him. At noon Oswald called the hunt off and they rode back with the dead men, and Stigmund, lashed onto the backs of the horses. At the clearing where they had been ambushed they found the theow they had left with the injured soldier and the thegn. The soldier had died during the night. They took their bodies also and came from the forest and rode back to the manor.

It was like a journey in a nightmare. Stigmund, half conscious, moaned as the horse jolted him and the other horses, nervous under their burden of dead men were hard to handle, shying at each sound, and baulking at every shadow. At the crossing of the Tweed, Stigmund came momentarily to his senses and cried for water. Madaah halted and climbed down from his horse. He felt a blow across his shoulders and when he looked up, Oswald was above him.

'What is this, monk?' Oswald cried.

'An act of charity,' Madaah said.

'Charity!' Oswald screamed. 'He is my prisoner, Monk, mine. Touch him and I will cut you down where you stand.'

'The boy is dying.'

'He will live long enough—long enough. Now, get back!'

There was nothing Madaah could do. He looked at the soldier but his face was blank. Helplessly he remounted, but he rode with Stigmund, trying to steady him as they crossed the river. That night Stigmund was tied on a wooden yoke and stoned to death. Then Madaah decided to kill Oswald.

Chapter 15

Madaah sat in a dark corner of the Hall. A fire flamed in the middle but he was away from its light. Oswald and his thegns were sitting by the fire. They were drunk and getting drunker. Madaah was content to wait. When they were drunk to insensibility, he was going to kill Oswald.

There was laughter from the fire and Madaah looked up. A thegn was kicking Cedric's gleeman to his feet. The minstrel, who was as drunk as the others, flicked his fingers discordantly across his harp.

'Silence!' Oswald commanded. 'Silence!'

The thegns fell quiet and the minstrel began chanting some old song, one full of blood and fire, and of brave men who fell fighting against all odds. It was not without nobility but Madaah stared at the minstrel with hatred and contempt. The song was about honour, and that had gone from Northumbria. The Kingdom was like a rotting carcase, torn by dogs from the outside, and gnawed by maggots from within. Oswald being a maggot.

There was another loud bray from the fireside. The song had ended and Oswald was laughing at some remark. Madaah stared at him with a fascinated intensity. How could a man with such deeds on his hands sprawl before the fire at ease, and laugh? And how could the thegns, supposedly dedicated to honour, join in the laughter?

Madaah had appealed to them when Oswald had made known his judgement but not one had answered. Then he had gone to Tuda but the priest had refused to intervene. It was the law he had said, and it was not for the Church to come between the criminal and his punishment. That was true enough, but Madaah had thought of the words of the Gospel. 'Let he that is without sin among ye throw the first stone.'

The laughter died away. Oswald was on his feet. He held his sword high.

'Thus I struck!' he cried. 'Thus!'

The thegns shouted their approval. One rose and waved his drinking horn.

'I drink to Oswald. Worthy son of his father. He knows his sword and his axe, and so do his enemies!'

The men cried again in salutation and drank deeply. Another thegn stood. 'I drink to the great Cedric, that he will tear down his enemies as a wolf the deer.'

A third man raised his horn. 'To the honour of this house, the greatest in the Kingdom. It will be greater yet.'

All drank, the minstrel sang again, the men drank, and drank. Madaah sat in his dark corner, twisted with hatred. Wolves they were, more bestial than wolves, lower than animals. And where was Anna? He felt a wave of nausea. Where was she now; lost in the forest? On the moors beyond the land of Northumbria? She was gone from his life, of that he was certain, but at least she had been saved from Stigmund's fate. Aella's courage and honour had done that, but who was there to drink to him, and his bravery—or his son's.

The men by the fire were falling silent, torpid with beer. They were sprawling on the benches now, and first one, and then another fell asleep. The servants crept away, and the Hall, usually so full of noise and bustle fell quiet. Madaah waited on watchfully. From the benches came drunken snores. Only Oswald remained awake. He was muttering to himself, a long drunken gabble. Now, thought Madaah, now is the time. He slid the dagger from out of his sleeve and stood up. With infinite care he moved along the dark wall. Just outside the light of the fire he paused. Oswald was staring glassily at his hand. Madaah waited patiently. The fire flickered and glowed, throwing a red stain across Oswald's hand. Then Oswald dropped his arm and his eyes closed.

Madaah gathered his gown around him and took a step forward. His hand was slippery with sweat and the dagger turned in his hand, as if it had a life of its own, like the old sword of so long ago. Another step—no movement from the inert figures on the benches. He raised his hand to strike—and as he did so, its shadow ran across the floor and one of the dogs raised its head, its attention caught by that little shadow. Its yellow eyes stared into the darkness where Madaah lurked, and the bristles on its heavy neck began to rise. Madaah held his breath and stood motionless. A vein in his forehead began to twitch and he had a sour taste in his mouth. The dog's mouth wrinkled back and from deep in its throat there was an ominous rumble. Madaah and the hound looked at each other for a long moment, then—as the dog began to rise—Oswald fell forward and his cup clattered to the floor. The noise distracted the dog and Madaah flicked back into the shadows. The clatter woke Oswald. He stared round stupidly. The dog moved to him and he struck at it with his foot.

'Dogs,' he mumbled. 'Dogs—we will drive them into hell.' He laughed his crazy laugh. 'The King's dogs will yap, but I shall tame them.' He raised his hand. 'I drink to Oswald, King of Northumbria.' He raised his empty hand to his lips, and gazed at it in a dazed way. Then he bellowed, a servant ran in, the thegns roused themselves, and Madaah's opportunity was gone.

The next day he took a horse and rode back to the hamlet. He went into the forest and followed the track. He rode through the glade where the thegn had died, on to where Aella had made his last heroic affirmation of his freedom, and beyond. After a mile the track ran into a huge bog. His horse sank to its knees in the green swamp and it was with difficulty that he got it clear. He left the horse and dragged his way round the swamp. 'Anna,' he called, 'Anna'. There was no answer. Only the leaves rustled and birds whistled and called. He spent the night in the forest, and another day and night, but in the end he was forced out. The women had gone.

When he got back to the Hall, it was to find Oswald had gone, too. Guthrun was in a passion of anger with Madaah, but Madaah ignored him.

'Where has he gone?' he demanded.

'He has gone where he wishes,' Guthrun spluttered. 'What business is it of yours? Get back to work now.'

He asked the servants but they shrugged. 'Gone,' they said. 'Who knows where?' In the end he found out. The soldier who had been at Aella's killing told him.

'You are looking for Oswald?' he asked. Madaah said he was.

'He has gone South, with ten thegns.'

'To Hexham?' Madaah asked.

'No. Lord Cedric is there, he is calling his men together. We go tomorrow. But Oswald has gone to York. You wish to follow him?'

Madaah did. He wanted that very much. The soldier nodded. He walked casually out of the stockade. 'You will need a horse.' He jerked his thumb at a copse in the arable. 'Maybe there will be one there tonight. You could have trouble crossing the Tyne; up river would be easier.' He turned on his heel. 'Thank you little Brother. The words of the Church are always welcome.' That was for the benefit of the guard on the gate. As Madaah followed him back, he heard one of them laugh.

'So Aelfwine has religion! The days of miracles are still with us!'

That was how Madaah heard the soldier's name. He never saw him again.

The night was overcast. Madaah slipped over the stockade and made his way to the wood. There were many camp-fires glowing in the stubble, but he made his way around them. In the copse he found a horse, a thin wiry beast. There was a sword lashed to the saddle. Madaah mounted and moved out of the trees. He knew the surrounding countryside like the back of his hand and before dawn, after riding south-east, he was on the road the Romans had made so long ago, and hammering after Oswald.

The road was straight. In places the turf which covered it was churned away from the stone but it was good going, and he moved at a steady canter through the clear dawn. At times he was challenged by troops but he had a story ready for them. He told them he was from St. Wilfred's going to Hexham with important news, the Abbot had died. It was an effective lie. The death of an Abbot, even one from so humble a place as St. Wilfred's, was important news, and to delay it a grave matter. Madaah's youthful appearance and monastic dress helped too. So some thegn would listen to Madaah's tale, often cross himself, then wave the rider on. In the early afternoon, as he came to the Wall, he was even given a fresh horse by a particularly pious thegn.

At the Wall he halted to consider his plans. Aelfwine had said he should go West about here, up the Tyne. He thought about this. He could go to the coast. There would be help from the Abbeys there, those that were left that was, but he would still have to cross the river and Cedric would have the bridges guarded, and the river was wider there. He decided to take the soldier's advice and he went West, over the moors. After an hour or so he realised that the plan was no good. From a distance the moors had looked inviting; long elegant curves that looked smooth and gentle, rising and falling, mile after mile in the evening light. The reality was different. The purple heather was made of great brushes which were hard to push through and every few hundred yards a stream cut a ravine which meant a slippery descent, and a hard slog up the other side. The horse began to flag and Madaah found himself being forced down to the banks of the Tyne far sooner than he had hoped. But if he had to come down, at least he had come to the right place. Ahead of him, across a water meadow, was a bridge—but it was guarded.

Madaah pulled his horse into a thicket on the hillside and considered what to do. If he crossed here and told his tale he would certainly be sent to Hexham, probably with a guide, and Hexham was where he did not wish to go. The alternatives were not good, though. He could not cross the river in daylight, and finding a ford at night would be impossible. In the end he decided on the bold course and, in the dusk, he came out of the thicket and rode to the bridge.

He was hailed roughly as he approached and he halted, docilely. A soldier asked him where he was going and when Madaah said, to Hexham, told him to stay where he was. The soldier went over the bridge and came back with another man. Madaah looked at him carefully through the dimness. He was dressed in a mail coat and carried a sword. A petty thegn, Madaah thought, probably some local landlord. He lied again, confidently. The thegn nodded assent, then—

'If you are from the North, why are you coming this way?'

Madaah was taken aback. 'Er, the road—' he fumbled for words—'I missed my way.'

'That road comes from the Tyne gap,' the thegn said sharply. 'From Carlisle.'

Madaah tried to bluster. 'What is the meaning of this?' he demanded. 'Why am I being questioned?'

The thegn was not overawed. His voice was hard when he answered. 'Nothing to you, priest—if you are a priest.' He called for light, and a soldier came with a burning brand. The thegn held it towards Madaah.

'You look foreign to me,' he said. 'Where are you from?'

'I have told you,' Madaah said. He had an inspiration. 'I have been on the moors, there is a hermit from our Abbey, a very holy man. He had to be told and coming back I missed the road and came down here.'

The thegn was unconvinced. 'If there is a holy man on the moors up there, I have yet to see him. Monsters and outlaws more likely.'

'Very well,' Madaah spoke boldly. 'Take me to Hexham, that is where I am going. The Lord Cedric will have thoughts on this.'

'It may be he will.' The thegn turned to the soldier. 'Take the monk to Hexham. Hear the Lord Cedric's words.'

'No need for a guide,' Madaah cried.

'Guard, not guide. A move from you and there will be a spear through your ribs. On!' The thegn waved his hand and Madaah clattered over the bridge. The soldier mounted a horse and followed him, his spear at rest in the crook of his arm but the point at Madaah's back.

They jogged along for a while then Madaah cried over his shoulder, 'How far to Hexham?'

'Four or five miles,' the soldier said. 'Now no more talk.'

It was full dark now. The shadow of the hills cut them off from the moonlight which shone on the waters of the river rushing below them. In the darkness Madaah reached under his robe and drew his sword. He held it under his robe and tugged his horse to a halt. Immediately he felt the nudge of the spear against his back.

'Move on,' the soldier barked.

'No need for that,' Madaah answered. 'My horse is lamed.'

The soldier's dark bulk drew level with him. 'No tricks,' he said. 'Lame or not, move!'

As he spoke, Madaah slid the sword from under his robe. 'No trick,' he said and raised the sword swiftly and rested its point against the soldier's side. He leaned against it gently.

'Drop your spear,' he said.

The soldier gave a grunt of surprise. 'The spear!' Madaah repeated. There was a clank as the spear hit the ground. 'Now, down,' Madaah leaned on the sword a little. 'Down!'

The soldier swung off his horse and looked up at Madaah. 'What now?' he asked.

'No harm to you. Back to your master.'

Madaah kicked his horse forward but he underestimated the soldier. As he moved off, the soldier jumped forward. Madaah swung the sword at him back-handed, but the blow was feeble

148

and glanced harmlessly off the soldier's helmet. The next moment the man had his hands under Madaah's feet and had heaved him out of the saddle. The horse lunged forward as Madaah fell and the soldier sprang round it and grabbed at Madaah. He was very strong, but heavy, and Madaah, who had his own wiry strength half wriggled from his grasp. The horse loomed above them and one of its hooves caught the soldier. He grunted with pain and rolled forward. Madaah almost got clear but was grabbed again and dragged down. Madaah struck at his adversary savagely but his blow merely bounced off the soldier's leather tunic. Then he felt himself being dragged to his feet. The horses jerked nervously and below them the river, glittering in the moonlight, roared ominously. Madaah gave a huge wriggle, like an eel on a line, and his robe ripped open. The sudden giving of the material caught the soldier off balance, he staggered backwards, pulling Madaah with him, and together they went over the bank and into the river.

Madaah crashed into the water, dazed and confused, rolled over, and felt a current pull at him. He staggered to his feet and then the dark bulk of the soldier rushed him again. Madaah was caught off balance and went backwards, the soldier with him, but this time they had fallen further into the river, into a deep pool. Madaah felt the bed disappear from under his feet and kicked out frantically. A hand grabbed him again but he struck it away. In the moonlight he saw, just for a moment, the soldier's face and heard a shout of despair, then the soldier was taken away by the river. Madaah was taken too, but water was a native element to him. He struck out, against the current, and crashed against a boulder. He grabbed it and, although his hands slipped from its weedy sides, he found ground beneath his feet and managed to scrabble onto the bank.

He lay there for a time, exhausted and battered, then dragged himself up the steep bank. He staggered along the path at the top and came to the horses, which were nibbling peacefully at the grass. He mounted one and let it pick its own way forward through the darkness. After a mile he halted. There was a dim glow ahead that must be Hexham, surrounded by the camp-fires of Cedric's host. There was no sense in going further that way. On his right was the dark bulk of a hill. He dismounted and led his weary horse up the dark slope. It was the hardest part of his journey. The hillside was dense with bushes, and his horse slipped and slithered. Madaah had to fight to avoid falling back into the valley again. At last he rounded the hill and fell to the ground in a stupor of weariness. But he had crossed the Tyne, and he was South of Hexham. Before him lay country wild enough, but he was free from Cedric's lands.

The next day he went through rugged foothills, but by evening he was at the crossing of the Tees. He spent the night with a priest and the following day, the second of his journey, he was back on the road and riding along the Swale. His horse foundered within six miles of York. He left it and went forward on foot taking his sword, wrapped in his cloak. For the last mile he was given a stirrup to hold by a young gallant, dressed in blue and yellow, and that took him through to the walls of York. As the bells were ringing for Compline, he reeled through the gates of the Abbey and fell into the arms of the gatekeeper.

Chapter 16

Madaah sat outside the Abbot's room. He had been waiting a long time. Bells clanged through the Abbey and there was the familiar clatter of shoes down the stone corridors. The day was slipping away in the unchanging order of the Church. Madaah was near to sleep. Images flicked across his mind; Oswald, somewhere in the town, smiling his hateful smile, the face of the soldier drowning in the river, Anna—but his mind turned away from that, as from the unthinkable. More bells, distant now; more clatter, muted by his tiredness. As if from a great distance he heard monks chanting . . . he drifted into sleep.

He was woken, not ungently, by a hand on his shoulder. Looking up, he saw Sigulf, the Master of the Novices—his master. Sigulf smiled at him. 'It is good to see you safe, Madaah. Welcome. The Abbot wishes to see you now. Are you well enough?'

Madaah rose stiffly. 'I am ready,' he said. 'And it is good to see you, Father.' He went into the Abbot's room. Edwin was standing by a small fire which glowed in an iron basket. He stretched out his hand to Madaah who knelt and kissed it. Edwin raised him.

'We are well pleased to see our faithful servant again,' he said. 'The Church is well served by such as you. And now we take you back into our bosom.'

'Thank you, my Lord,' Madaah said. He staggered a little and the Abbot caught him by the arm.

'Sit!' He pressed Madaah onto a stool. 'We shall not forget your services, Madaah, but we are surprised to see you. We had thought you were at Lord Cedric's Hall still. We do not remember sending for you.'

'No, my Lord.'

'Then why are you with us now?'

Madaah blinked drowsily at the glow of the fire. Why was he here? In the tension of his journey he had half forgotten. He opened his mouth to say Oswald, but cut the word short. He could not tell the Abbot that he had come to kill Cedric's son. That was a private matter, between himself and Oswald. The Church could find that out later and then exact what penance it wished.

'It is because of Cedric,' he murmured. 'He is ready to move against the King. He is at Hexham now with his host.'

'This we know already. Our Brothers at Hexham have told us.' Edwin stretched his hands to the fire. 'You are sure Lord Cedric is going to attack York? Quite sure?'

'Positive, my Lord. The land North of the Tyne is full of his soldiers.'

'The country everywhere is. These heathen from the North—every Aetheling and Ealdorman has his host out.'

'It is not just that,' Madaah was adamant. He remembered the night in the Hall. 'I heard the thegns boasting, and I heard Oswald drink a toast,' he frowned as he tried to call back the exact words. 'He said—I drink to Oswald, King of Northumbria.'

'But Cedric—' Sigulf began to speak from a dark corner.

'Oswald would be his heir,' the Abbot said. He turned again to Madaah. 'Those were the words he used—you are sure?'

'Yes my Lord.'

'Then it is so,' the Abbot stared into the flames. The firelight flickered across his face making it hard to tell his expression. Madaah shook his head—he must have been mistaken, but for a moment it might almost have been satisfaction.

Edwin raised his gaunt face and stared at Madaah. 'Again we thank you. Tomorrow it may be that we shall wish to speak to you again. Till then, rest.' He held out his hand and Madaah pressed his lips against the blue veins.

Then Sigulf took him and led him through the Abbey to the dormitory where he sank onto a bed and slipped into a black oblivion.

When he awoke it was broad daylight. A novice was standing by the bed. Madaah blinked at him. What was his name? Osric? Something like that. Osric gave him an uneasy smile.

'Madaah? That is your name, is it not?'

Madaah yawned and said it was.

'Sigulf said that you were to sleep as late as you wished but I have brought you some food.' Osric handed over a bowl of broth. 'I am glad you are back—sincerely glad.'

So am I, thought Madaah, most sincerely.

'You have come from the North?'

Madaah nodded and Osric leaned forward eagerly. 'Is it true that there are soldiers coming from there?'

'It is true that there are soldiers.' Madaah was annoyed at Osric's questions. He had the feeling that he had been woken not to be given soup, but to be asked questions.

Osric's eyes were round with fear. 'These are bad times. No-one is allowed out of the Abbey. I think there is going to be more fighting.'

More fighting—what did Osric mean?

'Oh, before you came here, there were battles, when King Osred was overthrown, and before that, when King Alfwold was murdered. The last time some soldiers broke into the Abbey and killed a Brother.'

Madaah said, soothingly, that he thought things would be better this time. If there was trouble, the Abbey would be safe.

With a forced smile, Osric agreed. 'Yes, I think so too.' He lowered his voice. 'I think Lord Cedric is going to give us men to guard us.'

'Lord Cedric?' Madaah was puzzled. Why should Osric think Cedric would guard the Abbey?

'Well,' Osric said, 'his son has been here these past two days. Why else should he be here?'

'Oswald?' Madaah exclaimed. 'Cedric's son?'

'Why yes, he has been with the Abbot a great deal and—'

'Get me a robe,' Madaah climbed out of bed. 'Quick!'

Osric ran down the dormitory in a flustered way, but he brought back a gown. Madaah snatched it and slipped it on. It was far too large and billowed around his slight figure. Holding it up he ran from the dormitory and through the Abbey to the Abbot's room. He hammered once on the door, then burst in. Inside was the Abbot, Sigulf—and Oswald. Madaah gaped at the three men.

Edwin frowned angrily at Madaah. 'What is the meaning of this?' he shouted.

Madaah blinked at Oswald who was lounging in a chair. He pointed at the young nobleman. 'He—last night—I thought—' With an effort he pulled himself together. 'I did not make myself clear last night, my Lord.'

'Have we sent for you?' Edwin's harsh voice was harsher yet. Madaah shook his head. 'My Lord, he and his father are planning to revolt. I thought last night I told you but . . .' His voice died away before the grim stare of the Abbot.

'We heard your words. Now, go.'

'But I was in the Hall when he spoke of the revolt.'

'These matters are none of your concern,' Edwin snapped. 'Leave us at once.'

For a moment Madaah was shocked into disbelief. 'None of my concern?' He took a step forward. 'I do not understand, my Lord.'

'These matters are nothing to you,' Edwin turned to Oswald. 'I apologise for this my Lord. Sigulf—' the Abbot jerked his chin and Sigulf seized Madaah's arm.

Madaah stubbornly held his ground. 'You do not know,' he cried. 'He—that—' Madaah spat the words at Oswald, '—that tied a boy up and stoned him to death.'

'One of the Church?' Sigulf's voice was sharp.

'No, just a boy.'

'He had committed a crime?'

Oswald broke in. 'He was a runaway theow, and he had killed a thegn. The penalty was in the law.' He waved a languid hand at Madaah. 'My Lord, must we?'

'He was dying,' Madaah cried. He turned to the Abbot, unable to believe that his words were not being heeded. 'He was dying when they tied him up.'

'Enough!' The Abbot's face was a mask of anger. 'Take him away.'

Sigulf pulled at Madaah's arm. 'Come,' he hissed, and Madaah yielded to his strength. Sigulf walked firmly to the door and pulled Madaah through the doorway. As the door swung to, Madaah heard Oswald's empty giggle.

In the corridor Sigulf spoke severely to Madaah. 'You must speak to no-one of this. These matters are not for you, or me either.'

Madaah stared blindly at him. 'You do not understand. He has done terrible things.'

'Then God will punish him. Now come with me. I will place you under Ealdred. He needs help. You are to stay with him and speak to no-one else. Is that clear to you?'

It was clear enough. Madaah walked with Sigulf through the Abbey and up the familiar steps into the Library.

It was a different scene from the one Madaah knew so well. The shelves were stripped of books, monks were hurrying about the room, their feet clattering on the stone floor, the little cells where the illumination had been done were deserted, only the ancient smell of musty parchment and ink was the same. Sigulf marched down the room and then Madaah heard his name called. In turn he went down the room and came, face to face, with Ealdred. Sigulf left them and Ealdred looked hard after his retreating back. Then he faced Madaah and smiled.

'So, you have come back to us again?' His smile faded as he saw Madaah's expression and his own turned to one of concern. 'Sit down, my son.' He led Madaah to a bench, half-smiled and waved his hands at the scurrying monks. 'You can see we are busy. I am moving the books down to the cellars. If there is trouble they must be kept safe.

'I must talk to you, Ealdred,' Madaah said.

A monk came up and asked a complicated question about the catalogue. Ealdred gave some quick instructions then turned to Madaah.

'Will it not wait? You can see—' He looked more closely at Madaah's face. 'Very well, come.'

He led Madaah into his small cell at the end of the library, sat down and listened to Madaah's tale. For a while neither spoke, then Ealdred sighed. 'We are all sinners, Madaah, some more than others, but Oswald . . .' His voice died away.

'He is a monster,' Madaah said venomously.

'It would seem he is.'

'Then why is he with the Abbot? What has he to do with the Church?'

Ealdred's face was grave. 'It is a question which has been asked many times, not just about Oswald. The Church should be pure and holy but the world is made of pitch, and it is in the world. How can we stop defilement?'

Madaah ignored the question. 'Oswald is evil.'

'Yes, yes indeed he is.'

'And he is under oath to the King, he and his father both. Is that not so?'

Ealdred stirred restlessly. 'I should not be talking of these matters.'

Madaah was relentless. 'Is it not true what I say?'

'Yes.'

'And that oath is valid under God—is that not so too?'

'Yes, you have not forgotten your lessons in reasoning, Madaah.'

'It was you who taught me. But I am not doing my exercises. Did not the Bishop himself witness the oath? And the Abbot? In this Church?'

'It is true.'

Madaah brooded sullenly. 'Then we are breaking the word of God. We, the Church. We are worse than the Norsemen. They keep their oaths.'

The Librarian placed his hands on his knees and leant close to Madaah. 'This I should not tell you, but perhaps it is right that you should know. The King is dead. He was murdered three days ago.'

Madaah stared unbelievingly at Ealdred. The King dead? Aethelred? He of the tawny hair and the quiet deceptive face who had ruled through fire, and blood, and terror?

Ealdred nodded affirmation. 'He was slain while marching from the coast to meet Cedric. This Kingdom has no King.'

Madaah could not grasp the fact. 'But who killed him?'

'Cynwulf, the thegn.'

Madaah cried in disbelief. 'But he was the King's own man!'

'He was his own it would seem.'

Madaah was still incredulous. 'But when I was chosen to go to Cedric's Hall he was with the Abbot and gave approval. I thought he was speaking for the King. And at Hexham, when the King wished me to stay with him, Cynwulf spoke to him and then Aethelred let me go.'

Ealdred averted his face. 'You were sent to the Tweed to be the Church's eyes, Madaah.'

'That I know. I accepted it. I was to see if Cedric would rebel.'

'No. In this evil world—' Ealdred's voice fell into a whisper and he spread wide his white scholar's hands. 'Madaah, there was nothing so certain in this world than that Aethelred would be killed. Nothing so certain that there is going to be a struggle for the throne. The Church cannot be ignorant of these matters. It must know. Madaah,' the Librarian's voice was sad. 'You were not sent to the Tweed to tell us if Cedric would rebel, we knew what was in his mind—as did the King. You were there to tell us if he was not going to rebel. We had to be sure.'

The skin on Madaah's forehead began to prickle. 'You mean the Church knew?'

'We did not know. Many men have said they would rise

against Aethelred—some have, some have not. Until now we have supported the King but Cedric is strong and so—'

'And so the Church made a bargain with him?'

'Not a bargain. We were . . . aware.'

'And Cynwulf—was the Church aware of his plans too?'

'Not the plans he had. We thought he would support Cedric.'

'And the King—what did he know of this?'

'Aethelred? He knew everything, and nothing. But no matter now if he did or not. He is dead and Cynwulf holds his Hall. He took it two days ago and he is calling in his followers. He who wishes to hold this Kingdom must hold York, so Cedric will come here and there will be fighting. Cedric will win, we think, thanks to you for that knowledge Madaah.'

'And he will be King?'

Ealdred looked thoughtful. 'I think not. Cedric has a claim to the throne, but Eardwulf's is better, and there are many in this land who would serve under Eardwulf who would not accept Cedric. He is not of the stuff of which Kings are made. Besides there is one Torhtmund, the King's minister. He has sworn to avenge Aethelred and he is one to do it. Cynwulf has made a mistake, I think. He cannot fight Cedric and Torhtmund. But we shall see. It is interesting in its way.'

'Interesting?' Madaah gave a bitter laugh.

'Why yes,' Ealdred's voice was gentle. 'All these matters affect us, but they are not our concern.'

'And Oswald? He has ambitions of his own. Is that interesting, too?'

'I would not concern myself with him. He will be dealt with, that I do believe.' Ealdred rose and went to the window. The light caught his pale face and accentuated his pallor. 'These affairs of men come and go, as restless as the sea. The Church alone remains, stable and enduring. Like the wise man's house it is built on stone, on a rock. And there are the books. The labour of centuries lies in them, and the wisdom of the world. They are worth saving I think, be the price what it may.'

'No!' Madaah spat the word out. 'They are not worth the life of one man.' He stood up, shaking with rage. 'A family has died because of me.' His voice cracked with despair.

'That is foolish talk.'

'If I had not gone to the Tweed, I would never have met them, and they would not have died. That is not foolish.'

157

Ealdred sighed. 'Yes, the price can seem heavy at times.'

'Seem! Why was I chosen—why?' It was less a question than a cry of despair, but Ealdred answered it.

'It was not of my choosing that you went, but you were chosen because you knew how to survive. You survived the Heathen. Not many have done that, or could do.'

'Survived them!' Madaah gave a bitter laugh. 'I was a heathen. Before I landed on these shores, I had never heard of God, or His Church!'

'We knew that, Madaah,' Ealdred stared at Madaah through his green eyes. 'We have known it since you went to St. Wilfred's.'

Madaah stared back incredulously. 'Known it?'

'Why yes, the fathers at that Abbey were not foolish. Leofric wrote to us after you arrived. But what matter. You are not a heathen now. And the Bishop himself wishes to baptise you.'

'Me?' Madaah burst out laughing. It was not a pleasant sound. 'I do not wish to be baptised,' he shouted.

Ealdred flushed deeply. 'You dare not say such a thing.'

'I dare. I have seen things done—and the Church would not lift one finger.' His eyes filled with tears.

'It is this Anna you are thinking of. Madaah—' Ealdred turned in appeal. 'Madaah, before the Church came to this land, there were darker things than that. A man could be bought and sold like a beast—and a woman too. You are thinking of your own sorrows, and your own desires, but the Church rises above them. It holds the sorrows of the world in its hand, and it is its only salvation.'

'I have been used.'

'Yes, you have been used. We are all used, that is what service in the Church means.'

'I have been betrayed,' Madaah cried the words out in agony of despair. 'And I have been a traitor.'

'That is not so. You bear no guilt for what you have done. The Church will carry the burden of your sins.' Ealdred went to the doorway of the cell. 'I will leave you now. When you are calmer you may help us with the books.' He paused for a moment. 'Madaah, the world lies before you. You could be a second Alcuin, a great scholar, a great leader. Our Saviour said Render unto Caesar what is his due. You have done that, the Church has done that. Now render unto God what is His.'

158

After Ealdred had left him, Madaah went to the window and stared out onto the Abbey. The courtyard was full of hurrying monks carrying the Abbey's treasures to the vaults and crypts. Beyond the Abbey walls rose the gables of the King's Hall. That too would be full of scurrying figures as Cynwulf marshalled his men for the coming battle.

It was early evening and the sky was flecked with red and gold clouds. Through a huge rent in them Madaah could see the sky beyond. He looked into the delicate blue infinity. God was up there in that pearly eternity, with his son on his right hand; both crowned in majesty on thrones that would endure for ever. That was the teaching of the Church, and he had accepted it, believed it, but now—his mouth twisted in a grimace of contempt; more lies, more deceit. It was the Bishop and the Abbot who sat robed in their purple palliums on thrones of gold that were everlastingly secure. But he, and others like him, were used to keep them there.

He leaned against the window-sill full of sick bitterness at what he had learned that day. As the light faded in the West his mind grew darker too, as if the shadows of the night were falling across his soul. And in that gathering darkness some gentle growth of trust, and kindliness, and affection, which had begun to turn toward the light, withered, and in its place a fouler growth of malice and hatred began to sprout and ooze. He would be revenged; of that he was sure. He would kill Oswald first, catch him somewhere in the Abbey and destroy him—then he would avenge himself on the Church. Somehow he would repay the evil done him, and if it was repaid by evil—so much the better.

It was almost dark now. Outside the Abbey someone had lit a great fire. Its flames leapt high and illumined the carvings on the King's Hall. The plants carved on the gables seemed to move as the firelight rose and fell, seemed to writhe like living beings, like coiled snakes. It was an omen, Madaah thought. His sign had been the Fish, let it now be the Snake. He liked the thought. The snake was a symbol of evil; in the Garden of Eden a snake had brought about the fall of Man, and all his generations—but he had once mastered the power of the serpent, long ago when he had subdued the snakes on the sword. Now he would be a snake himself; he Madaah, scholar and viking, monk and magician he would become a serpent and bring about a second Fall.

He heard a sound behind him, and turned to see Ealdred. The

Librarian beckoned, and Madaah left the cell. The Library was empty now. The hurrying figures had gone and the shelves were bare. Ealdred looked around.

'It will be full again,' he said. He put his hand on Madaah's shoulder. 'I did not disturb you, sometimes one needs solitude.'

They walked down the long room. It was lit only by a long line of candles that glowed along the table. One by one, Ealdred put them out. At the door he stopped. 'Sigulf says you are to go to the dormitory and stay there. He says you are not to be left alone, but I think I can trust you. You will go there?'

Madaah nodded.

'Good. Then I shall see you tomorrow.' As he leant forward to blow out the last candle, he looked sideways at Madaah, his green eyes glittering in the light. 'Oswald has left the Abbey. He slipped out at dusk to join his father. I thought knowing that he is not here might help you to sleep better. Now go, say your prayers and forget your words of this afternoon.' He blew out the candle and the room became dark. Then he left, quickly. Madaah followed him out and watched his figure go down the corridor. For a moment he felt an impulse to shout after Ealdred and tell him of his thoughts, but then the Librarian had turned a corner and had gone.

Madaah walked slowly down the long corridor to the dormitory. It was dark and there were not many people there; one or two huddled figures, the youngest of the novices. The rest of the Abbey was hard at work. He felt under his bed, where he had hidden the sword, he took it out, still muffled in his cloak, and left unobserved. His original plan had been to find Oswald in the Abbey, kill him, then leave and go—where? Somewhere, to the North anyway, to Strathclyde—to Anna. But now Oswald had gone, so first he would track him down, as Oswald had tracked down Aella, and then the reckoning would be paid.

He pulled his hood over his head and stole through the Abbey. He went through the kitchens, dark and deserted now, and out into the square at the front of the Abbey. He stood in the doorway and listened. There were voices in the square. As his eyes grew used to the light, he saw men. They were not monks and they were armed; retainers of the Abbey brought in for its protection. A bell pealed and the main gate was opened. Men on horseback trooped in, more retainers. Through the open gate

160

Madaah could see the dancing light of the fires outside. In a strange way it was reminiscent of the day he had first arrived at St. Wilfreds; when he had stood before the dark gate and seen, as it opened, the light in the square beyond. But the light then had been steady and clear, luminous—revealing. Now it was red and wavering, casting as much shadow as it gave light. Then the gate swung to and the light was gone.

In the darkness Madaah slipped from his door and slid along the wall. At the end, where the wall met the Abbey stockade, there were tumbled blocks of stone which were to be used for the Abbey extensions. He climbed up them, seized the edge of the stockade, swung over and stood, balanced on the timbers. He was looking down now, out of the Abbey. On his left was the town, dark and silent, and on his right the King's enclosure. Inside it the huge fires blazed and cast out tongues of flame, and shadow. Armed men moved around the square, their armour and weapons glowing in the firelight. There was talk, but it was subdued; brief calls, orders that hardly drifted to Madaah in his eyrie. The gates of the Hall were open and light streamed from them, but there was no sound from there—no cries of revelry or calls of defiant boasting.

One of the soldiers heaved a log on the fire and there was a crackle of burning timber and a stream of sparks gushed into the sky. Long yellow tongues of flame leapt out and the men turned their heads away and laughed. Madaah crouched like a cat on the Abbey fence and listened. The town was silent with a heavy, unnatural quietness, but, as he stood poised to jump, there was a wild screaming from the darkness and the thunder of galloping horses. Streaks of flame curled across the dark streets and the bells of the Abbey began to toll wildly. Cedric and his host had arrived at York.

Madaah crouched on the stockade as a wild mob of soldiers rushed below him, howling like wolves. He pressed back into the shadow as they stormed past, swinging crude weapons; clubs and hammers and sickles. This was the first wave of Cedric's shock attack; peasants, hastily armed and flung against the stockade to batter down the defences. Behind them came the thegns, mounted and armed in mail-shirts, and waving battle-axes and swords. The peasants smashed at the gates of the stockade, and the thegns, dismounted, swung their axes at the wood. The Hall was ablaze with light. Men poured from it and formed a line of shields across the square. Cedric's soldiers were climbing over the stockade. As they came over, they were slashed to their deaths by Cynwulf's warriors, but for every one who fell two more came over. Flames began to curl from the thatched roofs of the houses outside the stockade. In the streets there were bloody, hacking battles as Cynwulf's men, who had been quartered there, tried to fight their way back to the Hall.

Then the gates gave way and the thegns smashed into the square—and at the shield-wall of warriors. There was no hush in the square now. The air was full of the sound of battle; men screamed and howled, horses gave long agonised squeals as they slipped on the bloodied ground, and swords and axes clashed with a tortured scraping of metal.

Before the onslaught of the thegns, with Cedric at their head, the shield wall was driven back, leaving a line of bodies before it. The thegns leapt over the dead men and swung savagely at the living. Twice Cynwulf's men drove the attackers back, but twice in turn they were hammered back again by the weight and numbers of the thegns from the North. They were trapped like animals, but they fought with the blind courage of animals, too. None fell but before a blow from an axe and every gap in the line of shields was filled when a man died—but each time, the line grew shorter.

The peasants were out of the fight now. They filled the square behind the thegns, finishing off the fallen warriors. Then Madaah heard a wild hammering below him. He looked down and saw a mob beating at the gates of the Abbey. He gave a great cry in the darkness. He knew who they were down there—the drunken rabble of Cedric's host, after plunder. Good! He would make that task easy. That would be his revenge on the Church. But then, as he was ready to turn and jump back inside the Abbey he saw Oswald. He was against the wall and, though armed, well away from the savage fight across the square. Madaah stretched down and grabbed a chunk of stone. He stood upright on the edge of the stockade and raised it over his head. 'Oswald!' he screamed, 'Oswald! Murderer!' and hurled the stone down. It missed Oswald and crashed at the feet of his horse which swung round wildly. Oswald dragged its head back, looked upwards, and saw Madaah.

For a moment both stared at each other, their faces distorted with rage, then Oswald leaped clear of the stirrups. He dragged his sword from his scabbard and shook it at Madaah. Madaah bent to seize more stones, but when he straightened, Oswald was running along the stockade to the gate. Madaah jumped down into the darkness of the Abbey. As he landed, someone grabbed at him but he shook the hand off and ran to his side of the gate. He crashed into a line of soldiers who were drawn across the square, their swords out. A voice challenged him and he darted across to the kitchens. By the corner of the stockade was a small wicket gate. In the anxiety of the night there was a chance that it would be forgotten, and unguarded. It had been. Madaah scraped at the bolts and threw it open.

The noise of the battle roared into the hush of the square, and a glow of light fell across its darkness. From the main gate there were cries of alarm; a dark shape rushed through the wicket, then more, and Madaah fell back. The shapes were drunken ruffians from Cedric's army. They whooped as they rushed through the gate, and then the soldiers caught them. There was a wild and confused fight taking place in the darkness but then, silhouetted in the light of the door, Madaah saw Oswald.

'Here,' Madaah screamed. 'Here, murderer!'

Through all the noise of the battle Oswald heard that high pitched scream. He lunged through the gate, swinging his sword, and came after Madaah. No-one noticed them in their dark corner. It was as if they were in a small and remote corner of some private universe, which only one would leave alive. Oswald lurched forward in the dark. 'Where are you, Monk?' he cried.

'Here!' Madaah's voice was steady as he answered. Then Oswald rushed him. He slashed at Madaah but in the gloom misjudged his blow. The sword swept by Madaah's face and struck sparks from the wall behind him. In turn Madaah jabbed but his sword was deflected by Oswald's mail and then Oswald swept his weapon down, across Madaah's sword, and smashed it from his hands. Madaah backed away, helpless now. He tried to dart forward to retrieve his sword but Oswald was too quick for him. Again the sword slashed at him and Madaah leapt back against the wall. Behind him he felt a door. He turned and opened it and as he did so the sword slashed at him again, and caught his gown. He jumped through the door blindly—and ran. Behind him he heard the sound of running feet and Oswald's voice shouting crazily. His one thought now was to keep clear of the slashing sword until he, too, had something—anything—

with which to turn on Oswald. He ran on down a narrow passage, and a flight of steps. At the end of it was a door. He scrambled at it, forced it open, and came into a chapel. At one end a candle burned in a huge metal candlestick. Madaah realised that he was trapped and turned desperately, to see Oswald in the doorway.

Oswald kicked the door shut with his heel. It was hushed and still in the chapel, and Madaah could hear his breath, rasping out in harsh spasms. Oswald clasped his sword in both hands and swung it over his shoulder. For a moment he stood, almost idly, as if closing the door had cut them off from time, but then he nodded.

'Now, Master Priest,' he said. 'Now, your time has come.'

He walked towards Madaah, who felt an almost overwhelming desire to drop on his knees and ask for mercy. Oswald was nodding his head in a jerky way, as if agreeing with some invisible speaker. Madaah watched him with a sick intensity. Oswald was only a yard or so away now and in the circle of candlelight Madaah could observe every detail of his face. It seemed very large and vacant, devoid of any vestige of emotion or feeling, a huge white vacuum. He held out his hand, whether in defence or supplication he was not sure, but Oswald was beyond recognition of anything. His mouth was twitching and he made a strange grunting noise, like a pig, and in the corner of his mouth a little bubble of froth had gathered. As if responding to a sudden command from that invisible speaker he raised his sword high. His pale empty eyes stared blindly at Madaah, his mouth opened and gave forth that high-pitched giggle; then— as he swung at Madaah—a figure jumped from the darkness. Oswald screamed and slashed at the shape. Madaah stared incredulously as the figure fell away from the blow, but as Oswald ran his sword deep into his attacker, Madaah moved. He dragged the candlestick from the wall and crashed it against Oswald. For one second he saw Oswald's face twisted in amazement, and then he struck again—and then again—and Oswald was dead.

Madaah let the candlestick drop and stood, trembling, over the two bodies. He turned over the body of Oswald's victim, and gave a cry of despair. It was Ealdred.

'Ealdred!' he cried, 'Ealdred!' But Ealdred was beyond his voice, far away in a last struggle of his own. Even as Madaah watched him, the green eyes grew dim, and the scholar's hands

slackened from their death grip and fell loosely apart. On his
knees, in a bitter parody of prayer, Madaah cursed Oswald, and
the Church, and the Kingdom of Northumbria and all in it. He
mouthed a stream of blasphemy which echoed around the silent
chapel, while from the walls the pale faces of the saints looked
down, impassively, on the bloody scene.

At last Madaah rose. He left the chapel and crept up the stairs. Half-way there was the body of a peasant and from beyond that the sounds of voices, harsh and unyielding. Obviously the Abbey had been cleared of the mob. He thought for a moment, then went back down to the chapel. He took the candle, went to where Ealdred had rushed on Oswald, and found a small door. He went through it and came into a vaulted chamber. It was dark and he lifted the candle high. Around him lay the Abbey's library. From the door behind him a draught blew and the leaves of the manuscripts stirred and rustled, as if they were being turned by the hands of innumerable, and invisible, readers.

Madaah wandered down the crypt. There was the Great Testament, illumined with gold, bound with silver, the work of generations, and yet unfinished; here was a psalter, the work of Ealdred's own hand, written on the finest vellum. Madaah picked a book up and glanced at it—'The Song of Caedmon'. He read a page, almost casually, as if he were a visitor passing an idle moment. 'The Father of Glory,' he read, who had made for men, 'Heaven for their roof, and then the Earth—' he threw it down casually, to the floor.

For a long time he stood holding the candle, staring at the books, then he went back into the chapel. He lifted Ealdred and dragged him into the vault and placed him in its centre. Quickly he went round the shelves, pulling down the books and throwing them round Ealdred's body. He piled them high; the commentaries, the laws, the grammars, the lives of innumerable saints, the Rule of Benedict, and then he found a box. Inside were unbound leaves, glowing with colour, green and red, blue and yellow, but all framed with a brown, charred edge. He looked at them sombrely. They were the pages he had gathered at Lindisfarne, when books, and learning, and the Church, had seemed a way to a future beyond the bloody miseries of this narrow life. His hand clenched and the page crumbled and flaked away. He took the box and threw the pages, like autumn leaves, over Ealdred; then he took the Great Testament and ripped away a page and held the candle to it. It browned around the edges, lightly at first, and then a fringe of light appeared round it, like a halo. As it caught fire the lettering discoloured and cracked. 'In the beginning was the Word,' it said, and then disappeared in flame.

He held it down to the books around Ealdred and walked round the body, lighting the manuscripts. As they burst into flame, he backed away into the chapel. He took Oswald's sword, went back into the vault and edged round the flames. He found his way through the cellars and up into the Abbey. At last he found a window which looked out onto the darkness. He climbed through it, dropped lightly to the ground, and ran into the vastness of the night.

PART THREE

Chapter 17

Madaah sat on his horse at the edge of the forest. He peered through the foliage at the fields and at the village beyond. It was quiet and peaceful; a dozen or so peasants were mowing the meadow, a boy was tending a few cows and a herdsman was driving the village flock of swine away from the forest.

Someone muttered behind him. He turned and looked coldly at the man and the muttering stopped. For another half-hour he stayed watching, motionless. Nothing happened; the men in the fields worked on, a cow-bell clanked, the swine and their herdsman disappeared behind a copse. Satisfied at last, Madaah moved from the shelter of the forest and into the arable, ten mounted men at his heels.

One of the peasants saw them as they moved through the wheat. He gave a cry of alarm and dropped his hoe, but he did not move. The men with him stared dumbly at the riders. One of them turned and began to run to the village but one of Madaah's followers cantered easily after him and buffeted him to the ground. There was a burst of laughter from the riders, but Madaah's face remained impassive as they trotted from the fields into the village.

There was panic in the village as they rode in. A woman screamed somewhere, others ran wildly across the dusty street into their houses, snatching up children as they went. Then there was silence. Madaah's followers began to dismount, but, at a sharp word, stayed mounted. Madaah rode his horse around the village and through the gate in the thorn fence. He cantered round the fence. There was nothing to be seen, only the arable, and then the forest with a gap in it where a path ran to the next clearing. Then he rejoined his men.

'Bring them in.' He jerked his thumb towards the fields.

Two men swung away, then Madaah nodded. 'All right.' He

climbed down from his horse and stretched himself. Guthlac, a vast shaggy man stood beside him. He grinned, showing strong yellow teeth.

'Satisfied?' he asked. 'It was not worth waiting, eh?' He laughed heartily taking any possible sting from the words.

Madaah shrugged. It was always worth waiting, always worth taking extra care. That was why he was still alive, and Guthlac, and the others, and the thirty-odd more men back in the forest. Yes, it was always worth taking care, but whether the occasion was worth it was another matter. This time he doubted it; they were taking a risk, as they always did when they moved from the shelter of the forest, but for what? To spend a night in this miserable little village, to get drunk? What had brought him, he wondered. Not the thought of a drunken riot. That had brought the others, but himself—was it the wish to be back among the Folk again? To live as a human being? To take off, for one night, the Wolf's Head? Perhaps.

He was brought from his thoughts by cries from the men. The peasants were trooping into the village. They were boys and old men, not one able-bodied man amongst them. The oldest hobbled forward and held his hand out in a supplicatory gesture.

'Master!' he cried, then fell silent, as if that one word had exhausted his language and his thoughts.

'Where are the men?' Madaah asked him.

The old man stared at him speechlessly. 'The men!' Guthlac shouted.

One of the boys stepped forward. 'The thegn has taken them. Two days ago. The Ealdorman has called all the freemen together. There is fighting somewhere.'

There was always fighting somewhere in Northumbria, thought Madaah. The Kingdom was falling apart.

'Where is the fighting?' Guthlac demanded.

The boy shrank from the harshness in Guthlac's voice, but he answered. 'Over there,' he pointed to the East. 'It is a big battle.'

The old man found his tongue. 'It is not as it was in the old days. Then we sent so many men according to the law. Now the thegn takes all if he wishes. It is not like the old days.'

Guthlac and the others laughed, and even Madaah gave a wry grin. No, it was not like the old days. The Aethelings and Ealdorman were fighting each other, the coast had to be watched against the Norsemen. Inside and outside the Kingdom was menaced, and every man made his own law. That was why he, Madaah, and the others, lived as they pleased, were here today—because they made their own law.

Guthlac turned to Madaah. 'It is so then,' he shouted. 'Nothing to worry us. I knew it was true. Did I not say so?'

Madaah nodded. Guthlac had spied the village and seen there were no men in the fields, and guessed why. 'You spoke the truth, Guthlac.'

Guthlac laughed, a great jovial burst of sound. 'And now, beer! And meat!'

The old man swayed forward in a bow. 'We have beer, Master, plenty of beer, but no meat.'

'No meat?' Guthlac shook with mirth. 'I saw many cows in the fields. They are meat, old man.'

'No!' The old man's voice was serious. 'They are the Thegn's, Master. Once we had cows of our own but that was in the old time, now—'

'Now things have changed. They have, they have.' All Madaah's men laughed heartily at Guthlac's reply. 'We will leave a message telling him who has eaten his cow.'

'Who shall I say, Master?'

'Say?' Guthlac's voice changed from mirth to a savage growl. 'Tell him we ate it. We of the Wolf's Head. And tell him we will come again—and eat him! Now bring the cow, and the beer—or we will eat you!'

The cow was brought in and butchered. The women brought out the beer and the outlaws drank and ate before a huge fire. Before they got too drunk, Madaah said they would have a guard on watch that night. Guthlac was indignant in his loudly humorous way.

'A watch! No need for that, Madaah. The Thegn is far away, fighting great battles, over there.' He waved his hand dizzily and fell to the ground, shaking with laughter.

Madaah crooked his finger. 'Fridewith.'

Fridewith rose obediently and followed Madaah outside the fence.

'The moon will rise soon. You will watch until it is there,' Madaah pointed to a tree which rose above the others. 'Then you will call me. I will call the next man.'

Fridewith gnawed at a bone he held. 'Guthlac said.' He

170

stopped speaking as he saw the expression on Madaah's face. 'Until the moon shines there,' he said.

'And stay awake.' Madaah's voice was quiet, but it had that sound in it which made Guthlac's bluster seem harmless.

Madaah turned to the fire. His followers were gorging themselves but he wanted neither meat nor beer. In the three years he had been living the wolf's life, he had tamed his desires. Twice in his life he had given way to them, and what had been the result? He had betrayed Anna, and the Church had betrayed him. It seemed to him that trust was an illusion, love a weakness, and the only way to live unhurt was to cut oneself off from humanity. But as he had turned away from mankind, become a ghost, a phantom, haunting the forest, living in darkness, so, like a foul and perverted appetite, his need for attention grew. Wounded and warped, he struck at what he considered to be the wounder and the warper, although with every blow he struck, he destroyed yet more of himself. If there were books to be burned, he burned them; if there were churches to be destroyed, he destroyed them, seeking, in his own black way, to be revenged on the Church which had first breathed into his ear a promise of a better life.

And yet he was still a spiritual being, although his spirit moved in darkness and fed on revenge. Buried within him there was a feeling yet for the intellect which could be resurrected by wanton actions of stupidity. As now, when one of his followers threw a burning brand on the thatch of a cottage; he was the first to put it out, and, with Guthlac's brute strength behind him, quick to strike the man.

'We drink and eat,' he said, 'we leave them their homes.'

'That is so. It is as Madaah says,' Guthlac's voice boomed. And so it was as Madaah said.

They sprawled again around the fire. From the doors of their cottages the peasants peered at them anxiously, but Madaah's actions had calmed their fears, and, timorously at first, they came out to join the outlaws. Guthlac with his easy joviality made them welcome. 'We are all of one kind,' he said. 'All poor folk. Tonight we will eat our bellies full. Here—' he thrust a huge chunk of meat at an old woman— 'Eat up, mother.'

The woman cackled and munched at the meat. A child ran forward and Guthlac scooped it up. 'A fine child!' he cried. He stuffed a piece of fat meat into its mouth. 'Let it grow strong on the Thegn's meat!' He thrust the child back in its mother's arms and strode around the fire, throwing meat to the villagers. A cask of beer was brought out and broached, and the old woman shuffled after Guthlac pouring out the drink. The fire roared cheerfully, the women laughed boldly at Guthlac, and the children ran around the outlaws playing games. To everyone's surprise the raid had turned into a feast. Then, from the dusk, there came a shrill piping and Fridewith ran into the village.

'There is someone coming,' he cried.

Madaah was first on his horse. He lashed it forward through the gate, ready to fight—or run—whichever the odds favoured. He leaned forward and gazed into the dusk, his sword out. From the forest track a voice hailed them. 'Peaceful coming,' it cried. 'Peaceful coming.'

A man came out of the forest. By his side ambled a strange creature. It had massive shoulders and a long pointed head, and it moved in a queer swaying prowl. As the man saw them, he struck the beast which rose on its hind legs and staggered forwards a few yards.

Behind Madaah, Guthlac swore. 'By the saints, what is that?'

'It is a bear,' Madaah said, 'a dancing bear. I have seen one at—' he cut his words short. Nothing to Guthlac where he had seen it, but it was at the Hall of York.

The man came to the dark group and looked at them uncertainly. 'Masters,' he wore a hood and he doffed it and bowed. 'My name is Penda, my Lords. I travel with my bear through this land. He dances and folk laugh. Sometimes they give me money.'

'You have come through the woods?' Madaah looked beyond the man to the forest.

'That is so, my Lord. I was looking for the Thegn's Hall but lost my way. Are you the Thegn, my Lord?'

'Did you see anyone in the woods?'

'No-one, my Lord. Truthfully I was not looking. They are not places to be in at night.' The man looked carefully at Madaah and the others. His voice was soft and coaxing, full of the rhythmic patter of one used to telling many a tale, and deflecting a blow with a soft word. 'Although I do not think there is anyone there to do a poor man harm; a poor man who has known hardship, and has no money, with only a beast for company—Hup, Caesar!'

He struck the bear with his stick and it rose to its hind-legs,

172

waved its paws uncertainly, then fell to its feet. 'Caesar was the name of a great King,' he explained.

Guthlac got off his horse. 'A beast that walks! Come!'

He waved the man into the village. Penda went forward jauntily enough but his eyes flicked back and forward at the men beside him. The villagers were still by the fire but as he approached them they stood up and backed away. Guthlac called to reassure them, and strode into the firelight.

'Bring the beast here,' he commanded.

Penda hurried forward, pulling the bear. It jerked its head away from the flames, which made its eyes glint redly.

A chorus of 'oohs' came from the villagers as they saw the bear. Guthlac faced them with a proprietorial air. 'It walks like a man!' He cried. He was lost in wonder. 'A beast that walks.' A thought struck him—'Does it talk?'

Penda shook his head sadly, apologetically, as if the bear's failure was in some way his fault. 'Alas, no, Master. But he dances. See!'

He fumbled in his cloak and took out a pipe of wood. 'See!'

He blew a note on the pipe, a shrill bubbling air, and the bear rose, and, swinging its huge head, began an awkward shuffle in time to the music. The villagers, and the outlaws burst into roars of laughter, all except Madaah and Guthlac. Guthlac was lost in wonder, like a child.

'Look, Madaah,' he said. 'Is it not a marvel. A dancing beast!'

Madaah was unmoved. Beasts who behaved like men, or men who behaved like beasts—what was the difference?

The bear danced again to Penda's pipe, and fell to the ground. 'Is he not a fine beast, my Masters?' Penda cried. 'He has danced at the court of Offa in the far kindom of Mercia, and he has made the king of the East Saxons laugh. I caught him myself in the Frankish lands and—' he paused for dramatic effect,—'he has danced before the Great Charlemagne, and the Pope in Rome! See—' he rushed the beast forward to the ring of peasants. The children screamed and ran behind their mothers, who laughed with a mixture of fear and laughter.

'See!' He forced his fingers inside the muzzle and pulled at the bear's mouth, revealing long fangs, as yellow as Guthlac's.

'Those teeth would eat a man! But he dances to my tune. Is it not a wonder?'

It was, the peasants agreed. It was the greatest wonder they had ever seen. The old man shuffled forward.

'I have seen a man fight with a bear. It was in the days of King Oswulf, when the law was obeyed by all. A thegn fought a bear in the King's hall. It was a bigger bear than that,' he added.

'That would be something,' Guthlac turned to Madaah. 'To have fought a bear. A man would be remembered for that.'

'The thegn was a great warrior. I rode with him to the battle of Winchanheale when Aethelwold Moll was overthrown. He was slain there, but he was a mighty man.'

'No greater than I!' Guthlac stood up and stretched his massive arms. 'I will fight the bear, now!' He appealed to Madaah. 'Would that not be a great thing?'

Madaah shrugged. If Guthlac thought so, let him do it. It was nothing to him. Guthlac took Madaah's silence as assent. 'Very well,' he cried. 'I will fight it. He strode across the circle of flame to the bear. 'Loose it.'

Penda put out his hand appealingly. 'Master. Caesar—he is not a thing to fight with!' He looked around the faces of the watchers, seeking support. 'This is a time for merriment. Tomorrow perhaps.'

Again he looked around, and this time stared directly at Madaah. For one moment Madaah met his eyes, then turned his head away. Penda shrugged helplessly and dropped his hand. He turned to Guthlac who was scowling horribly.

'As your Lordship wishes.'

He released the chain from Caesar's neck. Then he turned. 'The muzzle too?' he asked slyly.

Guthlac frowned in thought, then turned to the old man. 'This thegn, when he fought the bear, was it muzzled?'

The old man was silent for a long moment, struggling to recall the memories of forty-four years ago. 'Yes, it had a muzzle,' he agreed. 'And the thegn had a seax, but it was a bigger bear than that.'

'Then leave it on,' Guthlac ordered. 'But I will not use a knife. I will fight it with my bare hands. Make it stand.'

Penda glanced round once more in a mute appeal, but met nothing but the uneasy stares of the peasants, the eager anticipation of the outlaws, and Madaah's indifference. 'Hup, Caesar,' he called.

The beast staggered to its hind-legs and wavered uncertainly. It was plainly weary but it looked formidable like that—nearly as tall as a man, saliva swung from its jaws, and its eyes shone in

174

the firelight. Guthlac screamed suddenly and jumped at the bear. His head caught it full in its chest and it fell backwards and rolled over. The peasants gasped and the outlaws bellowed applause. Between the noise and the fire the bear was confused. It backed away, shaking its head, pulling at the chain which was no longer there. Guthlac dived after it, shouting with laughter. He seized its loose fur and heaved backwards. The bear wriggled and shook him off and tried to pad away, but the outlaw grabbed its stumpy tail and with a huge pull lifted its back legs off the ground. 'Now it walks on its front legs,' he shouted.

The crowd laughed uproariously at that—but then the bear turned. A growl rumbled deep in its throat, an ominous sound, like distant thunder. It swung its head slowly, almost as if it was in thought, and then it growled again—the thunder drawing nearer—and wrinkled its lips, showing the long teeth. The watchers fell as silent, as if a command had sealed their lips. The bear moved forward a pace towards Guthlac, who crouched like a wrestler. Then, in the darkness, Penda rattled his chain and the bear heaved itself upright.

Madaah had a sudden feeling of disquiet, a premonition of disaster. For a moment he felt impelled to halt the fight, but he sank back. What was it to him?

The bear lurched forward a step. The light shone on its fur. It was worn and shabby and dull. Its claws were worn down by endless journeying, plainly it was an old animal, but then it growled again, a full throated roar. It was still a bear, still formidable, and then it hurled itself at Guthlac and seized him with its tremendous paws. For a moment the two, man and beast, were locked together, and then Guthlac fell beneath the weight of the bear. It scraped at him, its blunted claws dragged away Guthlac's tunic and left red weals on his skin. Guthlac worked an arm free and held the beast by its muzzle and forced its head back, then he gave a huge heave and the bear rolled over, into the embers of the fire. Penda gave a despairing cry, and the bear cried too, an appalling animal scream. It thrashed its way from the fire, its fur smouldering, and rushed at Guthlac—and it had no muzzle now. It caught the outlaw and bowled him over, turned with uncanny speed, and slashed at him with its yellow fangs.

Guthlac fought clear, but the bear caught him again by the arm and dragged him down. The speed of the bear's attack caught everyone by surprise, but then a man jumped forward and drove a sword into the bear's side. It turned, snarling, to meet this new foe and Guthlac grabbed the sword, shoved the man aside, and drove his sword into the bear's throat. In a last spasm Caesar came forward, onto the weapon, and then it gave a bubbling cough—and died.

There was a complete hush. Penda walked forward and knelt, incomprehendingly by his bear. 'He is dead,' he whispered. 'Caesar is dead.'

'And I killed him, and he was un-muzzled,' Guthlac held his torn arm and looked around proudly. The peasants dropped their eyes as he stared at them. Guthlac was puzzled. 'That is a great thing, is it not? To kill a bear?'

No-one answered—Madaah knew why. Ten minutes ago they had been laughing at the harmless animal, and the laughter had been a bond of humanity between them all; now, blood, and fire, and iron had entered the village. The poor mangy beast was dead, and it looked very small.

'What now?' Penda's voice was lost and bewildered. Guthlac did not understand.

'I will skin it,' he said. 'I will wear its fur and its head—and we will eat the meat. I have never had bear's meat before.'

He took a knife and pushed Penda away. As he bent over Caesar, he looked up and stared into the darkness. 'Who is there?' he shouted.

It was Fridewith. The moon was over the tree. Madaah went out to take the watch. Guthlac protested, but Madaah brushed him aside and walked out of the village, leading his horse.

He went away from the thorn fence and stood at the edge of the field, by the barley. An owl hooted in the forest and another echoed its call from the darkness. He leaned against the warm side of his horse and listened to the sounds of the night and the forest, as familiar now as the liturgy of the Church. From behind the fence voices came to him faintly, and he moved further away until he could no longer hear them. For the first time since he had killed Oswald, he felt a mood of deep regret. In the village, briefly, there had been a bond between them all, those in the law and those outside it, and it had been destroyed. He had felt a longing then to enter that life. For a moment he had felt at harmony with the laughing women and children, and the old men, and Penda and his bear; he had wanted to be able to share in their wonder, and laughter, and deep simplicity. But now it was gone—wiped away with the death of the bear.

He heard a sound behind him and turned sharply. Penda's voice called him from the darkness. Madaah asked him, curtly, what he wanted.

'Nothing, Master,' Penda said. 'I did not wish to stay in there.'

'What are they doing?' Madaah asked.

'They have skinned my bear. They have taken its flesh away and given the bones to the dogs. Caesar is gone—gone!' Penda sounded bewildered. 'I have had him for thirteen years. He was a very harmless bear.'

Madaah moved restlessly. In a way he, too, found it hard to believe that the bear was gone, and with it the warmth and humour of the feast.

'Where did you get the beast?' He asked.

'I won it at Winchester, playing dice. We have been together ever since.'

'And have you been to Rome, and the Frankish lands?'

'No,' Penda sighed. 'I tell the folk that—what harm in it? It makes them happy to think of such marvels. But I have travelled this land of England with Caesar for thirteen years. I have a paper which gives me leave. A prince of Offa's court gave it to me.'

'You have been in Offa's court?'

'Never in his Hall, but Caesar danced before it. Then the prince gave me the paper. What shall I do now without my Caesar?'

'Get yourself another bear,' Madaah said harshly.

'They are not creatures one gets easily. They come from over the sea.'

'Then travel alone.' It was a brutal answer, and Madaah knew why he had given it. When Guthlac had wished to fight the bear, Penda had looked at him in appeal and by ignoring it he, Madaah, had been guilty of the bear's death, and what it symbolised. He had known what the consequences would be. Of all the people there, only he and Penda had known that, and Penda had been powerless. He wished to drive Penda away, as if by doing that he would be driving away the guilt of the night.

Penda's face was sad in the moonlight. 'Alone? That is a hard way to travel. What will become of me?'

'What becomes of any man. You lived before you had your bear.'

'But then I was with my own people, with the Cymry in the far West.' So that was where Penda had got that sing-song rhythm in his voice. Years of wandering across England had blunted it but it was still there. Penda was of the old stock who had lived in the land before the English came and conquered them.

'Go back to your own people,' Madaah said, 'and be glad you have people to go back to.'

'I will need to buy bread, Master. And without my bear, how can I do that?'

'Guthlac killed your bear. Ask him for money.'

'He is not the one to ask, Master. He will not pay me.' Penda hesitated, waiting for a response from Madaah, but got none. He gave a hopeless shrug. 'Very well. May I go? I do not wish to stay here.'

Madaah jerked his head. 'I thought you said you were afraid of the woods at night.'

'There are worse things than those in the forest.'

'Then go.'

Penda bowed his head deeply, deeper than respect called for. 'Thank you, Master.' He paused for a moment then walked away into the darkness of the forest. Madaah watched him for a moment then fumbled in his purse. 'You—' he shouted—'here.' Penda turned and Madaah flung a coin at him. It glinted in the moon-light and Penda caught it with practised ease.

'Thank you,' he cried. Then he called out in some strange tongue, whether a blessing or a curse Madaah did not know—or care—and he disappeared into the night.

Madaah did not call the next watch. He lay on the ground and stared at the moon. He watched it travel across the sky, slowly and steadily. Even the moon had a destination, somewhere to travel to. Penda had a goal, too, even if it was only a struggle to die in his birthplace. What have I? he thought, where will my journey end? He found no answer, though he stayed awake until the dawn. Then he went into the village.

The peasants were indoors. Some of Madaah's men snored round the embers of the fire. Caesar's skin was stretched on a wicker frame and a few of its bones were scattered around in the dust. Madaah lay close to the fire and slept, too.

It was close to noon when he woke. Guthlac was scraping at the bear skin. He grinned when he saw Madaah rise, and threw

178

him a piece of meat. 'It is bear-meat,' he shouted. 'Eat it and become as strong as the bear. As strong as I am! Eat it,' he urged, 'and I will eat a fox and become as cunning as you!'

Madaah threw the meat down and Guthlac hurried over, full of massive concern. 'Will you not eat?' he asked.

'No. Get me beer,' Madaah said. 'Much beer.'

Guthlac looked at him curiously. 'Beer? You want beer?'

Madaah did. He got it and he drank it—mugfuls of it. His men were amazed, but they joined in. They built up the fire and drank until they were stupid. They laughed senselessly, wrestled with each other in the dust, leaped over the fire, spreading the wood further and further apart, until they landed on the hot embers and ran down the village howling with pain. Madaah got drunk, too. Only he knew why. He poured the heavy, bitter liquid down, blotting out his memories, drowning them in the beer. The outlaws were pleased to see him drunk. It made him as they were, creatures of the senses, and reduced him to their blind level.

After two or three hours Madaah tired of the village and the drinking. He lurched to his horse and mounted it. He waved the others up and they rode from the village a bawling cursing mob, quite different from the hard disciplined group who had cantered in the day before. Behind them, quite forgotten, they left Caesar's skin, hairy on its frame, paws outstretched, its eyeless sockets seeming to watch them as they cantered out.

Chapter 18

As they left the village, Madaah swayed drunkenly in his saddle. Guthlac caught his arm and steadied him. Madaah mumbled incoherently and the big outlaw grinned through his beard. Then the ripening wheat parted and a man with a spear jabbed at Madaah. The point caught him below the ribs, scraped upwards, and became entangled in his jerkin. He fell sidewards against Guthlac, who was being attacked from the other side. Madaah's drunkenness left him instantly. He dragged himself back on the saddle; the wheat field was alive with men, drawn in a cordon around the village. Guthlac had his sword out and slashed his attacker down, then set off at a gallop to the forest. Madaah kicked his own horse frantically and half broke through, but someone, quicker thinking than the rest, thrust his spear between the legs of his horse and brought it down. Madaah went crashing forward with his horse, through the wheat. His head slammed against the ground, and then he fell unconscious.

When he came round, he was being dragged by the legs down the village street. He was vaguely aware of peering faces, and harsh shouts, then he fell into the darkness again. He was roused by a sudden shock that brought him jerking forward. His head was full of a terrible throbbing ache and his side was raw and painful. As he raised himself, a foot caught him in the chest and kicked him down. Then he felt the shock again as a bucket of water was thrown at his face. He lay gasping for a moment, and looked blearily upwards. A man was bending over him. He was dressed in mail and his face had a look of hard authority. He was not young. His hair was scanty and streaked with grey, but his eyes were penetrating and his face was marked with lines other than those of age—lines of fierceness and ruthlessness.

Behind him the villagers stood in a group. The man asked them if Madaah had been the leader of the outlaws. Yes, they chorused, and the old man who had told of the bear fight came forward. 'He was the leader, my Lord. There was another—a big man— but he is not here.'

'And these?' the Thegn waved his gloved hand. Madaah followed the gesture. Besides himself there were six other captives. 'They were nothing, my Lord. Dogs!' the old man spat at the captives and aimed a feeble kick at the nearest. 'He—' a trembling finger was pointed at Madaah—'he was the leader. When he spoke, the others obeyed, even the big one who fought the bear— even he listened when that one spoke.'

The Thegn leaned over Madaah. 'Do you know me?' he asked.

'No, but I shall when we meet again,' Madaah stared unwinkingly at the Thegn.

'My name is Osred,' the Thegn said. 'And you will meet none other in this life. Depend on it.'

'They ate two of your cows, my Lord,' the old man cried. 'And they said that they would eat you, too.'

'Did they so?' Osred put his foot on Madaah's chest. 'Did they so?'

Someone in the crowd called out that they had frightened the children too, and the women. Madaah coughed and spat out a mouthful of blood. That was not so, he thought. They had frightened no-one, except Penda, maybe.

Osred pressed his foot on Madaah's chest. He looked down thoughtfully. 'It seems to me that I have heard of one such as you. A small man who speaks and others obey. My Lord Cedric has looked for long for such a one. They say that you are clever, a fox. But you are not so clever.'

Madaah agreed silently. They had been stupid—he had been stupid; stupid to listen to Guthlac, stupid to fall into such a trap, stupid not to have burned the village last night and gone back to the woods. It was Penda, he thought, Penda and his bear—and his own weakness, his desire—he recognised it now—for the warmth of ordinary life.

'There are more of you,' the Thegn said, 'beyond the forest. Where do they hide?'

Madaah did not answer. He turned his face away from Osred but the Thegn turned it back with his foot. 'I would flay you now, and place your skin next to that—' he pointed to the bearskin—'but there are those who wish to have you in their hands. But you will speak. You will tell us where your rats' nest is.' He

squatted on his haunches and pressed his face close to Madaah's. 'You will speak,' he said.

One of his men leaned over Osred's shoulder and whispered in his ear. Osred nodded. 'Yes, they would talk, easily, but this one— this fox—he thinks he can defy me.' He slapped Madaah lightly on the face with his glove. 'They are outside the Law, but this one thinks that he is above it. I know him. I have seen such men before; their pride drives them. They think they are more than other men. They believe that they know more than others, and they think that knowledge puts them above God's laws, and the King's. But today he will learn differently.' He tapped Madaah again with his glove. 'You will talk, and these—' he pointed to the peasants—'these will see that you are just a man. Then Lord Cedric may have you.'

The Thegn ordered Caesar's skin to be taken down from its wooden frame. The frame itself was brought down and Madaah was spread-eagled on it and tied down. At first he was silent, but soon he began to whimper and then gave terrible screams, and in the end he talked. He talked, and Osred listened, satisfied at what he had done. But the knowledge was of little use to him, for at dusk Guthlac returned with forty followers and destroyed the Thegn and his men, and when he saw Madaah's tormented body, he killed the peasants too, and burned the village. When he left, with Madaah across his saddle, there was no living thing in the village, or the fields, except the languorous moths that fluttered to the flames and were destroyed, too.

Chapter 19

The band of men crawled laboriously up the bare hill-side, their faces down against the rain which lashed against them. They crossed a stream and one man fell. He lay in the water, watching helplessly as the others stumbled past him. Two of the men were on horse-back, and the leading rider, whose name was Fridewith, pulled up in the lee of some huge boulders, green with lichen, and looked back. Two more men were down, stretched out in the saturated grass, and the others were barely moving, stumbling forward a few yards, then sprawling. The second rider pulled up beside him and Fridewith jerked his head towards the others.

'They are finished,' he said. As he spoke, a string of saliva swung from his lips but he was too weary to wipe it away.

The other horseman looked down the hill, but did not answer.

'What are we going to do?' Fridewith asked. 'Leave them?'

The other man did not speak, gave no sign that he had heard the question. Fridewith looked at him cautiously out of the corner of his eye. Hard to tell what he was thinking, what was going on behind that mask-like face. Fridewith spat the saliva over his cloak. It was the other man's decision. He was the leader. He squinted again at the indifferent face. What was the real name that mask bore? He had often wondered, but never cared, or dared, to ask. Some called him Snake, but he had heard him called Fox too, and he had been known as Madaah; but that was a name he did not understand. Snake, Fox or Madaah, the man beside him accepted them all equally, as if none meant more to him than another. No man Fridewith had ever known had felt that about his name—even the meanest man would stress his name, his right to a sound, at least, that was his own.

The first of the men following dragged himself to them and collapsed by the boulders. His face was slack and his limbs jerked with exhaustion—and he had thrown away his sword. Fridewith spat again. When men, and men such as they, threw away their weapons, it was the end. He had kept his though, and Madaah, or Snake, or Fox, had his too. That was a fine sword. Its hilt was inlaid with gold and on the blade there was writing. Once, when he was drunk, Madaah had told him what it meant. 'I was made for Oswald' it said. When Madaah had told him that, he had laughed for a long time, as if there was a hidden joke behind it. And he was a man who laughed rarely.

Fridewith's eyes were closing and he jerked awake and stared across the valley, through the rain and the swirling mist. Were they still being followed? The mist swirled—and swirled—and his eyes began to close. He heard a chink of metal and he jerked awake in panic, but it was only the sound of the bridle of Madaah's horse as he kicked it forward. They were going on then. He hacked viciously at his own horse and goaded it forward. It moved, but only just.

They moved on, under a towering wall of crag. They were in thick mist now. Far below them there was the sound of roaring water but they could see nothing. Madaah halted again and cocked his head like an animal, and listened. There was nothing to hear; no cries of men, no clatter of horses, no baying of dogs, only the sound of falling water. But Madaah had none, even, of Fridewith's faint doubts. They were still being followed; Cedric would never give up. Twice in the past week they had tried to double back, to slip through the long cordon of Cedric's troops, but each time they had been sighted and driven back into the wilderness, and each time Cedric had followed them.

Again they climbed upwards. Madaah's horse slipped and stumbled among the rocks, and Madaah wrenched its head back with an iron hand and raked its sides cruelly, forcing it on.

'Rest!' Fridewith's voice croaked behind him. 'Must rest.'

Madaah let his horse stop and Fridewith drew level with him. He was holding his side and he looked at Madaah from sunken eyes set in a narrow face, black with dirt. Madaah stared coldly back.

'All right,' he said. 'Get down.'

Fridewith half climbed, half fell off his horse and slumped against a rock. Madaah looked at him with contempt. Was that how he looked, he wondered, a scarecrow, ragged and filthy. A mere bag of bones held together by—by nothing in Fridewith, but by what in himself? Some pride? A feeling that he was different from the others; that he had horizons beyond theirs? At least he had chosen his life whereas they—the battered figures down the mountain—they were mere offal, unwanted scraps thrown away by the society in which they had once lived; like that Ceolfric he had once heard Aethelred cast out from the life of the Folk.

But Aethelred was dead, killed by Cynwulf, as Cynwulf had been killed in turn by Torhtmund, and Ealdred by Oswald and Oswald by Madaah himself. Now, of those days, only he and Cedric lived. There was a new King. Ealdred's words had come true. Eardwulf had been crowned, and ruled with a hand harder than Aethelred's had been. He had imposed a peace on the land that had freed Cedric to hunt down the killer of his son; and Madaah had made sure Cedric knew who it was. And now they were here, wherever that was—half way across Strathclyde in a wilderness where no man had ever been before.

Fridewith lurched to his feet and grabbed the bridle of his horse. Madaah looked down at him. What use was he? The scarecrow could hardly stand, Madaah doubted if he could lift his sword. And he had a horse. With two horses a man might just get over the mountain, over into new country, just conceivably shake off Cedric.

'What is that?' He said suddenly.

Fridewith jerked with fear. 'What?' he cried.

Madaah bent his head and lifted a warning finger. 'I thought I heard something. Go back a little, listen.'

'Back?' Fridewith's voice was a mere whisper. He looked up into Madaah's face, then staggered off, obedient to the last. When he had lurched into the mist, Madaah took the bridle of the other horse, stabbed his own gaunt beast into motion with his spurs, and moved away, up into the mist.

For the rest of the day he forced his way up the mountain. As the evening drew near, the weather cleared. From his vantage point, high on the mountain, he looked back. Behind, there was range after range of mountains, a wild confusion of rock and peat; beyond them a river curved, leaden in the evening light, and beyond that a darkness, almost purple, covered the lands of Northumbria. At evening he came into a high plateau, a wilderness of bog and peat-hags, and faced the westering sun. In the far distance a mountain rose, snow covered, pure and remote, lifting its crystalline head above the darkness of the moors. He

186

faced the mountain, and for an hour or two drove the horses across the black desert. Then, as darkness came, he fell from his horse and lay in the heather, shuddering with fatigue.

He had reached a point now of near total exhaustion. His back was jarred with a deadly throbbing pain, and his head ached dully, constantly. The coldness of the night gathered round him, but he was barely conscious of it. He lay face down, not awake, but not sleeping. Each tiny noise, the scratching of heather on his face as he turned restlessly, the furtive movement of an insect, became magnified into crashing thunderous noises, and vivid images of violence and death flickered across his mind.

At dawn he came to, hot and yet shivering. The black shapes of the horses loomed above him and he was terrified that they would trample on him. He called out in alarm and then wondered who had called. After a while he realised it had been himself and he laughed, a crazy, racking sound that ended in a dry rattle. He looked around furtively, as if ashamed, and then he laughed again. This time the sound amused him and he giggled feebly. He crawled forward to the horses on his hands and knees. As the sky lightened behind them, they looked blacker, bigger, strong and invincible, and Madaah felt strong, too. He stood up and took a step forward, then fell again. For a time he lay sprawled, mindlessly. His eyelids closed and he began to drift into a fitful, uneasy doze, but he jerked awake on hearing a cry. He dragged himself to his feet and stood with his sword out in a pure reflex of violence. Then he realised that the cry had been his own, and one of terror and despair.

Again he dragged himself to the horses. As he approached them, they moved restlessly away. They are frightened of me, he thought. The idea pleased him. He swung his sword feebly and gave a weak threatening cry. It was right that he should be feared—had not Northumbria feared him, thegn and peasant alike? After that day in the village, he had become one to fear; the last shreds and vestiges of humanity had been torn from him then as he had screamed and whimpered by the fire, stretched on the frame that had held the bear skin. Even Guthlac had been frightened of him after that. But Guthlac was dead—slashed down in that last hacking fight through the forest when Cedric had finally come down with his host, and his huntsmen, and his dogs, and driven them through the snow like wild animals. But he had survived, he was still here. The thought gave him fresh courage and he stumbled to the horses. Again they moved away, and he held his hand out imploringly, close to tears.

The beasts were as weary as he, and finally he caught a bridle. It took him a long time to mount. His foot kept slipping from the stirrup, but in the end he managed it. From his saddle he looked around. The moor curved away, mile after mile, and in the distance the mountain shone in the early light. Madaah began to ride. Every now and then he changed mounts, dragging his raw thighs across the saddle, and fighting off waves of nausea. All morning he went on, with ravens croaking about him, and hawks swinging across the sky. At first he looked back, expecting to see figures on the moor, and the glint of weapons, but as the day wore on, he forgot even his pursuers, and he kept his face towards the shining mountain. Somewhere beyond that lay the Western sea and, although he scarcely knew why, the thought of that beckoned him on, as if by reaching that restless infinity of water he would find something infinitely precious and long since lost. Although he did not know it, he was heading for his home.

As the horses plunged through the heather and the black clinging peat, they weakened. They began to stagger and heave, and, about noon, the first one collapsed. Madaah tugged weakly at its head but it was finished and he left it staring dumbly at him, and went on. An hour later the second horse collapsed. He left that too. Far to the west, beyond the mountain, there was a brightness in the sky, and he set his face towards it and reeled on. As he walked, his raw thighs rubbed against each other and a film of blood began to seep down his legs. At times he seemed to be floating and the moor began to lift and move slowly round. It made him dizzy and fall, and then he would come round and find himself face down in the clinging peat. He began to hear people calling his name and he shouted back, hoarse cries of defiance that were mere whispers in the silence of the wasteland.

Several times he heard the clash of weapons, and the cries of men dying in battle. He thought it was Cedric, and he thought he heard the panting of horses behind him. He staggered for a few yards until he realised it was his own breath, rasping in his ears. For long periods he simply lay, staring vacantly at the sky and the hovering hawks, and then he would jump up and move forward quickly as though late for a meeting, run on, and then collapse again.

Once he awoke and saw a raven perched by him. It croaked at

him and he knew that it was talking to him and he understood its language. It was Ealdred's ghost and it reproached him for burning the books at York, and then it flew away. He saw many ghosts after that. A grouse burst from the heather, and that was the spirit of Leofric, laughing at him. Then he saw a hare, its fur whiter than the mountain and he knew that it was Anna. He ran after it, calling and weeping, but it hopped away and hid in the heather. And then he saw a fox creeping around him in a circle. That was his own ghost, come from the spirit world to inherit his soul. Then his legs bent beneath him and he fell into a darkness deeper than any he had known before.

When he came to he was calm and rational. He was lying in a ditch. A little amber-coloured stream trickled down it. He drank some water and slowly pulled himself up the dark walls of the ditch. It took him a long time but at last he dragged himself from it and lay among the heather and the bilberries and gazed calmly round. His eyes were full of thick yellow matter, and he scraped it away. He saw then that his hands were cracked and raw, and that there were sores between his fingers.

It was evening. In the west, beneath the blueness of the sky, there was a delicately luminous green light. A little breeze caught his face and cooled his burning skin. It was quiet, only the wind sighed through the heather and in the distance a bird called, a long plaintive trill. Madaah knew that he was dying, but the mountain was near now, and he thought he could hear, far away, below the green horizon, the boom of waves; and so he lay, his head tilted against the wind, listening to the sound of the sea.

The green light faded in the West. The sky darkened, and stars began to shine above the white cone of the mountain, and his mind wandered away; he sat again in Ragnar's Hall and looked down at the Norsemen as they drank and boasted; heard once more the chanting of the monks at their devotions; slew Oswald yet again; whimpered under the hands of Osred, and then, as the moon rose serenely in the clear sky, he murmured again the spells and charms of his innocent youth, until even they died away.

But during the night his legs began to twitch and jerk in terrible nervous spasms, and his body rose, moving convulsively, and he staggered forward again. He was over the watershed now, shambling down a wide valley. The moon shone on him as he moved down, and down, like a living corpse. His mind was very far away, lost in a dim shadow of despair, and he went through the shadow, crying and moaning, his rotting hands held out before him as if in quest for mercy, but there was none to see, or heed him.

Then he fell by some boulders and lay still. After a long time a little red spider ran from the boulders onto his face. Under the skin a vein throbbed and flickered, although so faintly only the spider's delicate legs could have detected it. Frightened, it ran across Madaah's forehead, over the great scar there, across the blind eye, down the slashed and mutilated nose and came to rest on the cindered burns of his chin. There it crouched, as if listening to the sounds of the night; strange calls from the hills, the wind sighing among the boulders, and the lap of the sea against the stones where Madaah lay, fighting his greatest battle.

Chapter 20

Colum woke early. He clutched his old knees with his bony arms and tried to hug a little warmth into himself under his rough blanket. A grey light filtered through the cracks in the wicker door of his cell and the pool of darkness under the domed roof ebbed away. Colum lay very still, as he always did when he came from the darkness of his dreams into the blessed light of day.

He rose, reluctantly, creakily, stooped and crawled through the doorway. The air was chilly, and he shivered miserably. His feet arched with cramp on the cold sand, and he bent and rubbed them until they straightened. It had been a hard winter—harder than most. Once there had been snow on the shore for a fortnight, a fortnight, it was an unheard-of vexation.

Dutifully, but with an involuntary groan, he knelt to say his prayers. He would fast all day, too, although Lent was over, for something evil had entered his dreams last night and he had woken twice, his mouth full of saliva, and his mind full of images of food. He had knelt in prayer until his knees were sore, but when he had slept again, the thought of food had pursued him into his dreams—and worse thoughts than those—and he had woken in a state of deepest sin.

So, today he would fast and do all his religious exercises—all of them—he told himself firmly. He knelt before the boulder he had chosen as his altar and looked at the crude figure of Christ he had carved there. He crossed himself devoutly, but before he prayed he looked around. A white mist was rolling off the mountains and the greyness of the sea was altering, almost imperceptibly, to a delicate green. Somewhere to the East the sun had begun its long climb over the sleeping world. The Spring was coming, the world would be reborn and the bees would wake and there would be honey—honey—fresh combs dripping with sweetness; his mouth ached with desire. He would take the

honey-combs and—he checked himself sharply—there was the
Devil again, creeping up behind him even as he knelt at his
prayers. But in the daylight he would defeat him and his evil
ways. Today he would—he would drink no water even! And he
would think only of the most holy things. He clasped his hands
and closed his eyes and raised his hoarse voice in prayer;
   'Most mighty Lord, greatest of gift-givers.'
   His old voice quavered across the empty sea-loch and the wind
blew against him and ruffled his thin hair.
   'Shining shield against evil, light in our darkness.'
   Along the beach sea-birds were calling and screeching.
   'Look on me lonely, lost; rest me on thy right hand.'
   The birds were screaming very loudly. Colum closed his eyes
tighter and shuffled on to some pebbles. He concentrated as hard
as he could, but the noise went on and finally he turned, still
kneeling, and peered through his fingers. Up the beach, by a
jumble of boulders, a flock of birds wheeled and screamed. Colum
dropped his hands onto his thin thighs. What was exciting the
birds? Food? It could only be that. He realised he was licking his lips
and sighed. Perhaps it was not a day for prayer and fasting after all.
   He stood up and walked along the beach. If the birds were
going to disturb him, he would at least see what was disturbing
them. The tide lapped his feet as he shuffled along the sand. As
he neared the boulders, the birds rose lightly, like wood ash in a
wind. Colum kept his eyes on the birds—odd that they should
look so beautiful and sound so ugly! He rested his hand on the
boulders and tilted his old head back. The sun had gained warmth
now, and the waves breaking gently on the shore had turned
from green to blue. The mild breeze blew and behind it he felt
the delicate, inexorable pressure of Spring. He breathed deeply,
gratefully, and then, almost absent-mindedly, as if he had forgotten his reason for being there, he glanced into the boulders—
and saw the body!
   He stared down unbelievingly. A crumpled body slumped
among the rocks! Where had it come from? He looked around
wildly. There was nothing but the silent hills and the empty sea;
no horse, no boat. Above him the birds wheeled and called with
their flat, empty cries. He stooped and touched the body, and
then hesitated. A conviction seized him that there was something
black and evil about the day. He withdrew his hand and shuffled
from one foot to the other in an agony of uncertainty. Where

had the body come from? Not washed ashore—it was above the tide-line—not from the empty wilderness that frowned along the bay. Nothing human lived up there; only, perhaps, dark things better not thought of. Some said the wilderness was haunted by the rejected things of Creation—shapes from which God had turned away his face—the monstrous offspring of Cain! He shuddered, then screwed his courage up, placed his foot on the body and pushed it over.

For a moment he stared down dispassionately and then his mind, numbed at first, made sense of what it saw. 'Oh Jesus,' he whimpered. His face twitched horribly as he stared down. It was true then—the monsters did live in the mountains, and one of them had come to him.

He looked wide-eyed at the terrible face turned to his. It was swollen and pulpy. The eyes were the merest yellow slits in a mass of stretched flesh which shone redly. The nose was a monstrous pig's snout. A reek of decay drifted from the body, and then a little red spider scuttled from the charred chin.

'Jesus!' Colum shouted. 'Jesus Christ!' He put his hands over his mouth and ran down the beach, sobbing with terror. He ran to his altar and fell to his knees before it.

'Oh Jesus,' he cried. 'Save me, save me!' He mumbled the words over and over. 'Save me, save me.'

He stared at the figure he had carved and the figure stared back. Slowly Colum's nerves began to slacken, and his body ceased its trembling. It was the crudity of the carving which calmed him. The face of his Christ was only a blob, with the merest scratches for features. As he looked at it, he was reminded of that terrible crude mask he had just seen among the boulders. Was it possible that under that horror there was a man, as, under Christ's humanity, there was divinity—and they—could they share in that common humanity, and divinity? But then he thought of the red spider. Was it just a harmless insect, or a familiar—a devil? A great struggle raged in his mind. He lived in a world peopled with phantoms, a world in which a little ring of light was forever lapped by a sea of dark evil. He shuddered at the thought of the circle of nightmares which surrounded him, and his pale eyes filled with tears. But the face of Christ looked gravely down and he rose to his feet and trudged back to the boulders—and with every step he took, the tide of darkness ebbed a little.

At the boulders he paused again, and then, as if he were seized and moved by some vast hand, he leaned stiffly over the body. Surely it was a man. Disfigured, swollen with illness, stinking of corruption—but still a man! Colum stared down wonderingly, and placed his hand on that terrible face. It was hot, burning as though a fire raged beneath the skin. He sighed; the man was alive but before such a wreck he felt helpless. Where could he begin? What could he do? He shambled back to his cell and took the wicker door off and went back to the boulders. After a long struggle he got the body away from the rocks and eased it onto the door. Laboriously, he dragged it back down the beach. It was very tiring and he paused often, but he managed it in the end. He made a fire and put water on to boil, and then he stripped the body.

He cut away a leather jerkin, heavy with mail, and a woollen shirt. Around the body's neck was a gold torque. Colum clucked with amazement, then threw it casually aside. The body was seamed with appalling scars. He shook his head when he saw them. What suffering had the man—if it was a man—gone through? Then he screwed his eyes in concentration. The scars made a pattern, and he realised that they were letters. He put his finger on them and traced them out; an O, an S, R, E and a D. Osred. Was that the name of the thing which lay before him? The letters had been burned on the body; surely if it was a man, it had done some terrible evil to have had such a punishment. The pulse in his temple began to flutter again, but he pushed his thoughts away and gave up speculating.

He washed the body and wrapped it in his woollen blanket. Then he made broth and tried to feed it. One or two spoonfuls went down, he thought. He tried to remember what he could of medicine, but he knew that what he, or anyone else, knew, would be useless anyway. He went to the altar and prayed.

All day he sat and watched the body, and at night he pulled it into the hut and sat by the door. In the night he heard long keening cries and he built up the fire. What were the noises but wolves, he thought. He had heard them before, but tonight they seemed like calls, like summonses from the hills to the dark shape behind his shoulder. When the dawn came, he pulled the body out and laid it in the sun, fed it with broth and prayed. At night he took it back into the cell and sat again by his fire.

For a week the body lay inert. Somewhere, deep inside it, remote from the sun and the wind, a pulse beat, hardly perceptible but as stubborn and as regular as the waves that beat along the shore. They were days of fear for Colum. He sensed that whatever else lay before the door of his cell, death did; but the sun shone stronger each day. Along the shore the saxifrage and the gorse began to bud, and something deep inside the body

o

began to struggle to the rim of the dark pit in which it had lain for so long.

Then one day it stirred. Under the blanket its hand moved, a minute gesture. Colum held his breath, uncertain whether he had seen it or not. He sat quite still, hardly breathing, as if his slightest movement might inhibit the body's struggle. Nothing happened. With a sigh he rose and turned away, and then, from behind him, he heard the faintest sound and he stopped, frozen into stillness. His hair prickled and for one despairing moment it was as if the sun had gone out, the birds had screamed and flown away, and the loch turned into a lake of pitch.

Trembling, he turned round and stared down. Surely the body had spoken. The words seemed to hang yet, in the air, but it was not possible. He dropped to his knees and stared at the grotesque mask—and then again the mouth twitched and the words stole out. 'God, God.'

Colum flapped his hands fretfully. It was incredible and his fears revived again. There was something unnatural in the words dropping from the obscene mouth, and then the hand under the blanket moved again and the slight gesture seemed unmeasurably pathetic and defenceless. Colum took a cloth and wiped the terrible face, and the action of helping seemed to soften the brutish mask, and soothed Colum's fears.

Although he spent the next day, and the next, peering anxiously at the swathed figure it did not move again, but on the third day, as Colum turned from his prayers, its eyelids flickered and he knew that it was returning to this world, but whether for good or ill vexed him all through that night. The next morning the fever began to die away. The green sores on the fingers and the ears broke and scabbed over, the face began to shrink from its swollen mass and Colum poured broth through the cracked lips, and wiped and swabbed—and prayed more fervently than ever.

And then its eyes opened. Colum was prepared for this. He picked up a jagged rock he had carefully selected and stooped over the body. He was very frightened and his hands and legs were shaking.

'If thou art a devil,' he quavered, 'then depart in the name of the Lord Jesus Christ.'

He started back, fully expecting the body to turn into a writhing flopping reptile, or a monstrous spider, or simply to rot into corruption, but it remained enigmatically still, its eyes gazing at him with a bright, glassy stare. He leaned forward again, threateningly, but the eyes remained fixed upon him although the mouth opened and spoke. 'Christe,' it said, 'Christe eleison.' Christ have mercy.

Colum cast the stone away and sank to his knees. He nodded and smiled reassuringly and placed his hand on Madaah's forehead. He looked up at the sky and heard the larks singing on the mountains. Behind him the clear blue waves, laced with seaweed, broke on the shore in sparkling showers of light.

Chapter 21

Madaah sat slouched on the sand watching Colum. The old man was down the beach among the boulders, gathering shell fish. It was early evening and warm. There was a heavy swell, and the waves curled and broke on the shore, sparkling as they caught the sun's long rays. Little birds ran along the sand, chasing the waves as they retreated. Madaah watched it all—the sun, the sea, the birds and the old man,—with the same cold indifference. He was alive, and strong now; that stubborn vitality which had sustained him through all his journeys had not failed him yet. But his body survived at the expense of his spirit—something there had failed, and even the miracle of his survival after his journey over the waste land had not revived it.

A pot on the fire by the cell simmered and Madaah threw more wood in the flames. He did nothing else. The old man was content to cook the food—let him do it. Colum came down the beach and squatted by Madaah. He began to crack the shells he had gathered and threw the small molluscs in the pot.

'We will eat soon,' he said.

Madaah shrugged. It was of little importance to him whether they did or not. He was aware that Colum was looking at him, but he was used to that. Many people had stared at his wrecked face but few cared to question him about it. Colum had not either, although Madaah knew the old man was devoured by curiosity.

The sun was dipping below the sea and the fire glowed brighter. Colum bent over the flames and stirred the pot. 'It is not a rich meal,' he said, 'but it is nourishing. You will have eaten better.'

Madaah was amused, in so far as he ever was. The old man had finally tried to probe a little. In return he felt an impulse to tease the old man. A cruel little impulse.

'You prayed long today,' he said.

Colum was pleased that Madaah had spoken. They had exchanged few words since that day a week ago when Madaah had opened his eyes and looked at him with that bright, glassy stare. He was more pleased that Madaah had mentioned prayer. He quite missed the note of irony in Madaah's voice.

'I am very lax', he sighed. 'Sometimes I pray for a long time to make up for it, but I fear God would prefer regularity.'

'Does God listen to your prayers?'

This time Colum caught the mocking note in Madaah's voice. He looked thoughtfully at the mask opposite. It was hard to tell what emotions were stirring behind it. 'I am sure he does,' he said.

'And does God answer them?'

'Yes, I believe so. In his own way.'

Madaah poked the fire with a twig. 'How do you know that?'

Colum looked firmly at Madaah. 'Because I see with my own eyes. You are alive.'

'You prayed for me?'

'Yes.'

To Colum's dismay Madaah burst out laughing. It was a nasty animalistic sound, coming from that ugly, tormented face. 'I doubt if God heard that prayer.'

'You doubt?'

Madaah glanced sharply at the old man. There was a note of authority in Colum's voice that took him by surprise. Then he shrugged. 'I doubt it, yes. I would not be welcome in your Heaven.'

Colum gazed into the night. Nor will I be, he thought, with something like despair. He shivered and moved closer to the fire. 'Where did you learn Greek?'

Madaah was taken by surprise. How could the old man know that? 'I know none,' he blurted out—then clicked with annoyance. Of course, he must have muttered some in his illness. It was a stupid lie, and Colum knew it.

'Are you a priest?'

Madaah jumped up and walked away from the fire. From behind him Colum shouted.

'Are you?'

Over his shoulder he shouted back. 'No, no.'

Colum's voice was calm. 'Why lie?'

Madaah turned. 'I am not lying. I am not a priest.'

The old man smiled at him across the flames. Madaah raised his fist. 'I do not wish to speak of it,' he shouted.

'Then why boast?'

Madaah stared angrily at Colum. Boast! What was the old fool prattling about? The old voice creaked across the flames. 'You are proud that there will be no place for you in Heaven. That is boasting. Salvation—'

Madaah cut him off. 'There is no salvation, and I would be beyond it if there was.'

'No man is beyond salvation. Not even me.'

'You!' Madaah laughed again—his ugly jeering laugh. He looked at Colum contemptuously. He was just a harmless old fool. 'What terrible things have you done?'

'What terrible things have *you* done?' Colum asked in return.

Madaah stared through his single eye at Colum's calm face. The temptation seized him to tell the old fool everything. To shock Colum out of his calmness. It would be a fitting thing for himself to do—to repay good with evil.

'Very well,' he went back to the fire and sat down. 'I am a murderer. I beat out a man's brains with a candle-stick.'

Colum had averted his face and Madaah could not see what effect he was having. He prodded the fire and the flames leaped up beneath the pot; Colum's face was still lost in shadow, but Madaah could see his hands, loosely clasped together. Very well, he would stir those hands, make them clench with disgust and despair.

He leaned forward and told Colum of the years of his outlawry. He told him of the years of savagery when he had been worse than a beast, when he had turned, not just against the Church which had betrayed him, but against mankind; when humanity had been his enemy, and he had hunted it down with such fury that even the men he led, wolves themselves, had become afraid of him. Across the fire the black shape of Colum was very still and Madaah searched for some one thing that would shake that dark composure. Then he remembered the village priest they had taken and how they dragged him around the village at the heels of the horses, and then they had taken out the cross from the church and—but there his voice failed him. He bent his head forward, amazed at himself. Why could he not tell that? Why? He ran his hand blindly over his tortured face.

'You see this?' he cried. 'I was tortured—tortured, and none protested, none! But they paid, they paid, and the debt is still owing. Do you hear?'

Then Colum turned and Madaah saw the old face, remote and composed. 'I hear,' he said. 'And you are forgiven.'

Madaah could not believe what he had heard. 'What?'

'You are forgiven. I have heard your confession and you are forgiven. Go now and sin no more.'

Madaah was incredulous. 'That was not a confession.'

The calm voice came from the darkness. 'You were boasting? Boasting of doing evil?' Colum sounded politely puzzled.

Madaah gave an angry laugh. 'What about my penance? Give me one that will wipe away my sins.'

Colum was silent for a while, then he spoke. 'I think you have already done your penance.'

Madaah flung himself angrily away from the fire. Colum's voice followed him into the darkness. 'The confession you owed to God, and you have given it. Your penance you owed to yourself, and you have repaid that in suffering.'

'I owe nothing—nothing!' Madaah shouted. A thought struck him. He went to Colum's cell and took out the gold necklace. He threw it down before Colum. 'I owe you my life. Take that. Now I have repaid that one debt.'

Colum held the necklace. 'What use is this to me?'

'It is a king's ransom!'

'Not my King's,' Colum said, and threw it into the night.

Madaah stalked away, angry and confused. He sat on a boulder and looked out across the loch. The light had gone now. Stars were glittering in the heaven and the moon had risen from her dark bed. He turned and shouted at the orange flicker of the fire. 'I am heathen, a pagan,' he cried. There was no answer and he groaned in exasperation. Then he heard a laugh.

'Odin? Wotan? Thor? Hummin and Nummin?' Now the old man was teasing him. He flushed angrily and strode back to the fire. Colum was sitting there placidly.

'I believe in nothing,' Madaah shouted. 'The world is—is,' he searched for that word which would convey his paralysing sense of loneliness, and the bleakness of the world from which his beliefs had been whipped by betrayal. 'The world is empty. And if anything rules it, then it is evil,' he looked scornfully at Colum. 'But what do you know of evil?' He gave a jeering laugh. 'You have run away from evil. That is why you are here.' He sat down and looked triumphantly at the old man. 'That is true, is it not?'

Colum nodded. 'That is true. I ran away from evil.'

Madaah leaned on his elbow. He felt superior and at ease now. 'Yes, you have run away from your little sins. What were they? Kissing a kitchen-girl? Stealing bread from the bakery?'

'No,' Colum's voice was quiet. 'Not those, though they too are sins worthy of our concern—lust and greed.'

'What then?' Madaah was condescending, ready to harry the old man into some ludicrous confession.

'I murdered my mother, Madaah.'

'What?' For a moment Madaah thought he had misheard—must have misheard.

Colum did not heed Madaah's interruption. 'I come from an island, Madaah, off the coast of Ireland. There was always trouble; fighting and war. My clan had a feud with men on the mainland. My father had killed their leader, and one day they raided us. There was a host of them and they had with them strangers, the Dhu Gael—Norsemen you would call them. They slew all on the island. I was at the fishing, and when I came back in my little boat, I saw the bodies laid out along the shore like fish after a catch. They thought we had treasure hidden, and so we had, but I had seen that my mother and her children were not on the beach, and so I knew that they had hidden—and where they had hidden was where the treasure lay. They built a fire for the torture, and made their knives hot, and they took me to the fire—and so I told them. And they found my mother and her children and killed them before me. Myself they took to the mainland and turned me loose, as a warning to all others they said. And I wandered for many years, for something had gone wrong inside my head. Then the Church found me, and saved me.' His voice died away sadly.

Madaah looked into the glowing embers of the fire. 'I am sorry,' he said.

'It was a long time ago.'

'I meant for taunting you.'

'No, it is salutary to remember sometimes.'

Madaah felt a surge of shame, and from the shame came something like affection. He felt anxious to mitigate the old man's sorrow and guilt. He leaned forward. 'There is nothing to feel shame for. How could you help speaking. Anyone would talk under torture. I thought not once, but I . . . I—' his hand crossed his face trembling as it did so, 'I talked.'

Colum's voice cut across his. 'I was not tortured, Madaah.'

Madaah's jaw dropped. 'But you said. . . .'

'I spoke before they put me to the test.'

Madaah stared numbly at the fire, its embers glowed back, like red eyes in the darkness. 'I am sorry,' he mumbled.

'For what?' Colum's voice was still calm. 'Evil had triumphed. The men were never punished. Do not you believe in an evil world?'

Madaah lay on his back and looked into the infinity of the night sky. A streak of fire shot across it and he gave a little grunt of fear. Surely that meant something bad, something evil leaping from the blackness onto the Earth, to hunt and harry poor mankind. He felt, suddenly, defenceless.

'Perhaps they are good signs.'

Madaah twisted sharply and looked at Colum. How did he know what he was thinking? Then he realised, of course the old man had heard him grunt. What sharp ears Colum had.

'They have been falling for many nights now. Perhaps it is a sign of something good, rousing itself to come to our earth. They say a star shone when our Saviour was born.'

'What are they?' Madaah asked.

'That I do not know. Sometimes great lights appear in the North.'

'I have heard it said that they are giants, from the Land of Frost.'

Colum chuckled. 'You have heard many things, Madaah. I think you heard that among the Heathen.'

'It could be true. There were giants in the olden times. I have seen books which tell of them.'

'So I have heard, too,' Colum's voice was sceptical.

Madaah felt mildly annoyed. Why should the old man disregard what all men believe? 'There was one in the Bible,' he said. 'Known as Goliath.'

'Yes, and a child overcame him,' Colum rose and stretched himself and took the pot from the fire. He sauntered into the darkness and his voice drifted back to Madaah. 'So strength was overthrown by weakness—evil by innocence.'

Colum disappeared into the night and Madaah lay back again. The night was calm and clear, and the stars in their countless multitudes shone down upon him. He felt a curious lightness of spirit, and he stood up and followed Colum. The old man was standing by the shore, looking across the loch. The swell had subsided and the waves were calm and full of phosphorescence which sparkled like white fire.

'Why did you come here?' Madaah asked.

'It is a solitary place.'

Colum began to walk along the shore, Madaah with him.

'But why this solitary place? Why not an island?'

Colum laughed. 'They are all full up you know.'

Madaah laughed too but pressed his question. 'But why here? This one particular place?'

'God sent me here.'

'Why here and not somewhere else?'

'To hear your confession.'

Madaah did not feel angry now. 'You really believe that?'

'Yes.'

They walked on, under the stars. The waves curled in at their feet, sparkling, brilliant.

'When I came here,' Colum said, 'the Brothers at my monastery were afraid.' He looked sideways at Madaah. 'They said the hills were full of monsters. They said they would come in the night and eat me.' He laughed. 'Poor pickings!' They had come to the rocks where Colum had found Madaah. Colum stooped. 'There are pools here full of life. Flowers grow in the water. That is strange, is it not?' He peered closely. 'It is too dark to see them. When I found you, I thought you were a monster.'

Madaah was startled. 'A monster!'

'Yes. Your face was swollen. I ran away. I was very frightened.'

'But you came back.'

'Yes.'

'When I woke you stood over me with a rock. I thought you were going to kill me.'

'Yes. I was not sure, even then.'

'Why did you come back—when you ran away?'

Colum looked at Madaah's tortured face. It was strange he thought. He hardly noticed the disfigurement now. 'I saw Christ in you,' he said.

He walked on, and left Madaah staring after him. He was shocked by what the old man had said. Shocked that he could have been taken for a monster, and shocked, too, that he could be seen as Christ. And yet perhaps it was true. Maybe there was divinity and bestiality in every man—perhaps, even, and still—in him. He ran after Colum.

'And you think God sent you here to save me?'

'Not only that.'

'Then what? What else?'

'God sent you here to save me.'

Madaah looked stupidly at Colum. 'Save you from what?'

'From my sins. I have never confessed before what I have told you tonight.'

Madaah plucked at Colum's sleeve but the old man carried on calmly. 'It has been a great burden on my soul. Now I am free of it. That is why God sent me here, and you.'

'But how can you be free of it now? 'Madaah was bewildered.

'You have forgiven me for it.'

'No, I have no power to do that. I was only ever a novice.'

'But you do forgive me for it?'

'Yes—' Madaah turned in anguish, 'I mean no—I mean how can I forgive you?'

Colum clasped Madaah's arm. 'I think you are as close to God as I am, or any man.' Madaah looked closely at Colum's face. It was calm in the moonlight, and he knew his own was too. And it was true what Colum had said. He sighed.

'You place a great burden on me, Colum.'

'Yes.'

'Then I forgive you.'

'And my penance?'

Madaah laughed. 'I think you have done it,' he said. Colum laughed with him, and they stood by the shore, their feet lapped by the sparkling waves.

They walked back to the fire in silence and ate. When they had finished, Colum spoke.

'Soon a boat will come from my monastery.'

'Should I go on that boat?' Madaah asked.

'Yes,' Colum was firm. 'Speak with the Abbot. He is a wise man.'

Madaah nodded agreement. 'I will do that. Shall I find a remote place, too?'

'That is for God to decide. But you have many gifts I think, and you have done many things. You have lived with the

Heathen. It may be that you will return to them. There is no telling.'

That night in the darkness of the hut Madaah lay awake listening to the old man snore by his side. He thought for a long time, but before he fell into a dreamless sleep he knew what he should do.

Chapter 22

The man came over the brow of the dark hill, from a wilderness of rock and peat. The wind blew towards him and he could hear the surge of the ocean. He crouched by a boulder and looked down onto a bay.

Below him there was a small fort on a headland, and beyond it were a few houses. People moved in the small fields, sheep grazed, and drawn up on the beach were two long black ships.

The man sat watching for a long time and then he began to move around the boulder. At last he found what he was looking for. He knelt and began to scrape away at the peat. In the damp soil he felt something hard and rough. He moved the peat away and carefully lifted the object out.

It was the remains of a sword and he smiled as he looked at it. He ran his hand carefully over the hilt. The ornamentation had gone, rusted and flaked away.

He remembered his charm, how long ago was it? Twenty, twenty-five years? When he had bound a snake-skin around the hilt to make the snake's magic his own. He remembered, too, his fear, when he had buried the sword, that the snakes, deep in the cool earth would wriggle away, squirm to their own element. And they had gone, and now were a part of the eternal darkness of the hill.

The sword was thin now, merely two pieces of crossed iron. Perhaps that was a sign—and as the snakes had gone from the sword, so too had they gone from his mind.

Madaah stood up, and swinging the rusty cross, he strode down the dark hill Mamdorcha; down to the village, and the sea, and the long ships.